Tom Wasp and the Murdered Stunner

Tom Wasp and the Murdered Stunner

Amy Myers

FIVE STAR

An imprint of Thomson Gale, a part of The Thomson Corporation

Detroit • New York • San Francisco • New Haven, Conn. • Waterville, Maine • London

THOMSON
™
GALE

Originally published in German in 2001 as *Tom Dickens und die Geliebte des Malers* by Aufbau Taschenbuch Verlag GmbH, Berlin.

Thomson Gale is part of The Thomson Corporation.

Set in 11 pt. Plantin.

LIBRARY OF CONGRESS CATALOGING-IN-PUBLICATION DATA

Myers, Amy, 1938–
Tom Wasp and the murdered stunner / Amy Myers. — 1st ed.
p. cm.
ISBN-13: 978-1-59414-593-3 (alk. paper)
ISBN-10: 1-59414-593-8 (alk. paper)
1. Great Britain—History—Victoria, 1837–1901—Fiction. I. Title.
PR6063.Y38T66 2007
823'.914—dc22 2007012341

First Edition. First Printing: October 2007.

Published in 2007 in conjunction with Tekno Books and Ed Gorman.

Printed in the United States of America on permanent paper
10 9 8 7 6 5 4 3 2 1

To Dot
with love and thanks

ACKNOWLEDGMENTS

The London docks area has changed a great deal since Tom Wasp walked the streets with his chimney-sweeping brushes, but it is still possible to imagine how it once was from what remains. In particular, Wilton's Music Hall still stands, and despite many ups and downs in its career, is basically unchanged since the day of John Wilton. Run by the Wilton's Music Hall Trust, the Hall is still used for theatrical productions and is undergoing restoration. I am very grateful to Mr Brian Daubney, who some years ago showed me around the hall prior to any restoration and so vividly recreated its history for me.

My thanks are due also to my agent Dorothy Lumley of the Dorian Literary Agency, who has been such a firm supporter of Tom Wasp throughout my endeavours to record his adventures, to Five Star Publishing, and to my editor Alice Duncan, who dealt with Tom's idiosyncrasies so sympathetically.

ACKNOWLEDGMENTS

PROLOGUE

My name is Tom Wasp. Tom Wasp, master flue faker, at your service. Now you might wonder how it is I'm lettered, but that chimney's long swept and can wait a better time, for what I'm here to tell you today is the story of poor Bessie Barton, of how she was foully done to death in the year after the passing of Prince Albert, Her gracious Majesty Queen Victoria's consort. I heard tell yesterday, in the way we chimney sweepers do when at work in the big houses, that there's talk of a great memorial obelisk to the German prince. I said to Ned, 'Who's going to put up a memorial to Bessie, eh?'

Young Ned—he's my apprentice—thought I needed an answer, which I didn't, knowing it already. No one. He piped up, 'Mister Drake.'

'All them pictures of his, Ned, that your line of thought? Because he said "Cast Out" would make her live forever?'

'Yes, Gov.'

'Perhaps you're right, Ned. Bessie will live on in paint, but what about in Mr Drake's heart and mind? He means well, but he's putting Bessie behind him now, and who can blame him? Life's chimney was cruel to him.'

'Yes, Gov.'

I sensed Ned was losing interest, for he was casting wistful eyes at our money jar, indicating this was mutton pie night. There are some things more important than pies.

'Ned, we all of us start out up the same chimney. Some of us get sent up one flue, others another. Some draw the straight stacks of life, and other poor souls, such as Mr Drake, come across all manner of bends and flat sweeps, and go this way and that till they be fair wedged unable to climb to the everlasting light above them. Like the drying room chimney at Buckingham Palace they sent me up once. Fourteen bends it had up, *and* . . .' I paused impressively, '. . . down.'

'Did you get stuck, Gov?'

'Stuck? Why, they had to knock a hole in Her Majesty's own bedroom chimney to pull me out by my legs. Tom, she said, when out I pops like a stopper out of ginger beer, here's a golden sovereign for you, and you shall ride with me in my golden carriage to my coronation.'

'Did she, Gov?' Ned's eyes were as big as the iron ball I drop down a slanting flue to help my machine on its way.

Seeing that by such underhand means I had at last received the honour of his attention, I says to him sternly, 'They were bad times, Ned, before the Act was passed. They're still bad for some, so you thank your lucky stars I've taught you your letters and don't send you up nine-inch flues like the Walworth Terror.'

'I wish I was an artist,' was all the thanks I got.

'A picture can't travel round the world like Mr Dickens' stories, lad. It has to stay where it's put where only swells can see it.'

'I liked that picture of Bessie.'

And no wonder. Bessie was a stunner, and she shone out of that picture like she was going to walk out of it, saying 'Wotcher, Tom,' and winking in that way she had. But she couldn't. She'd stay there stuck fast in paint forever.

'That's only poor Bessie's face, Ned, not her soul, God rest her.' I could have cried for the pity of it.

Then it came to me what I had to do: set my hand to tell her story. I knew Bessie, I knew her life, I knew her death.

And as to who was guilty, twelve good men and true said one thing, but I shall tell you the facts that you may judge for yourself.

A NOTE FROM MASTER SWEEP TOM WASP

I want you to know Bessie's story, so I've done my best to write it in the way I was lettered, and if I mistake that path I hope I may be pardoned. Out here in London, there's a hundred languages and all of them could be called English. Each trade has its own language, and another binds the trades together. And scarcely a word spoken here would make sense to lettered folk.

I call 'here' London, for to my mind this is where our city's fire burns. Up West they have their own London, and see the East as a jealous canker on London's side, which heaves and pulses and rumbles with menace towards them. But the worst cankers live in the mind.

As poor Bessie knew.

Chapter One: In Which Poor Bessie Is Found

'Hey, sweepie, there's a dead 'un 'ere.'

Mudlarks must see in the dark, for the morning was still so black we should be invisible, Ned and me. The lamps by which we were making our slow way eastwards at Wapping—for we sweeps go about our business early—hardly lit the alleyways, let alone the riverbank. Yet many traders were busily at work in the mud, peeling their eyes in the dark with only pinpricks of light from passing ships and boats to aid them in their foragings. Swells still asleep in their beds, have no idea how many people work in the dark to make their lives run smooth, sewer men beneath, us sweeps above, street sweepers outside, all turning the wheels of a great city. Down on the riverbank work those that scavenge on others' leavings, and any morning you may be sure of finding mudlarks, sweeping boys, dredgers, old women up to their knees in mud, all seeking the means to live through to the next muddy morning.

Mud*larks?* I've never seen a lark but I've heard tell they sing most joyously. I never heard these nippers at the riverside sing as they dive in and out between the barges to steal scraps of coal to sell to earn an honest copper. Or, some would say, dishonest, depending on their circumstances in life.

There were four of them this cold March morning and in these parts, what's the point of hanging around for a pigman? The way I saw it though, the dead-un they'd found was some poor soul lying out there alone, and someone had to pay respect to that body.

'Ned, you run back to the Thames Police station, and fetch a pigman.' Even the Thames Police is better for my lad to face than a body. That's another chimney long swept, but its soot he'll carry with him always. Ned doesn't say much, but inside him are locked many scary monsters that lie sleeping until disturbed. I know about such monsters, and so did Bessie.

I am not a big man, having started the way I did in my trade, but I am sturdy for all I walk like a man half bent-kneed in prayer. My boots began to sink all the same in the mud of the mighty Thames riverbank.

'Dear Lord Jesus,' I prayed, 'You was a working man too. You must have known how valuable boots is. If you'd save mine I'd be much obliged, me being on a Christian mission, and not passing by on the other side.' (In case He'd missed the circumstances.)

The Good Lord was up early, however, to look after us humble folk, for the boots held fast, and I saw the body lying a few yards ahead, washed up by the river current. It was a woman's, clothes all ragged and torn, body bloated, bruised and attacked by fish, a common enough find in this river of ours. The poor souls throw themselves off the bridges and come down with the current.

It was then I saw the hair, full of weed and mud and entangled with the detritus of a noble city, but it streamed out unmistakably with its red-gold lighting the river mud. It was *her.* It was Bessie.

We chimney sweeps lead a lonely life, save for our fellow sweeps. The soot is so ingrained in us that even if we were to bathe once a week we'd never get the black cleaned off, and so most folk keep clear of us, not liking the way we smell. It's a hard life for a woman to share, respectable calling though I follow. I had a woman once; she died of the cholera and in respect

I ain't taken another. Ned's my family now, after I took his indenture from the Walworth Terror, now safely jailed for whipping the poor lad's feet and sending him up with fires in the grate, and tossing water on them to make him climb faster from the steam. Very tender is Ned still. He don't like water, and I don't force him to bathe, though it's been four years now. The subject ain't mentioned. His monsters, like mine, are private.

I was a climbing boy once, and remember full well the dark of the chimney. You never forget it. The smell of the soot, the darkness of the walls around you. Only the light above you guides you—that's in a straight flue, but what of those that slant, or are horizontal like the dead flats? What monsters may gather there?

I have a nightmare still, that I am wedged in the chimney, slowly wriggling upwards with bent feet and hands towards the pinprick of light above. And then it's blotted out; there's darkness above and the flames of hell beneath from those that light fires to make you climb the quicker. As I force myself upwards towards a dark sky I feel a hand reaching down to grasp me—not the blessed hand of God, but His fallen angel, my monster.

I used to wake up screaming then. Now, remembering Ned, I try not to, and retch out my guts in a shivering sweat instead. Ned's own monsters will only go if he has hope that grown men don't have them too. But they do.

Now looking down at that red-gold hair, the hand in the chimney reached out for me again and caught me by the throat. I knew that hair; I knew that ring on one of the few fingers that the fish had been kind enough to leave alone. I knew that dress. It was her Sunday best she was so proud of. My last hope vanished. The corpse was Bessie's.

Inside me, where there should be a man's fire, had been clogged up with soot, but the embers of humanity still glowed, and when I met Bessie they burst into flame. Now they burn my heart for the flame has been extinguished forever.

Let me tell you the story.

There's a touch of the wanderer in me, though don't get me wrong. I work my passage. For all I was born in the Nichol, but a mile or so from where Ned and I doss now, I had from an early age a liking to travel. At four I discovered there was a life outside the Nichol rookery, but I was dragged back. Boys of four were valuable commodities in the trade then, and still are. At five I was pushed up my first chimney, at a public house in Bethnal Green where the noise drowned screams. Bethnal Green was an eye-opener to me. It was yellow with sun and it had pie shops to thieve from.

By the time I found out Bethnal Green was not the world any more than the Nichol was, it was too late to travel farther. I was indentured as a climbing boy. I was one of the few lucky ones. I survived my indenture, and by the time I was too big to be of use I knew there were big houses and green spaces without chimneys in the world. I chose to stick to my trade once I was free. Why? Ah, that's a long story and I ain't here to talk of me, but of Bessie. I walked the streets of London, and by and by I bought a horse and cart to save my legs and feet, them not being in the same shape they were carved to come into this world.

The day I met Bessie, I had taken a fancy for Chelsea, where I could look at white houses overlooking the river, and where the sun weren't ashamed to shine. It's good for Ned, too, to see how the swells live. The chimneys are decent, though pots sprout like rotten potatoes on the rooftops, and the servants are a good class on the whole, and know what an honest working man looks for in the way of vittals after a job well done. Some of my brethren fall to sin, and this reflects badly on us all, since folk believe we are all being sooted with the same brush, if you'll excuse my turn of phrase. But I wander from the straight flue of my story, not being accustomed to the pen.

On that fine October morning, I let Ned call the streets from his grand position in the cart. 'Sweepie Soot Ho! Sweeeeup!' That often brings the quality folk out to see if I'm using a climbing boy so they can do their Christian duty and report me to the law. Then I has much pleasure in showing them my Smart's chimney cleansing machine, and Ned does a fine job, slapping his hands in the chilly air and saying with true pathos, 'Just one more chimney, then can I have my gruel, Gov?' 'If we've a halfpenny or two to spare, my lad,' I growl and before you can say God bless Her Majesty, Ned and me are tucked up in the scullery with muffins and cocoa, or maybe a glass of ale, which I'm not against, counting it more as food than the devil's temptation.

Ned's a lad of few words but his eyes does his talking as well as his looking. He's a thin scrap still, but strong now, thanks be to the Lord working through His humble servant Thomas Wasp. He looks like a scrawny angel with his yellow hair, washed only by God's rain, peeping under his cap, and blue eyes that shine out in innocence. Innocent he is in the eyes of our Lord, but not in the ways of this world.

Well, this particular day, in a house not too big and not too small, Ned and I and my machine had finished our work and taken down the tuggy cloth over the last fireplace. We were about to receive our pecuniary rewards when the parlour maid said to the butler: 'What about master's fireplace?' There had been one flue I was told to miss out.

'He's working. Not to be disturbed.'

'He did say that it was smoking and that's bad for him and his canvasses.' The parlour maid didn't care for the butler; that I could tell.

'Downdraught,' I said quickly, not knowing whether that were so or not, but not being averse to a further tuppence. 'Very dangerous. You take me to the master and tell him Tom Wasp does a clean job. No black stripes and never yellow—that's my little joke.'

She looked at me blankly, but led the way upstairs to a large room at the top of the house. Pressing herself back so she didn't get soot on her from touching me, she knocked and I heard an imprecation within to which I hope heaven was shutting its celestial ears. Then the door was pulled open abruptly and Mr Valentine Drake stood on the threshold, paintbrush in hand. He was hardly taller than I myself, and about ten years younger in age, myself being about thirty-seven, though I never rightly knew when I was born. He was striking to look at, with his long dark hair and fiery expression, but the vittals in this house must be better than the Nichol, for he couldn't be squeezed up any chimneys. He looked dramatic, almost as though he were performing at a penny gaff. His expression changed, however, and, bless my stars if his dark eyes didn't flash with excitement, even pleasure, as they fell on me. A rare happening.

'God has sent a miracle,' he shouted.

'Smoking's that bad, is it, sir?' I asked deferentially. 'I can smell it in the air.'

He stared at me as though I spoke a different language to his own. 'No, no, my health is good. I seldom take a pipe.'

'The chimney, sir.'

'Chimney? My dear sir, no talk of chimneys today. Immortality is to be yours. Pray step inside.'

Now I've heard a fair bit about immortality over the years one way and another: I heard it from preachers on street corners, I've heard it from missionaries; I've even heard it in the pubs come a Sunday when the churches want to drum up business. But I never heard a swell express any interest in my immortal soul, and I was most grateful for this promise of everlasting life.

'I'm much obliged to you, sir.'

'Tell him what you mean, Val. He thinks you're a Bible-thumper.' There was a rich chuckle, a woman's, and venturing into the large airy room I looked across at her, where she stood on a platform by the window.

I've seen pictures of Her Majesty, I've seen pictures of princesses, I've seen ladies in fine carriages and sometimes, in big houses, young ladies in ball dresses sweeping up and down staircases in their young beauty, but I've never seen a lady so lovely as this. She was posing for him in a white gown with no crinoline, so the skirt fell around her in graceful folds. A black shawl was over it, and her red-gold hair was caught up at the back and jewels set in silver upon it. And she was smiling at *me,* lighting me up with her warmth, as though I was a person, not a blackened sweep.

The young gentleman howled. 'You've broken your pose, Bessie. My masterpiece is *ruined.* I shall abandon all hope of it. You have deprived the world of my genius.'

'Nonsense, Val.' The lady did not seem upset at his shouting at her. In fact, she was laughing at him. 'Now tell us about your miracle.'

The young man promptly brightened again. 'My dear sir, pray forgive me. You see this canvas upon my easel? The picture—the best I have ever conceived—is entitled "Cast Out", and the lady is being driven from the house into the snow, having betrayed her husband. I wish to portray in the background an image of her future life, and you, my dear sir, are *it!*'

'Me?' Try as I might, I could not fathom his meaning.

'Inspiration struck the moment I saw you. The outcast. Who more so than a chimney sweep?'

'That's very true, sir.' I was gratified, for the swells don't usually think much about us sweeps. 'Greatly reviled we are for our black faces and line of work.'

'Yes, yes, you walk alone.'

'Now that ain't quite true, sir. We walks together, we sweeps, just as I'm sure you artists do. Why, we even have our own feast day, though it ain't regarded as it should be in these modern times.'

'Oh.' His face fell, but only for a moment. 'But there will only be the one of you in my picture. Black, in the background, a stark warning in a snowy street. I see you standing still as death, holding your brush as a symbol of what is to happen to this wretched woman.'

'I'm going to be a crossing sweeper, am I?' Bessie enquired cheerfully.

'You do not take me seriously.' Mr Drake was hurt.

'Bless you, Val, I do. But a smile never hurts, does it?'

Dear Bessie, even smiles can hurt. Somehow, somewhere, perhaps you smiled too often, and a clutching monster's hand came out to seize you. Did you see it coming, Bessie, did you suffer?

'Beg your pardon, sir, but why would I be standing still holding a brush in the air if it's snowing?' I was contemplating myself in my new role as a miracle.

'You are a symbol,' says he. Then, perhaps thinking I couldn't understand, 'Like an apple in fair Pomona's hand.' Now I couldn't follow him, but I got his drift like the first soft fall of soot.

'Suppose,' I said, anxious to be of service, 'I turn my back, hunched over a barrow, looking as if I was walking into a dark sort of future, with a chummy (that being a climbing boy) at my side?'

He gaped at me, and when he had recovered his wits after discovering that a nice layer of soot keeps a man's brains tucked up cosily, he rushed forward and, before I could stop him, pumped my hand up and down.

'Now you didn't ought to have done that, sir. You'll have soot all over those nice white painting hands of yours.'

He held them up before him, gazing at them as if in a trance. 'Soot is the symbol of fertility. Is it not considered lucky for a bride to see a sweep on her wedding day? What more appropriate than that "Cast Out" displays a sweep with his back turned to the woman who has fallen. Oh my dear sir, I shall pay you the price of twenty chimneys—each day.'

I sent word to Ned I was delayed and not to make a nuisance of himself in the kitchen (by which I meant he was not to fill his pockets uninvited) and not to forget to go out to see the horse was fed and watered. We'd left him tethered to the wooden rail that runs along by the trees bordering the riverbank on Cheyne Walk. Then I took my place behind Bessie, who smiled at me most kindly, even though I had to pass close by her. At first, I found the standing hard, for Mr Drake wouldn't let her talk so that I could listen to the bright voice, and my legs were used to moving, not pinning me up. I never knew it took so long to paint a picture. I stayed as quiet as a mouse, though why they say that I do not know, since every mouse I see is running like a dipper with the peelers after him, thumping through every bit of rubbish in his way.

I began to feel anxious; to be trapped inside a house for so long was not to my taste. I like to be coming and going, a free man, not surrounded by walls closing round me like a chimney. It was worth enduring for the sake of Bessie, however. I'd never met such a friendly lady, nor a lovelier. When Mr Drake told us we could go, I remembered the chimney, but he said not to bother, but to wait till the picture was done.

'Done? I thought you said you'd finished it, sir?'

'For today only. I shall need you again of course. Tomorrow, and bring the boy up with you too. And then the day after and after that.'

Well, as he was so good as to press two whole shillings into my hand, who was I to teach him his trade?

Behind a screen Bessie was changing into her own clothes, and I was so preoccupied with wondering whether my immortal soul was worth all this standing still, I forgot about her till she bounced out again. Had it not been for the hair, I wouldn't have recognised her, and even that was quickly bundled up and stuffed under a man's cap. She wore an old black skirt, neat enough, and a bright red gaudy shawl. You see many dressed like that, in markets and public houses, but not ladies like Bessie, although her beauty shone above it.

As I went, promising to return on the morrow, I heard Mr Drake say to her: 'Stay, Bessie, do,' and that laugh again from her:

'Now, Val, you know what we agreed.'

'I don't even know where you live, I don't know *anything* about you.'

'Windsor Castle will always find me at home,' she quoth blithely, as I heard her footsteps hurrying down the stairs after me.

She surprised me by accompanying me into the kitchen: 'Will your cart hold three?' she asked, as I lured Ned away from the cosy fire crackling in the kitchen range and the powerful smell of supper. I eyed his bulging pockets with suspicion, but decided to ignore them.

'A lady like you can't ride in a sweep's cart,' I said, most puzzled, as she walked beside us to the cart.

She hooted with laughter. 'Fine feathers make fine ladies. Look at me now. Do I look like a lady?'

'A lady to me, miss, and Ned and I are sweeps. We like the way we smell, just as Mr Drake must like his paint, but that don't mean we expect the same of others.'

'We all come into this world with the same smell,' she

declared. 'Anyway, I'm used to smells. So what makes a lady for you, Mr Sweep?'

I gave this my most earnest consideration, it being just the kind of question I like to ponder over, as Bessie hopped up into the cart, and off we went. Ten minutes later young Ned pipes up:

'A silk dress, and a clean face make a lady.' He was halfway through a muffin that had appeared from nowhere, for the pockets looked as full.

Bessie smiled. 'I have both, but do they make me a lady? No.'

'Education.' I produced the fruits of my consideration.

'You're educated, Mr Sweep, I can tell that. Does that make you a gentleman?'

I gave this my consideration too. 'To me, ma'am, it does.'

'Val would have me educated before he marries me, but I can't abide the thought.' Bessie wasn't smiling now as our old horse, proud of his very precious burden, plodded his way among the traffic past the Houses of Parliament, just as though he were a young stallion again. 'Val says he'll pay someone to make me a lady,' Bessie continued.

'Do you want that, Miss Bessie?' I asked, greatly daring. 'And seeing as how I just got above myself and called you Bessie, I'm Tom Wasp, at your service.'

'I don't know, Mr Wasp. Half of me wants to be a fine lady and ride a white horse, the other half . . .'

She broke off, and I said, getting her meaning and to save her from the embarrassment, 'He thinks highly enough of you to marry you even if you're not a lady born.'

'Too highly.' She grimaced. 'He worships the ground I walk on, he says.'

'But you're a good girl. I can tell that.'

'What's good, Tom Wasp?'

'That's one of those philosophical questions, Miss Bessie.'

'And the answer?'

Like Pilate before our Lord, I had no answer, so I turned away, making a remark about the falling night and the stars up above us.

Over the days that followed, we grew friendly, she and I, laughing and joking in a way that mightily upset Mr Drake. I stopped when I saw this happening, for he was a most serious young man, seldom joking himself—at least in his studio—though the mistress of the kitchen told me he laughed enough in his cups. Some evenings the other three Angels would come, she said. They were only mortal folk like the rest of us, I gathered, and there'd be drinking and singing and shouting all night long. They were Valentine's fellow artists who had formed themselves into a friendly group.

Bessie always came away with me; she never stayed with Mr Drake, so I got to know her, to be at ease with her, with her warm heart and striking looks. For all that, she never told me where she lived, or what else she did besides pose, nothing, and no reason she should. I often wondered when Ned or I handed her down from the cart in the Strand, just where she went each night.

I used to watch her as she bought a bunch of violets from the old flower-seller outside the great church of St Clements, and disappeared into the night, whirled away with a tide of humanity, none of whom cared a jot about Bessie Barton.

All that terrible day of Wednesday, the fifth of March, 1862, I couldn't help but think of Bessie's body on the riverbank. I was a-sweeping a regular chimney of mine at Paddy's Goose on the Ratcliffe Highway. I daresay you've heard of this public house, wherever you may be reading this, in America, China, the Indies; all those places even a hundred miles away or more, they'll know it, for matelots tell of Paddy's Goose the world over. A certain sort of matelot that is, and all the pimps and judies they could wish for. Not the sort of seamen as have seen the blessed light of course. I'd stop young Ned's ears and eyes up, but what's the use? He'll see it sooner or later. So I sends him up on the roof. 'Look up, Ned,' says I, 'first down in them alleys where the old devil is at work between matelots and their whores, and then up there to the stars and the sun and moon and heaven itself. Nothing can dirty them. They don't need hell-fire's chimneys.'

The preacher tells us turn away from sin, but I reckon he's never been in Paddy's Goose. It's easy enough to turn from sin in church, but out here 'tis better to keep your eyes wide open for sin, for else it comes a-creeping up behind and you don't recognise it for what it is. The landlord used to work for the press gangs during the late Crimean war, and now that's over he's turned his evil attention to the dockers. Still, even Paddy's Goose needs its chimneys cleaned, and my tuppence earned there is honest, even if nothing else is.

'They're only wapping,' says Ned in superior fashion, of what goes on in those alleys. He looks all worldly wise. I'm afeared Ned knows all too well what goes on, ever since he took up going to the penny gaffs. Those stewpots of humanity don't mind a sweeping lad amongst the other smells. I'm all for culture, but there's more going on in the audience than on the stage most of the time. I took Ned round to the workhouse one day and showed him the poor girls with their babies. 'That's what comes of penny gaffs, Ned,' I said. 'Most like you was started off in one yourself.'

I never knew Ned's origins. I bought him off the villain who sent him up chimneys, and Ned couldn't remember much before that. I like to think he was a kidnap baby, taken from a grand house to be sold, like so many, but more likely he was stolen from a workhouse, so all I can do is make sure he don't go back there by teaching him a decent trade. He knows enough of the other sort. The Walworth Terror taught him.

'Judies is only ladies who went up the wrong flue,' I reminded him.

Ned thought about that. 'Bessie wasn't like that.'

He had taken it hard when I told him whose that corpse was. There were tears in his eyes for the first time I remember. Tears on a sweep's face taste of soot as well as salt—I know, for they were on mine too. Ned fair idolised Bessie, and she was fond of him as well. None of his sly tricks while she was around.

Did I mention Ned was an expert dipper? Very skillful he was—or *is,* I regret to say, when times are hard. I was ill last winter with my chest and I can't say the sight of a fat wallet didn't cheer the spirit. The Lord tells us not to worry, for He shall provide. The way I see it, if this is the way He chose to provide in such dire need, who am I to dispute His almighty methods? I tried once to send Ned to the Ragged School, but he wouldn't be parted from me even for a morning. So we came to an arrangement. I would letter him myself, provided he went to Sunday school. He dodges it sometimes, but goes often enough to be taught the Lord doesn't approve of dipping (as a rule!).

That evening, the peeler from the Thames Police had told me to come to them at Wapping, down by the waterside. That's because I had told them whose the body was after Ned returned with two of them. They would have liked to take me up on suspicion, but there weren't no cause. Now it's a fair step to Wapping from the Nichol and the old horse needs his rest of a night, so I begged a lift from a Shadwell fish market man I know of. He don't mind the way I smell, because it makes a change from fish. All the same, I don't ask him too often.

The old horse had no name till Ned came, me never having got round to it. Ned called him Doshie.

'Why's that, Ned?' I said.

'He has to go a long way, Gov,' he answered gravely.

I remember how I laughed even now, though I wasn't laughing any more. My heart was heavy with the way of the world. All the fine things—and all the darkness. With Bessie gone, night had come indeed.

At the far end of the narrow alleyway that led to the front entrance of the River Police headquarters, I could see the old Thames, lapping by in its evilness, only the glow of the lights of passing ships to prick the darkness, and the lamp over the station door to show the water beneath, and I couldn't help but think of our Bessie in that dark sludge for days on end and no one knowing. What had made her do it? It was common enough, I told myself, girls jumping off bridges, and being washed up weeks later farther down along the old river. Poor lass, had Mr Drake taken advantage of her? Had she given in to him for the sake of an extra shilling? Or had she walked in the dark of the night once too often and come across some drunken matelot who forced her, then tossed her like a pail of slops into the river?

I walked along the alley past big placards about villains sought for misdeeds. The placards looked forlorn and unassuming, as though they knew full well they had as much chance of catching them here as winning the three-card trick off a broadsman. In this thieves' kitchen of the East End, one might as well arrest the whole blooming lot of us and release the few innocents.

The last placard made my heart stand still, though: 'Found drowned. Woman aged about twenty-five.' Just that, no mention of Bessie and her red-gold hair.

I went inside the wicket gate and up to the building. In the nearest room overlooking the river I found the Thames pigmen awaiting their turn at duty on the river, their warming toe-bags piled up beside them and snatching a bite of a pie and drinking beer, laughing and jeering. I wouldn't have known their faces from the matelots of Paddy's Goose, save for the lack of women hanging round them. They looked more like matelots than peelers, with their watermen's gear and hats, and they looked at me strangely, as though I'd popped straight out of a chimney; when I explained, one pointed me where I should go as though I contaminated the fresh stench of the river they thought they owned.

The old Thames belongs to no one and everyone. It belongs to the matelots, the bargemen, the mudlarks, the fishermen, the laughter-loving, and the lost and the damned. Our river's always there as the last loving arms for those that stagger out of the darkness of their rookeries only to find the whole world a rookery.

There in the section house where the cells were, I found Sergeant Wiley. I didn't take to him when he came to the riverbank with a constable; he was a cold sort of individual, suspicious as though he thought it strange to find a chimney sweep by his river. His boots had sunk right down in the mud, I was pleased to note, so he hadn't been praying as he should. He was a tall thin man, who didn't say much more than he had to, with a squint in one eye that made it look as though he was disbelieving everything you said. He had a regular police blue uniform on, but his regulation Wellingtons were still muddy from the morning.

'Didn't expect to see you again, Wasp.'

'Begging your pardon, sir, but I remember you asking me to come here most particular.'

He grunted. 'Just as well for you you did then.'

From the passageway came the sound of shouting and yelling and two peelers struggled in with a handcuffed drunk. Big man he was, with eyes like a glaring animal. It took three of them finally to get him in, and then he wouldn't shut up without a lot of persuasion from the peelers' batons. He was shouting and swearing so loud, Sergeant Wiley had to come closer to me to be heard. He didn't like that.

'What's to happen to Bessie?' I asked. 'Are you seeing that Mr Drake I told you of about the funeral? He'll want to know.' I had explained how I came to know Bessie when we were on the riverbank.

'We'll be calling on him right enough—now we know.' The one straight eye was on me.

'Know what?'

'The post mortem.'

So that's why they wanted me back. 'In the family way?' I asked, fearing the answer.

'No. But she were dead before she went in.' He must have seen my puzzled look.

'She was strangled,' he said, relishing the moment, and looking at me meaningfully, as though it could have been no coincidence I was the one that found her.

A great feeling of rage boiled up inside me. Later I might feel relief that she hadn't jumped in of her own free will, but for now it was anger at the ill-fortunes of fate, for the hand of our Lord is far away from such evil. He had not chosen to take her, but the devil had caused her to meet a matelot, or one of the garrotting gangs that were presently cursing this city of ours. They use a scarf or something similar to choke the victim so they can't object when their possessions are removed, and if they pull too tightly, and leave a corpse behind them, they aren't over concerned. But what would Bessie have to be stolen, except her own sweet body—and her life? No one who knew her would take that from her, and so I was back to my drunken matelot.

'She got a family, Wasp?' The squint now roved over me, and I racked my brains for anything she had said to me about that.

'She said nothing, sir, save she was born in a rookery.'

The picture had been finished three months since, and I had only seen Bessie once after that, though there had been talk of another picture, of me and Ned and Bessie all together again. I saw her only once more, in the Haymarket about a month ago, as I was going to the theatre there to offer my services. I'd been treated most royal there last winter, having settled a little problem of updraught. Finding this gentleman behind me in blue livery when I packed up my machine, I asked him, most courteously, for my dosh, and he vanished. Now this ain't unusual in my trade, but this gentleman did it before my very eyes by walking through a wall. It turned out I'd asked the theatre ghost.

Bessie didn't vanish though. 'Tom!' She didn't look herself, but she greeted me friendly enough that day in the Haymarket. 'Did you know our picture's to be hung in the Academy Rooms in the National Gallery? Val's submitting it for their summer exhibition.'

'That's good news, Bessie. I'd best see if they need a sweep. And what about our new picture? Are you posing for him again?'

She hesitated. 'I don't know, Tom, and that's the truth of it.' She seemed about to say something more, but then someone hailed her from a private hansom cab. 'Bessie,' this toff called, though I couldn't see his face. She ran across to join him, and I hurried to open the door for her. She paused before she stepped up: 'Take this, Tom,' and be blowed if she didn't put a golden sovereign in my hand.

'You can't afford this,' I protested.

'Oh yes I can,' she said, though she didn't look happy about the fact. 'It's stained money. I'm glad to get rid of it.'

That was the last I saw of her, till she fetched up on the riverbank.

I was in a pea souper over what to do when I took in the meaning of what Sergeant Wiley had told me. A real London particular. Murder—and I'd been the one to tell them of Mr Drake. I know the peelers. If they got it into their heads Mr Drake must have done it, nothing would stop them. I realised he should know of it before they visited him. Now I still had that sovereign, hidden in the fireplace—one place no sweeps look at in their own lodgings. Not that Ned would pinch it, but I don't believe in putting temptation his way. Mr Drake should know straightaway about Bessie; after all they planned to wed. What better use to put Bessie's gift to?

I couldn't find a hansom whose jarvy didn't turn up his nose, pretending he couldn't see me, so I took a four-wheel growler, and he only carried me when I showed him the colour of my money. But go I had to, and quickly.

I rode along like a prince up in the growler among the carriages and nightlife of London. The West was more lit up than the Ratcliffe Highway music halls, not that I go to them more than once or twice a year after my bath. Even though they are cheap, to have a bath and wash of clothes at the Whitechapel public baths for three pence halfpenny (and they don't exactly welcome me either), added to a shilling for the hall and a penny for ale makes an expensive evening.

Even the river seemed different up West, as though it were keeping itself more respectable by behaving itself in front of the toffs' houses. Here were swells in evening dress and opera cloaks and ladies in crinolines sweeping the pavements cleaner than my chimney machine. If it weren't for Bessie I'd have enjoyed it, but all I could think of was her poor mistreated body lying all cold in the Wapping mortuary. Cast out by life, poor lady, just like Mr Drake's picture.

I clambered down from the growler outside Mr Drake's house, and the jarvy, quick as a dipper, was there in case I took it into my head to jump in the river myself before paying his fare. There was a little bother over this delicate matter before I could get to see Mr Drake. The jarvy told me what I should give him, and I told him it was daylight robbery, when we were both working men. An honest fare according to the book was what I'd pay. One shilling. He agreed we were both working-men, but said he worked harder carrying me because of the smell. I said he wasn't getting any more, but he produced a most powerful argument in the shape of a fist, so I agreed there was logic on his side. Even so, I felt I'd let Bessie down by wasting her money on a gonolph.

It was after ten o'clock. By rights I should have gone down to the area entrance, but the servants wouldn't thank me for interrupting their evening cocoa, and they might refuse me entrance. I had an important message for the master, so chimney sweep or not, I had a right to knock at his front door.

Parsons, the butler as he calls himself, though he had to turn his lazy hand to most jobs, answered the bell, eyes popping out of his head like a brush from a chimney top when he saw who it was. He opened his mouth, but I got in first.

'Urgent message for Mr Drake, if you please, Mr Parsons.'

It didn't impress him. 'He's not at home.' He's never taken to me, has Parsons. He being a tall man and me not being advantaged that way, he looms over me like one of them ravens in the Tower of London flapping his big black wings. A Parson by name but not by kindly nature.

'I can hear him well enough.' I could. The sounds of laughter and snatches of song were coming from what I knew to be the dining room. The gentlemen were in their cups, but that way I knew there'd be no ladies present and I could speak freely. 'Who's dining?'

'If it's any business of yours, it's the regular meeting of the Angels, and Mr Drake is not at home.'

Although he hadn't joined the Band of Angels until a year

and a half earlier, Mr Drake had once explained to me that the other three had worked together for seven years or so. They believed that the Pre-Raphaelite Brotherhood did not go far enough in its portrayal of realism. It was the Angels' aim to rise above the darkness of life by combining good and evil in their work. By the time Mr Drake joined them, they went further. The Pre-Raphaelites had lost their purpose and early ideals. The Angels considered themselves their successors. They resolved on strength through unity. They would be loyal, Mr Drake explained (waving his paint brush so enthusiastically a splatter of black joined the soot on my old pegtop trousers), both to each other and to their great ideals.

The Angels claimed they had a message for mankind, but Angels or not, Bessie commented, that didn't stop them showing their appreciation of earthly beauty in the form of stunners. She didn't say anything more, but her eyes went dark and I had the impression her life wasn't easy. And now she was dead, and I was filled with unreasonable rage that the Angels joked on regardless.

'Oh yes, he is at home,' I roared, so loud they must have heard me over the sounds of 'The Ratcatcher's Daughter.' The words they were using would have brought a blush to the Ratcliffe Highway.

By this time, bent knees or not, I was inside the house, and before Parsons could seize hold of me, the door of the dining room opened. Mr Drake himself almost fell out, tripping over the mat.

Quick as an eel who didn't fancy being jellied, I was there steadying him.

'I know that smell,' he hiccupped.

'Tom Wasp, sir, with sad tidings.'

'Leave this vagabond to me,' Parsons said grandly to his master, all righteous.

'This, Parsons . . .' Mr Drake waved a hand in grand manner, tipping my stove hat askew in the process. '. . . is no vagabond. He is to be a model for my new masterpiece, "The Judgement," or perhaps, following the triumphant success I shall undoubtedly have this year at the Royal Academy—' Here another hiccup interrupted his flow '—with "Cast Out," I shall call it "The Lowest Room." '

' "When thou art bidden, go and sit down in the lowest room," ' I quoted, knowing my *Apostles* as well as any Angels.

Mr Drake clapped me on the back. 'Thou art well lettered, Tom, and a good man. So now, I say unto thee, "Friend go higher, thou shalt worship in the presence of them that sit at meat." Furthermore thou shalt join us in a glass of port. Come in and welcome!" ' He seized me by the sleeve and dragged me into the dining room.

'Gentlemen,' he announced with pride, 'the model for my next masterpiece.'

Three pairs of bleary eyes regarded me. Then one of the party, with hair the colour of Spitalfield's rotten apples, beard to match and a middle-aged belly as big as his arrogant smirk, came to life and raised his glass to me. 'The sweep again,' he roared. 'By George, the lowest indeed. Pray join us, sir.'

'Much obliged,' I replied amiably, as the dark thin-faced Angel put a glass in my hand. Not being used to drink stronger than porter, I put it down again when they weren't looking, bearing in mind the reason I was here. The third stranger, the youngest of the three, though some years older than Mr Drake, did notice. He picked it up and handed it back to me with what seemed a malicious smile on his handsome face. Golden curls and blue eyes don't necessarily mean the soul is pure, for all I'm sure Ned's is.

'What are these sad tidings of yours, Tom?' Mr Drake asked. 'You've been thrown into the street by your wicked landlord?

Ned has run away from your cruel servitude? Or have they sold the last of the mutton pies from the pie shop?' He knows my little weakness. He resumed his seat, and left me standing, as it should be in the presence of my betters. But I felt like Judgement myself, looking down at them, so mightily pleased with themselves and happy in their cups.

'It's Bessie, sir. She's dead, and you ought to know it.'

For a moment I thought they did not hear me. It was like one of their own pictures, so still they all were, like the apostles at the Last Supper being told there was a Judas amongst them. They weren't looking at each other; they weren't looking at me. Each was busy with his own thoughts.

'The police will be coming,' I added.

'Police?'

I don't know whether it was Mr Drake or one of the others who spoke, but the word was taken up and ran round the table like an echo in a Tudor stack.

'It looks like she was murdered, sir.' I pushed it home like the whalebone in my brush that finds its way into the tin pipes and chimney pots to clear out all the soot.

Was there soot here? There was no sign of shock, no revulsion, just a tension.

The golden-haired Angel fiddled with a glass, the bearded rotten apples reached for the cheese board, and the thin one for the decanter of port, but still no one said anything more than that one word. Valentine sat absolutely still, white-faced. Yet I could almost feel Bessie's presence in that room, so strongly was she telling me to be on my guard. Had Bessie modelled for the other Angels too?

'They'll want to know about her family, for the funeral,' I said at last.

The silence was immediately broken, almost as if I'd put their minds at rest. 'Of course, of course.' Valentine Drake glanced at his fellow artists. 'Thank you, Tom, I'll be ready for them.'

He rose, just as if I were a gentleman born, to see me out. But it wasn't for manners' sake. I could tell that, because when we were in the hall he put his hand on my shoulder, just as if we were pals.

'I loved her, Tom. Don't ever think I didn't.'

Then it struck me, why it hadn't occurred to me before I don't know. These were the only words of regret—if you can call it that—I'd heard, though it was as clear as the Thames is dirty that Bessie had been known to them all. They had been shaken and shocked, not because Bessie was dead, but because the police were coming and she'd been murdered. Even Mr Drake.

I walked home, my heart bleeding for Bessie. I wouldn't waste more of her money. I might need it. I'd plod along the old river, which had seen evil and good since the world began. I'd follow it from the waters of Chelsea, which suddenly seemed not so clean after all, down to the black stench where the likes of me are at home. But for all that, out East we are farther towards the cleansing sea.

On the far side of the Thames the buildings were silhouetted against the sky to the right and trees to the left. Here and there a light glowed. Those lights were a world away, for in between us was the ever flowing dark river.

'I'll mourn you, Bessie,' I vowed. 'I'll find out who did this to you, never fear. You'll rest in peace.'

Chapter Two: In Which I Size Up the Chimney

'Where to start, Ned, that's a problem.'

'Breakfast?' suggested Ned, sensible-like.

Most days we take our breakfast at Spotted Dick's coffee-stall in Cable Street with a coffee and two 'thin,' that being bread and butter, me having a liking for Dick, warts and all. It's worth a penny. Chimneys is one thing, but a man and a lad need something hot inside 'em on days like this when brain-work is called for, this being unaccustomed labour off Rosemary Lane. Our lodgings are in Hairbrine Court, tucked away from that rogues' meeting place, nice and quiet—save when the liquor flows, or when Mrs Parsnip, who lets the rooms to us, is having a spot of trouble obtaining her rent from the pair of costers above us. A very nice lady is Mrs Parsnip, save when crossed.

'We sizes up life's chimney flue by flue,' Ned suddenly pipes up, his mouth full of 'thin.' 'Like Mr Christian.'

'That's very true, lad.' I was gratified that at least some of my teaching stuck. I always thought Mr Bunyan's *Pilgrim's Progress* was much like a chimney. Pilgrim didn't just go along the flat; he was like us sweeps who climb upwards to heaven, meeting flats, slants, even downward turns as we go. At last we see the light and the Good Lord beaming down on us, saying: 'Well done, thou good and faithful chimney sweep.'

'He put the wicked captain in a lifeboat.'

I was mystified, not recalling any such adventure in Mr Bunyan's tale, but then I remembered telling Ned the stirring story of Captain Bligh and how the crew took command. I sighed, but then Ned's only a lad.

'So how do we size up our chimney, Ned?'

'Experience, Gov?'

'Truer than a flash note. Do we start at the fireplace or the chimney pot? What do we know about Bessie? We don't know where she lived, we don't know *who* she was. We can ask Mr Drake about the chimney pot end of her life, but the fireplace where she began is different. Was there soot on that part of Bessie's flue?'

'She didn't want us to know.' Ned opened his big eyes at Spotted Dick in the hope of more 'thins,' but Dick looked the other way.

'You have it, lad.' I bought him one of yesterday's half-price pies to reward him. 'She came from a rookery, so she said. But which one?'

There's still rookeries all over London, south, north, east, even west, for all they try to sweep them away with new roads and other good works. Swells in their grand houses look down from their front windows on the broad busy thoroughfares beneath. Why do they never look down from the back, and see some of the poorest folk in London clustered in rat-infested hovels beneath them? There's places so bad within a stone's throw of New Oxford Street that pigmen don't walk there, and which the missionaries have long stopped visiting. St Giles they call it, though to my mind it's an insult to a good saint. And take the Nichol—it's not so bad as it was when I first saw the light of day. That's a figure of speech, because there's no light there, down in tiny alleys and courts where the houses press so close the sun never gets a look in. And if he did, he'd shut his eyes quick enough when he saw what went on there. There's precious few born in a rookery as ever get out, especially women. But I did—and Bessie did.

'Flowers,' Ned said suddenly.

'Eh?' For a moment he had me lost up my own flue, thinking of rookeries where no flowers grow. Then I took his meaning: the flower seller on the steps of St Clements in the Strand. Every day, Bessie had bought a bunch of violets. 'She bought them at night, Ned. Not in the morning like most folks for their buttonhole. How do you fancy cleaning a flue or two up West today? We'll take Doshie and the cart.' Doshie was stabled close by at the Bear and Staff pub, whose chimneys are kept nice and clean in return.

'Not them Courts of Justice,' said Ned quickly.

'No, lad.' It's unfortunate that big public buildings have the worst chimneys, all bends and angles. They're machine and ball jobs now, but in my day we went up them, down them, along 'em, and were lucky if we got one with a register built in so we could get out if stuck. Ned never said, but I think he had a bad experience at the Courts. 'Don't think I'm going to push you up, do you, lad? You know me better than that.'

'No, Gov.'

He was very quiet and I wondered what memories he had. I could guess. On a bad night, when the monster comes for him, does he remember, like me, the cap over the face, being stripped of shirt and trousers to save space, back against the flue, your feet braced on the side facing you, left arm on the side to your left, brush above your head with the other hand, and wriggling up like a maggot? Oh yes, I remembers it, the dark and the soot, and the heat.

'Sometimes, Ned, you've got to face the dark beast before he'll go away.'

'What dark beast, Gov?' He knew right enough.

'We all have a dark beast of our own somewhere, lad,

sometime. He'll either come from outside or inside you, but he'll come'

'Did Bessie have one?'

'Maybe even Bessie.'

Ned went very quiet, and I thought for a moment he might speak of his dark beast, but he didn't.

I like the Strand. It's a street with purpose. It takes you from the West out East, like the old river itself, but it flows both ways. Even at seven in the morning there is no use calling the streets here. In this din no one would hear you for omnibuses, delivery carts, and the sound of hooves. The pavements are crowded, early though it is. No black-suited gentlemen, for they come later, and their crinolined ladies later still. What we have now is the clockwork that keeps them all going: milk carters, postmen, boilermen, street piemen, costers—all with their parts to play before they melt into the army of office workers.

The old flower-seller had had a pitch outside St Clements for as long as I can remember. Violet-sellers are usually little girls or comely young sparky wenches, tossing you a smile along with the violets. Not this one. She was old with the sadness of life and too tired to raise the corners of her mouth.

'Oranges and lemons'

'Say the bells of St Clements . . .'

Fruit's what old women usually sell in London streets, and I wondered why this one was different. Did she cling to what she knew, and to her youth and memories? Her violets were fresh bunched from Covent Garden, but few seemed to buy them, and it occurred to me that's why Bessie made a point of going to her. She looked up at me now. There wasn't even hope in the one eye she possessed, the other being closed by disease. 'I'll take a bunch, ma'am,' I says firmly.

She made a movement as if to say please yourself. She was wrapped in a rug, dirty but warm, but her boots had so many holes you could grow violets in them. I grinned at her, and seeing I meant what I said, she croaked: 'God bless you, mister.' She held out her hand for the dosh first though, not all sweeps being known for their honesty.

'I'm looking for a lady who always buys a bunch from you.' No use crying for Bessie's death here, where it can come as a friend with such ease.

The long hairs on the warts on her chin wobbled as she grunted. She'd like me to believe so many ladies stopped their carriages and climbed down in their crinolines to buy from her that she couldn't be expected to recall them all.

'Every evening about seven of the clock,' I continued. This meant little to her, being born with a world where time was a matter merely of light and dark, and cold or hot. 'Not long after lamp lighting time. She has red-gold hair, like the autumn sun. Tall.'

The head inclined toward me. 'I know 'er.'

'What of her, ma'am? Where can I seek her out?'

She shrugged and the blanket slipped, revealing a grimy bare shoulder through the ragged black gown. Then she cackled.

'I don't ask for their addresses, mister.' She was overcome with her mirth, and this seemed to give her a fondness for me, for when the tears had been wiped from her cheeks by a corner of the blanket, she volunteered more information, perhaps out of respect for someone who could make her laugh. 'She said she were a flower seller once, like me.'

Bessie, a flower girl? I could see it, the basket on the hips, tall, proud, that wink, that way of walking. Perhaps I wanted to believe it, fearful I might find she had some other, less sweet-smelling, trade.

'You never knew her then, did you, ma'am?' It could be twenty years ago.

'No, I wasn't always a flower-seller.' She glared at me. 'I were a milliner.'

And then probably followed the usual path from hat-shop to street, I thought sadly, though all I said was: 'I'm much obliged to you, ma'am. Anything else she told you?'

What she replied, startled me. 'I could see she were scared.'

'Of what, ma'am?'

But this she could not say.

I pressed her. 'How did you know?'

This nonplussed her. Even if she knew the answer, it required words not used every day. Slowly her head turned first to the right, then to the left, and I took her meaning. She was looking over her shoulder into the dark of the night.

'Was there anyone there?' I asked hoarsely.

'No.'

As I turned away, she caught my arm. 'She gave me this.' She pointed to the blanket with her free hand. 'And this,' she indicated her warm bonnet.

Yes, that lady was Bessie all right.

'Ned, we're on our way.'

'Where to, Gov?'

I'd be meaning figuratively that I now knew two things about Bessie, but Ned is of a more practical turn than me. He's a lad of few words, but he must be doing, whether it's sweeping, dipping, or munching pies. Me, I can leave the doing some considerable time while I has a good think.

'To Covent Garden, lad. The market. Where else than where the flower girls get their bunches?'

Ned thought this over. 'Why should they remember?'

It was a long thought for Ned, and there was some sense to it.

'When there's only one flue you do that one first,' I told him firmly. 'Get down the soot bags, lad. We'll earn a penny or two where we can in Bedford Street.' I still have a weakness for the Garden. There's vegetables a-plenty in Spitalfields, even in Rosemary Lane, but the Garden is the heart of it. When I was a nipper I sometimes slept back here in a cellar area, snug under my soot cloth, my pillow a soot bag. Even through the stink of the soot I could smell them vegetables. Heaven must be full of vegetables, I decided. The Good Lord would know that flowers are all very well in their place but you can't eat them like vegetables, and that knowledge makes the smell special. The fresh whiff of apples snatches at your nostrils quicker than charred logs, and add to that the shouting and hollering, the baskets borne on heads, girls running to and fro, barrows decorated gay with brasses, and big bustling country women in shawls and scarves, their menfolk in their smocks and straw hats—why, everywhere you look tells you that London is the hub of this huge land of ours.

Somewhere there is a place called country I'm told, though I never seen it myself, but their farmers and traders have broad accents and use words as strange as any Lascar seaman. I like to watch when a ship docks at Tobacco Wharf or London Docks, and the sailors swarmed off to the dens and brothels of the Ratcliffe Highway. I keep myself from their path, though being a sweep can be a protection. No gentleman could go there without losing all his belongings, and his clothes stripped from his body. If he left with his life, he could count himself lucky, for some end up meeting their Maker in Nightingale Lane, that runs between St Katharine's and London docks. But even seamen know sweeps have nothing worth the stealing.

All was colour in the market. Barrows and vegetables sprawled over road and pavements. Greens, reds, yellows, all colours, heaped wherever you looked. Here a pile of parsnips looking like one of those Egyptian pyramids I saw pictured in

Mr Drake's studio, there a heap of cauliflowers looking like bonneted white faces.

If I could get a chimney here and climb up to the roof, as I have to sometimes, and look down, what sights would I see? God looks down from His heaven, anxious to keep an eye on us, ants scrambling everywhere. Only we're not so orderly as ants. I would look down from my rooftop and see the market with its grand piazza and colonnade by St Paul's church. I'd see the promenade in the avenue too, where the superior fruit shops can be found, but they cater for those that shop at a later hour than this, and so all the noise and swarm of bodies was centred on the open market itself.

I liked to think that Bessie worked here, to think of her alive and warm, not as I saw her last.

A sweep has no trouble pushing through crowds. 'Like Moses we are, Ned,' I said grandly, as the Red Sea of humanity parted on either side of us to let us through.

'He don't go out.' Ned looked puzzled.

It took me a moment before I recalled Moses Daniels, a master sweep who broke his back when he was run over by a carriage in the dark and never worked since. His wife sells pickled whelks from a stall down Limehouse way.

'He who was given the Ten Commandments,' I said severely. What were Sunday schools coming to?

'Thou shalt not kill,' he piped up, anxious to please.

Tell that to Bessie's murderer, I thought, but did not want to remind Ned of what we were here for. There were one or two flower girls round the water pump, but most of them were sitting on the steps on the far side, nearest to the great theatre, bunching up violets, and giggling as girls will. The youngest was about eight, the oldest perhaps eighteen. Oh, the perfume as I approached. It made me think of my poor dead woman, and then once more of Bessie.

'Bessie Barton,' I asked them, sweeping off my hat and affording them a deep bow. 'Name mean anything?'

'A sweep, is she?' one asked pertly.

'No, gal. A dead body, that's what she is now. A friend of mine. Murdered. I want to find out who done it to her.'

They were instantly sober, for they all lived close to the sudden terror that could strike from the night for working girls, even respectable ones.

'No one here like that,' the eldest told me, after they'd listened to my description.

And then it struck me. The eldest was not more than eighteen, and it could be ten to fifteen years since Bessie was here, if indeed she ever was. She might have sold violets from a barrow or even one of the swell shops.

'It might have been a year or two back.'

They had already lost interest. A year or two back was to them as remote as Old Boney. Napoleon, that is.

'Try old Annie,' one offered hastily when I had the idea of stepping closer within nose range.

'Old Annie?' I moved another step or two.

'On the cabbages.'

She pointed across the piazza, and we forced our way through to a cabbage barrow. Old Annie might be about my own age I reckoned, but it's a hard life, so she could have been younger. She had the sharp eyes of a woman who knows her business, and the body of the countrywoman she might once have been.

'Plenty of heart, mister,' she declared with weary pride, picking up one of her wares.

'I'm looking for a friend, ma'am. And perhaps one of these fine cabbages. I'm partial to a bit of raw cabbage.'

'I sells 'em by the sack full, sweepie.'

'I'll find a nice fat pie then to go with 'em. All the better for my poor lad's rickets.'

Ned obligingly bowed his legs. 'If you please, ma'am, we would like to find our friend Bessie.'

There are times when a young boy's plea can achieve more than a man in the full maturity of life, and this was one of them. Her whole face crinkled in what might have been a smile.

'Bessie who, luv?'

'Barton, we think. Red hair. About twenty-five now. She sold flowers.'

'No one here of that name.'

'Some years ago, perhaps,' I said. 'Maybe ten or more.'

'I never knew a Bessie Barton. There was Lizzie Watkins though. Red hair, dark blue eyes, tall and a way of smiling at you crooked and winking.'

'That's her!' I cried, excited.

'She's gone, mister. Years ago.'

'Can you tell us about her?'

She shook her head. 'She were a wanderer, she were. She wandered here and then wandered off, or ran, more like.'

'And why was that?'

'She ran away *from* someone, if you ask me. She was only a slip of a girl when she first come, maybe eleven, but she stayed a year or two, till she scarpered. From her father. Someone come looking one day after she'd gone, that I do recall. My memory's good for an old 'un. Maybe it was the peelers she were afeared of. How would I know? No one asks questions here. You can hide in this mob.' Annie looked at the seething mass of bodies before her with gloomy pride.

'Why run then?' I knew Bessie. She wasn't a runner by nature. She was a sticker. What had scared her so?

'I'd help if I could, but it was years ago.' Annie sounded aggrieved, as she groped back through the mists of time amidst the cabbages of the present. 'I got it!' There was triumph in her voice.

'The cove she was scared of?' I cried eagerly.

'Yes.'

'*Who* then?' I was in an agony lest she knew the name but not the face.

'She called him Moonman.'

Moonman. I was back stuck fast in my chimney, with the light blotted out. The sky was dark up there, but the fear was darker. I felt sick in my stomach as we walked to the cart and it wasn't from the sack of cabbages. There was something about that name that made me face up to the fact that by following Bessie's footsteps I'd been drawing closer to that clutching hand.

We were lucky enough to find a six-flue job in Wellington Street, followed by a nice Georgian, and went back east the more cheerful for it with a tuppenny 'block ornament' of meat from a butcher's counter in our bellies cooked in the tap-room of the Golden Lion. Small, but very fine.

My conscience told me I should honour my pledge to sweep the chimneys of the gin-palace in Rosemary Lane. Rosemary Lane it will always be to me and Ned, though the authorities are trying to change its name. It being gone one of the clock now, the lane was a-bustle. Rag Fair, as we call it, is chiefly known for its largest collection of old rubbishy clothes, stuffed birds, bits of old metal; so much selection you'd think the old Thames had dumped it all there on a high tide, but enterprising costers have brought in vegetable and oyster stalls. You could say the same of its tradesmen. There's an old legend told in the Rag Fair pubs that it was a bloke from Rosemary Lane who cut off the head of our noble King Charles I. I can well believe it, if he was wearing a nice crown. It would have been in the local dolly shop before the day was out.

One chimney led to another, and it was growing dark by the time Ned and I found our way to Hairbrine Court and home.

'The moon has two faces, Ned,' it occurred to me to say, looking up at God's own lantern in the sky, 'and Bessie saw the dark face. But that was years ago. It ain't likely Moonman would still be chasing her, is it?'

Ned said nothing, but I saw 'im shiver. My heart bled for him, but all I could do was hide my own terrors and tell him God's Word will see him through the darkness. But he doesn't believe me yet, and at times like this I don't believe myself. There are hidden flues in some men's minds that get so choked with soot they can find no way out, and if Moonman's hidden flue was Bessie, it was all too possible he might be the evil shadow that still pursued her.

'Where next?' I asked.

'The pigmen?'

'They're not interested, Ned. Bessie's just another body dead by the garrotter's hand to them. All they want is to bury her and have done with it.'

Ned said nothing but I saw him looking down every court and alley to see if there was anyone lurking. Not only him. Not only London, but maybe all England too, were in a panic about the garrotters. Gangs that walk by night are no respecters of persons or places from Kensington to Kennington, Putney to Poplar, and Bayswater to Bow.

Then it struck me, thinking of public panic. 'My lad,' says I, 'I'll seek out Mr Joseph Tompkins, that's what I'll do.'

'Shall I come, Gov?'

'You've done enough, Ned.' I felt in a kindly mood. 'You get the fire going and buy a bite for supper and beer. Or cook one of these cabbages,' I suggested without much hope. 'I'll be back in an hour or so.' Ned doesn't like Tompkins. Nothing personal. He just doesn't care for loud voices, and that being Mr Tompkins' trade, he tends to give him a wide berth. It all comes of Ned's former master being a big loud man. If there's one thing makes being stuck in a flue worse, it's hearing the master roaring up from below what he'll do to you if you don't get yourself out.

I set out unwillingly myself, if truth be told, but when one's brain obliges with a good idea it's only polite to pay it proper respect and act on it. It wasn't hard to find Joe Tompkins. He was back outside the gin palace, that being a profitable pitch for a patterer. His voice could be heard even over the hubbub of the market, with all the costers yelling out their late bargains.

'Murder, 'orrible murder,' Joe was pitching loud. 'Respectable gentleman foully done to death in tavern gardens.' A cunning fellow Joe; he knew the touch of tavern gardens, the East's own pleasure grounds, would bring shivers to the spine and halfpennies to his pocket.

He wasn't too impressed when I said I wanted a chat. His chaunter played on. He was a young lad of Ned's age, who played the fiddle for Joe's patter, which was half sung (or bawled) and half spoken in dramatic hushed tones, like I hear through church windows.

'Murder,' I shouted firmly. 'Just what I want to see you about.'

The patter briefly stopped. Being a teller of the news, in the hope that some innocent passer-by might be taken in and buy his out-of-date periodicals and broadsheets, he couldn't afford to stop shouting for long.

'Something in it for you,' I added. I told him about Bessie, forcing myself to highlight the gory details, and ending with a sob. 'Our Bessie, beautiful artist's model, garrotted to death and thrown into the water.'

Joe is a man easily moved. He has to be in his trade. He has to believe in the pathos of what he's pattering about, and that takes some doing for most of it's lies. He was a big man; his frock coat only fastened over his stomach by one button. Goodness knows what goes on inside that huge stomach of his. It can't be food, for a patterer's life is very hard, even if you're as crooked as Joe. Perhaps he stuffs rags round his middle to keep him warm.

'I want you to spread the word of this murder, Joe, both in your patter, and on to your fellow patterers.'

He was fair weeping when I finished telling him the awful story. 'I will, I will, Tom. As God's my witness.'

'And He is, Joe. He is. He's looking down and blessing you for your goodness.'

'He is?' Joe contemplated his goodness for a moment, then said, 'What's in it for me?'

'Bessie had rich and powerful friends.'

'Then why aren't they finding out about her?'

This was a good point, but it was no concern of his, when I *was*.

'Suppose,' I hissed, 'it were one of *them* done it.'

His eyes gleamed and he grew more enthusiastic, seeing more material for good patter. It would be all round London soon that a garrotting gang of swell artists murdered sweet Bessie Barton. There'd be a nice ballad in it, too, that could go for years to come. I could see it all happening, but you have to start somewhere.

He leaned over me and hissed down, conspiratorial-like. 'Where shall I tell 'em to come? Can't be your place. Needs somewhere respectable.'

I took his point, though I thought he might have phrased it better.

'I'll send my lad to see your chaunter, and we can call on them.'

'What about having a broadsheet done up? A real one.' Joe must really be hooked. 'They cost money, mind. Your money,' he added, in case the point eluded me.

I thought of the jar of pennies at home whose level went up

and down like the Thames tide, only not so regular. The lean summer season was coming too. But it had to be done. Maybe I could ask for help. I recalled the words I spoke so glibly. *Suppose it were one of them?* I remembered the group round the table that night, and the funny silence when I told them about poor Bessie's death, and the lack of shock when I mentioned murder. I went quite cold as I realised we didn't *know* the Moonman had caught up with Bessie at last. What about that swell into whose hansom Bessie had stepped that day? You don't find the likes of Moonman in hansoms. Suppose one of the Angels, even Mr Drake himself, did her to death?

On Saturday, we chose a route eastwards so I could call at the Wapping's Thames Pigmen station. As it happened, they needed a sweep so it all worked out cosily. Only after I heard Ned's cry that the brush had appeared at the top of the last flue, and I'd removed my soot bag and was unpinning the tuggy, did I remind Sergeant Wiley that under my black mask of soot was the same sweep who'd reported Bessie Barton's dead body.

'I've been looking for you,' was all he said.

'Then you are in luck.'

'No, I ain't. It was for the inquest yesterday, and it's over.'

I'd been so set on how I was the only person interested in Bessie's death, I clean forgot there'd be an inquest. I didn't know whether to be glad or sorry I'd missed it.

'I sent a Charlie round to your place Thursday.' Wapping is honoured by still having some of the old parish constables to 'guard them.' They tried to get rid of the Charlies when the peelers came, but the old ones refused to go, and still plod up and down with their lanterns. 'You was out,' Pigman Wiley added, sounding most aggrieved.

'I'm a sweep.'

'I can see that.'

We were getting nowhere quicker than an honest man in Rosemary Lane. I put on my politest voice to ask the verdict.

'Death by an unknown hand,' Wiley grunted.

'Was Mr Drake there?'

'The gentleman was kind enough to attend, yes.'

He made it seem this was a big improvement on sweeps who couldn't be found at home on a working day. But as for his attitude, I couldn't make the man out. He was as cold as a dead eel at Billingsgate.

'What about the funeral?' I couldn't bear to think of it, but I had to know.

'Monday, Wasp. St George's in the East. Ten o'clock.'

I had to ask this too. 'A pauper's funeral?' All the pennies in my jar couldn't change that, if so.

'Mr Drake and his friends are paying.'

That was only right and proper, wasn't it, I thought. After all, she'd been their model, and there'd been talk of marriage between her and Mr Drake. All the same, there was an uneasy taste in my mouth, which hadn't come from soot. If the Angels were paying, it seemed to me they had something on their consciences.

'Have you found out any more about her death?' I ventured to ask.

'Why are you interested, Wasp?' He squinted at me suspiciously. 'You sure you don't know more about this business than you're saying? If you do, it'll be the worse for you. We don't know no more, but then we don't need to,' he said airily, as if trying to ruffle my layers of soot to see what's underneath. 'She weren't a lily-white Madonna, if that's of interest, so the PM said.'

I knew Bessie's soul was lily-white, whatever her poor body said, but he was looking at me in a kind of triumph.

'Forced?' I managed to ask.

He shrugged. 'Don't know. Ask the fishes.'

I wanted to smack my brush in the middle of his uncaring face, but that does no good. All I said was, quiet-like, but with meaning, 'Ain't you even *looking* for her murderer?'

'Maybe we are, maybe we aren't.' He left it till I trailed frustratedly out the door with my soot bag, then called out after me, 'Ain't you forgotten something?'

'What's that?' I hobbled back, hoping for a useful word.

'Your dosh.' He flipped a joey and a few mags at me. Four pence and a few halfpennies was all I got from the pigmen.

That evening, even Ned couldn't cheer me, but though I took him to see the Fantoccini man to cheer *him,* them little dancing dolls just reminded me the more of Bessie, and what would be happening at St George's on Monday.

St George's is a handsome church, set back in its garden from the Highway. The Ratcliffe Highway it will always be round here, for all they call it St George's Street now. Even St George would run from the dragons he met here. Afterwards Ned and I went to the Whitechapel baths, to show respect for Bessie's funeral next day. Ned said he'd washed his face, which was a big step for him. I couldn't expect more, even for Bessie. Up we turned in our Sunday clothes. I wore my check trousers acquired from Rag Fair of course. There was only the three gentlemen, excluding Mr Drake, me, Ned and Sergeant Wiley. The sergeant's presence surprised me. Ned and I were the first to arrive, being anxious.

'What you doing here?' says the verger, sniffing. Our trade was obvious despite our best efforts.

'I was hoping to find our Lord at home,' I replied with dignity. 'I see he ain't, but I'll wait till He comes.'

He didn't have nothing to say after that, but still turned his nose up at the smell. It always lingers.

We few rattled around in that big church like dried peas in a pod. I looked at the coffin, listened to what the preacher said, stared at the red roses on the coffin, but it didn't seem to have much to do with Bessie. I was too anxious to keep Ned on the right track of when to kneel and when to stand up to do any grieving for Bessie. But when we went outside to the graveside, then the grieving started. Ned threw in the bunch of violets we'd bought, and that brought a few sniffs of disapproval too, as the roses had been laid aside so they could be admired afterwards. But we wanted our violets buried with her.

After poor Bessie's coffin took her body to the worms and her lovely soul straight up to heaven, the sergeant hurried away, but Mr Drake stopped to talk to me, and the other gentlemen waited with him.

'A sad day, Tom,' said Mr Drake. He'd make a good model himself for a picture called 'Grief.' He looked terrible, pale, and worried.

'That it is, sir.'

'I should still like you to model again, Tom. Would you come tomorrow?'

You could have knocked me down with a puff of soot. Model? I hadn't taken him seriously that evening when he was in his cups. What did he want me again for? I ain't no Bessie. Still, this fitted in with my plan to seek out Bessie's murderer, so I rapidly agreed. 'What about Ned, sir?'

'What about him?'

'He's under my care, sir, being my apprentice.'

He took my point. 'Bring him, by all means. Mrs Holly can look after him if I don't need him. Now, Tom, I want you to meet . . .' Evidently not considering my call at his house that evening constituted a gentlemanly visit, he introduced me formally to the three other Angels. An odd word when I was considering whether one of them had fallen indeed.

It's said all sweeps look alike because of their sooty skins, but to my mind so do gentlemen, and no more so than at a graveside, dressed solely in well-tailored black. Even when not at a graveside, you can tell a gentleman by his uniform. In *my* London there's individuality, a scarf, a weskit, bare feet, a straw hat. It's true to say: dress a coster in Savile Row instead of Petticoat Lane, and he'll pass for a gentleman. I've seen a coster girl dressed up in a lady's cast-off crinoline and a spoon bonnet and you couldn't tell her from Her Majesty herself.

I looked most carefully at these three swells now they were sober and not in their cups. The thin-faced dark one had an intense look, something after the style of Disraeli, whose chimney at the Houses of Parliament I had the honour to sweep, though this gentleman was not, I think, of the Jewish faith.

'You will recall, Edward, that Tom posed for "Cast Out"—with Bessie.' Mr Drake raised his voice as he mentioned the name, almost, if I were a fanciful man, like a warning. 'And now he's agreed to model for me again. It will be a great work.'

All three of them were looking at me most curiously. They must be wondering how many pictures can accommodate sweeps for a subject, I told myself, but I failed to convince me. They were nervous, which was odd. Mr Edward Harwood-Jones bowed as deep as though I was the president of the Royal Academy himself.

'Tom.' Mr Harwood-Jones then clasped my hand between his, although I had no gloves, and peered intently into my eyes as if he would save my soul. 'Our Lord blesses you for your respect for Bessie.'

Most obliging of him, I thought, to convey the Lord's message as though he were the Archangel Gabriel.

Then I was introduced to Mr Frederick Fairfax. He was the younger, golden-curled gentleman, with delicate and refined features. He bowed. 'An honour, Mr Wasp, to meet again the genesis of "Cast Out." '

Well, I didn't know what he might mean by genesis, but being honoured to be compared to Holy Writ, I revised my earlier opinion of him.

The third gentleman, Mr Laurence Tait, he with the beard and hair the colour of rotten apples, did not bother to disguise his disapproval and looked at me for what I was, a sweep from Rosemary Lane rookery. Still, he was a gentleman, so as Mr Drake had introduced me formally, he had to bend that neck of his at least a quarter inch towards the ground he thought I crawled on. Perhaps his stoutness and big belly made it difficult for him to bend properly, I thought, being a charitable man.

It isn't every day, however, that a chimney sweep is formally introduced to three gentlemen, and doubtless Our Lord had His purpose in arranging it. Perhaps Mr Drake did too. I watched him now. You'd think he'd be relieved it was all over, but he was still tense and anxious, for all he shouted, 'A glass at the tavern in Bessie's honour.' There was a chorus of approval and Ned and I followed them to the roadside, not having anything else to do.

I saw that Sergeant Wiley hadn't left after all. He was waiting by a carriage, trying to look casual. I decided it was time that Tom Wasp set the cat after any rats that might be around, while the sergeant was still here. I owed it to Bessie.

'Did you all know Bessie?' I asked loudly, so he could hear.

Well, that brought a chimney or two tumbling down. Mr Drake looked at me so kindly, I knew I was on the right track. But the others were taken aback, perhaps at my boldness. Perhaps for some darker reason: they thought, with her coffin gone, Bessie was dead and buried. Not while Tom Wasp's around.

Mr Harwood-Jones answered after a moment: 'We all had that privilege, Mr Wasp.'

'As our model,' Mr Fairfax said lightly. 'Not in the Old Testament sense.'

Now had I meant that? Perhaps I had, for it was in my mind.

'You used her for your "September Falling," didn't you, Laurence?'

Mr Tait looked most put out. 'Did I, Frederick? Of course,' Mr Tait continued, 'yes, you are correct. An early work, unsuccessful work,' he explained to everyone but me. 'She was too brash.'

I didn't know the word, but I was sure Bessie wasn't what it meant.

'I most certainly used her for my "Jezebel," ' Mr Harwood-Jones informed me. He took pleasure in it, obviously thinking I wouldn't know who that lady was.

'Biblical,' I remarked.

'Yes.' He didn't like me speaking as though I was an equal. 'Although I put her in a modern setting, as I do all my works.'

'What about your "Circe the Enchantress?" ' Valentine Drake laughed.

'A failure,' he said shortly. 'Like Laurence's, a very early work.'

'Only a failure to you. It comes of having a clergyman as a father.'

So that explained the way he greeted me. I should have realised, having seen the missionaries down at the Shadwell workhouse.

Mr Harwood-Jones reddened. 'An artist is an independent spirit.'

'Spirits,' roared Mr Drake. 'How about that drink?'

It came to me that they were talking *at* me, but not *meaning*. It was an act, like those in a penny gaff, for all three of them. Soon they'd be off, the curtain would be pulled, and amongst themselves they would speak freely. But what would they be talking of?

They climbed into the carriage, ignoring me, ignoring the sergeant. They appeared just four young gentlemen in search of a bit of light relief—or so they wished it to appear. Mr Drake stuck his head out at the last minute. 'Tomorrow, Tom,' he called, and off they bowled.

That left the sergeant, Ned and me.

Wiley squinted at me malevolently. 'Popular for a sweep, ain't you?' he sniggered.

'They all knew Bessie,' I said inconsequentially, feeling I was on the right road for more than a spot of dinner at the coffee-stall. 'I'm going to find out who did this, and when I do, I'll come back to see you. Never doubt that.'

He looked at me almost kindly. 'How?'

'I'm starting at the beginning, and working my way up the chimney to the top.'

'Interesting.' He might or might not be studying me. Hard to tell with his squint. 'Policemen start at the end and work back. What's a beginning got to do with it?'

'It made her what she is.'

'*Was*, Mr Wasp.'

Is to me, I thought. So long as her death remained unavenged, I'd know Bessie was right by my side. 'Go on, Tom,' she's saying, 'and never mind the soot.'

Next morning Ned and I turned up bright and early at Cheyne Walk. I knew from experience Mr Drake wouldn't be ready before ten, but that meant all the more chance of a spot of free breakfast for us both, not only Ned. I needed to know more about those three gentlemen, and what Bessie had meant to them. What's more, though I didn't like to think of it, there was Mr Drake himself. Moonman could have passed from her life years ago. Mr Drake and perhaps these other three men had been her current life. There was something to what the sergeant had said, I admitted. No harm in working the chimney up *and* down.

'Take a growler, Tom,' Mr Drake had said to me yesterday, only he omitted to give me the wherewithal, so it was the omnibus for us with two changes, not wanting to keep Doshie waiting all day. Ned gets excited about omnibuses, but it came on to rain, and as chimney sweeps naturally have to sit on the benches of the open top deck, I wasn't sorry when the second bus picked us up, there being intervals in the timetables and us not having waterproofs. There's times I've been as wet as the salmon in the Thames before those buses condescend to plod up. They must pick those horses very carefully to make sure they got the slowest in the land, and even then the cad's face (he being the conductor) changes when he sees a sweepie. You'd think the rain would wash the soot off, but this world being cussed, it prefers to clog it on.

I knew something was wrong as soon as the tradesmen's door in the area was opened. Mrs Holly was crying, her plump pink cheeks all puckered up.

'The master,' she sobbed when I asked her what was amiss. 'There's police here.'

There was no sign of Mr Parsons, so I left Ned with her and boldly went up to the studio on my own. Only I didn't get that far. Coming down the stairs were two policemen, a constable with his leather stock, collar and chimneypot hat, and one who looked of very superior rank, Mr Drake, and behind them all Sergeant Wiley.

To my shock, as I stood aside, I saw Mr Drake was handcuffed to the constable. His eye fell on me like I was St Christopher.

'Tom,' he cried, '*you* know I wouldn't touch a hair of Bessie's head. I loved her. *Tell* them.'

'Many a man kills in passion,' Wiley observed, looking at me, after a muttered aside to his superior to tell him who I was.

'They're arresting me for *murder,* Tom,' Mr Drake shouted back up the stairs to me where I stood, stunned with shock. 'Find out the truth, won't you? It's lies, Tom, all lies.'

The police didn't say a word to me after that. Model or sweep or Mr Drake's friend, it was all one to them. That's the trouble with pigmen, and their strength too. They only see one flue to a chimney. I could see, too, it was out of Sergeant Wiley's hands now. He was Thames Police and this would be the responsibility of the Chelsea V Division police. What worried me was that they must be very sure of their ground to arrest a famous swell like Mr Drake. I couldn't believe it. He loved Bessie; he was going to marry her.

The front door banged behind them and Parsons reappeared the instant it did so, from the morning room. We stood looking at each other, like two cocks at a cockfight, summing up the situation, him, tall, staring down, me, short, staring up. *Tom,* I says to myself, *take control.* So I did.

'You heard what he said,' I says to Mr Parsons. 'And I'm going to do it. Back to the kitchen. We're all going to have a nice talk.'

And breakfast too, I hoped.

Chapter Three: In Which the Chaunter Sings

I intended to be a spider in the middle of a web, for the whole world is made up of spiders' webs. Rich folk spin webs with other rich folk, artists spin with other artists, boatmen and sailors cling to their like, sewer men and scavengers with theirs, sweeps to sweeps—and servants to servants. How could I, a sweep, knock on the door of those three gentlemen, friends of Mr Drake, and announce I'd like to talk to them about Bessie and saving Mr Drake? They'd have me thrown out, and I've got my reputation to think of. I considered offering them my services as a model but decided against this. If any of them knew anything, they wouldn't talk to me. The more I thought, I realised webs were the way.

Once I'd explained to Mrs Holly, the housemaid Ethel, the parlour maid Nelly, and the odd job boy Percy, and Mr Parsons had grudgingly agreed Mr Drake had instructed me to look into the matter, they were all eager to help, once a certain matter had been discussed.

'Why should we help?' asked Percy, him not being very bright, and obviously resentful of Ned's presence.

'Who's going to pay your wages if Mr Drake gets topped?' Parsons asked. Behind the green baize door he seemed almost human.

'Oh, Mr Parsons,' Mrs Holly moaned. 'What a thing to say.'

'He's right to say it,' I said, 'now Mr Drake's been taken up. The police don't like letting go once their teeth is in. What I want to know is what proof they have.'

They looked at each other, nonplussed. 'We didn't tell 'em anything,' Mrs Holly said, self-satisfied. 'Mind you, there were nothing to tell.' It seemed to me she added this rather too quickly.

'Did Bessie ever stay here overnight?' I'd never known her to do so, but I wasn't here all the time.

'That's the master's business,' said Mr Parsons haughtily.

'And the jury's,' I came back quickly, and Nelly, who couldn't be more than seventeen, screamed. 'Now see here, I needs to know how much soot there is up this chimney. So tell me the worst. Then we know where to start.'

'A slice of this beef pie, Mr Wasp?' Mrs Holly broke the silence that had immediately fallen.

'I will,' said Ned, but I wasn't in a mood for pie just yet, for all I'd been hankering after breakfast.

'Bessie told me the master wanted to marry her,' I said.

A snort from Ethel, a lady of perhaps twenty years with decided views and chin. 'Scheming hussy. Marry indeed!'

'Bessie believed it, and I heard Mr Drake say it myself.' I kept my temper, despite what she says of Bessie.

'What men says and what they does is two different things.' Mrs Holly sniffed.

'You're right, Mrs Holly, but Mr Drake seemed most fond of Bessie. Now, did she come here at other times than to model?'

'Sometimes when them Angels were here,' Mr Parsons said. 'But I never knew her to stay overnight.' He sounded almost disappointed.

'Who's to know what went on in that studio?' Ethel put in gleefully, and Nelly gasped.

Ethel was right, of course. Sin is as easy at midday as at midnight.

'Mr Drake's a nice gentleman,' I said. 'If we find out we're wrong and he did it, he'll answer to us as well as our Lord.'

'She did come one evening,' Ethel volunteered aggressively. 'It was your night off, Mr Parsons. Late last month. I let her in. Hussy. I knew what she was here for, although she'd come for her wages, she *said.*' Ethel sniffed.

In love with Mr Drake herself, more like, I thought. Perhaps she was jealous because he chose Bessie, not her, to be a model.

'That would have been—' Mr Parsons cast his head back in thought, 'Saturday, twenty-second February.'

My heart sank. That could well be the last night of Bessie's life, and unless I could find someone who had seen her alive after that date, it looked black for Mr Drake.

'They was quarrelling,' Percy put in, eager to show that he had a role of importance in the household, 'when I went to the hall to put out the candles. She come out in a temper and he came rushing after her, and told me to scarper.'

'Did he ring for her to be shown out?' I tried to be business-like, remembering all I could about how grand folk lived. You pick up a lot along with your soot bags.

'I didn't hear anything. She was only a model,' Nelly said.

I didn't take to Nelly, all big eyes and simpers. I'd met her sort before, all talk and no heart.

'Nor me,' Ethel said.

'And none of you told the sergeant about this call?'

From Ethel's face, she only wished she'd thought of it, but no one admitted to it.

'Mr Drake wouldn't have told the police himself,' I pointed out. 'So why *did* they arrest him?'

They all looked at each other, nonplussed. Now we'd cleared that soot, I knew what came next. 'Mr Parsons, you and everyone here are clever people, and much respected, I daresay, in this neighbourhood. Suppose you ask around the servants' halls of the neighbouring houses if they know anything? They'll be only too anxious to see you once news gets out that Mr Drake is taken up.'

I should have been a magsman, not a sweep. I reckon I could talk a bishop into the three-card trick if I tried. Mr Drake's servants couldn't wait to get started.

'We need to know *anything* about Mr Drake and Bessie, good or bad,' I warned them. 'And how about . . .' I went careful here lest I slip on the ice. '. . . taking it further? *Someone* did it, and what about those other Angels? Did she model for them?'

'How could we help there?' Mrs Holly looked troubled, though willing enough.

Parsons knew. He was eager to be at the forefront of this army of salvation I'd just prepared. 'I can find their addresses easily enough, Wasp.'

'Call me Tom,' I says, Wasp making me feel like a bad-tempered bee without the Mister.

'Good. And when we've got them—'

Mrs Holly had grasped the idea now. 'The butcher!'

'And the milk-sellers. Maybe get to talk to their servants in the pub,' I suggested.

They all looked shocked, as though the idea of going to public houses was a new one to them. Maybe it was to Mrs Holly, but Parsons looked sheepish, and Ethel giggled.

'A photograph of Bessie might help. If Bessie was model to lots of artists, she might have gone to a spring-me-up photographer and had one of these newfangled Cartes de Visites made. Or there might be a print,' I suggested, 'of one of Mr Drake's pictures of her in his studio.'

'We couldn't look *there!*' Even Ethel was scandalised. 'He'll have lawyers and his family coming.'

Mr Drake had never mentioned a family to me, but Ethel was right. There might be parents, brothers, sisters, descending on the house. (As it turned out, his parents lived in foreign parts, and he only had one sister, who was a missionary in Africa.)

'All the more reason to look quick.' Parsons was turning out a real pal. In another world, we might have got quite chummy.

'And when you get an introduction to the Angels' homes, you might recommend a good sweep,' I added, as a touch of inspiration.

That evening I walked alone through the dark streets—they're not over-generous with gaslights in our part of London—and the dim lanterns burning in the shops were my guide. I watched the grey spirals of smoke from the chimneys lifting into the air as if they would follow Bessie upwards. Step by step. I'd two webs spun now, but there was a third yet to spin.

As I said, we sweeps stick together—since no one else clamours for our company in the evenings. So once a month we master sweeps congregate for professional talk (and drink) at a public house. We come from far and wide, so we can take over the whole pub and not upset the landlord by driving his clientele away without compensation. Around forty pairs of eyes in sooty faces looked up as I came in, weary now, for it had been a long day.

'Wotcher, Tom.'

A glass of porter was in my hand before you could say the Walworth Terror. It's fortunate that, being a Christian man, I gets on both with crooked and honest in our trade. The crooked ones know I won't give 'em away, the honest ones have a respect for me being lettered, and even the villains that still send the boys up at least keep quiet and listen, which means some day I might do a bit of good for the lads.

Tonight I looked at them and raised my glass. 'I got a job for you, lads.'

And so my third web was spun, and perhaps the most important. There are two types of sweeps, as I have indicated, those with their regular beat and those who wander. Both could be useful in seeking news of Bessie, once the newspapers spread the word of Mr Drake's arrest. Strange, isn't it, how this world works? Bessie's death was nothing until a swell was arrested for her murder. Tomorrow the whole of London would be talking of her.

I got back to Hairbrine Court very late, and crept softly onto my mattress so as not to disturb Ned. But he was still awake, wanting to hear the news, anxious about my late homecoming. He doesn't like the dark.

'I'm here, lad, and weary.' So tired, very tired. 'I'll tell you tomorrow all about it.'

There was a silence. Then: 'I put a slice of pie under your pillow, Gov.'

'I'm much obliged, Ned, for your kind thought.'

But I was asleep before I found it.

Next day, with rent day looming as high as the mountain of rubbish that dominated the Nichol, which was so high it tried to block out God Himself, I had to revert to our trade, so I sent Ned to see Joe's chaunter. He returned to me speedier than a March wind down a tallboy. His eyes was bright with excitement, and not just because I could tell he'd been up to his tricks again, since his hand was jingling money in his pocket. 'Eight Friar's Court,' he says.

'And what or who might be there?' I decided this was not the time for moral talk of good and evil.

'Dan Truebottom.'

'Who might Dan Truebottom be?'

'He's news of Bessie. He's a purefinder.'

'He's *what?*' I groaned. If there's a class of men less well thought of than chimney sweeps, it's purefinders. There aren't many of them, and that's hardly surprising. However delicately they deal with their task, there ain't many willing to shake the hand of a man who collects dogs' muck for a living. However, if Bessie knew him, she must have seen something in him. There's one thing about purefinders—they're sure to be found home most nights. Dark evenings aren't the best time to follow dogs round. Early morning is their main collection time.

I knew Friar's Court. Everybody did by reputation. It was in the centre of the Nichol. The Nichol ain't what it was, thanks to a lady who's making it her business to get rid of Rubbish Mountain, but it's only raised itself a quarter inch above the stinking quagmire of humanity it used to be. It's found the effort too great, so there it's stopped. It still boasts the worst slums in London. Even St Giles has bettered itself a little since New Oxford Street were cut through it. But while this bettering's going on, those that have no hope simply stay where they are, for there's nowhere else save the workhouse to go. And they prefer their cheap lodging-houses, the stinking alleys, and filthy living conditions to what they see as a living death. Their time's their own, if nothing else, and they can live with their families instead of being separated in the workhouse. So on they go in the Nichol, still living ten or more to a room.

I kept to the chief street, Club Row. At least the danger's out in the open there, not lurking to grab you by the throat from a doorway. It was a gathering point not for the real villains, but those that were trying their paces. I marched past gangs of them while they looked at me, passed the hovels of vice you couldn't honour with the name of public house, from which the white faces of them that had given up the fight for a decent life stared out hopelessly. And so I came to Friar's Court.

The first thing I wondered about Daniel Truebottom, when I climbed to his room at the top of the house, was how he managed his job with only the one hand. The other ended in a stump. Purefinders need two hands, one for the bucket, the other to pick up their smelly finds. Who am I to talk about smell? I grow used to the smell of soot; purefinders may find a pleasure in dogs' muck. There was only the one room but he seemed to have it to himself. A straw mattress for a bed, two rickety-looking chairs, a fireplace, a table, and a number of upturned wooden fruit boxes, one of which held a basin. A bucket of water at his side. There was one unusual thing though.

He followed my eyes. 'My mother.' His eyes lingered on the daguerreotype of an elderly lady, quite smartly dressed. 'I weren't always a purefinder,' he said angrily, reading my thoughts. He indicated the stump. 'Till this, I worked in a mill—a good job too. After it happened I came down south to look for another. This is what I come to, and even this is not so good as it was. There's too many of us in it, and only so many dogs. The tanning and bookbinding leather trade can't use all the dung we get now. I gets six shillings a week, mostly. It does for me.'

'And your mother?' I was curious.

'Dead these two years. But here, not in the workhouse. It was Bessie done that for her.'

'Tell me, if you please.'

'When trade went slack, I couldn't keep us both. It broke my heart to have to say it, but "Mother," I said, "in the workhouse you get fed. Here we both starve." Then one day, about two years before Mother died, I was following my trade outside the Dragon music hall down in Bermondsey—nice and handy for the tanneries there—when Bessie flies out of the door and knocks the pail from my hand in her haste. When she saw what she done, she insisted on helping me pick it up herself. Laughed, she did. Serve me right, she said, and these were old gloves anyway. She left them with me, and I washed them up nice for Mother. When she found out Mother was ill, she came to see her. She couldn't spare much, she said, but what she could would keep Mother out of the workhouse. And it did, till she died of lung disease. I still saw Bessie but I wouldn't take her money. For all I'm an honest trader and don't mix brick mortar with the dung, I can get by. Till it's my turn for the workhouse.' He paused. 'The patterer said she was dead. Murdered.'

'Yes. And I'm to find out who did it.'

'Dead,' he repeated. 'Ah, well. It's the same wherever you go. The good never last.'

'In heaven they do,' I said stoutly.

Daniel reflected on this. 'I followed Him when I was in the mill. Here, it ain't easy to track Him down.' He looked at the stump.

'This music hall you mention, sir,' I asked quietly. 'Was she visiting it?'

'Working there. That would be about four to five years ago.' He hesitated. 'I was up West today—better pickings up there, because the dogs get more to eat—and I heard them shouting, "Man arrested for model's murder." Was that Bessie?'

'Yes. I knew 'em both,' says I, 'and it's my belief Mr Drake wouldn't hurt a fly.'

'Bessie were a woman,' Dan said, and we were both silent, knowing what we was both thinking. It put us in accord.

'Did Bessie still come here to see you?'

'No. We met at a coffee-stall, by the Tower. Last time would have been about six weeks ago.'

'Do you know where she lived?'

'She never told me. Like me, she knows it's best to be alone. She were born in a rookery, she said, like the Nichol. I was surprised, for I had set her down as a rich lady at first. That made her laugh when I told her. "No, St Giles it was for me," she told me.'

So now I knew that at least. 'Anything else she told you of herself?'

'Only that she was an artist's model again. When Mother died she was still at the Dragon, but then she left to try modelling. That didn't work, so she went back to the halls and stayed there till some swell artist came to persuade her back. She'd been his model for about a year, the last time I saw her.'

'Did she mention Mr Drake?'

'No. She had something on her mind, though. "You're free," I said to her, "you can walk away when you like." "Not always, Dan," she said. "Life isn't as easy as walking away." "Oh, it is," I said, foolishly. "Did you walk away from your mother when she were spitting up blood?" she asked, and I had nothing to say to that.'

'She was scared of someone once,' I said. 'Know who that was?'

'Not me,' he said humbly. 'But you're right. She wouldn't come to the Nichol after Mother died, and when I said I'd escort her, she wouldn't have it. That's when we fixed the coffee-stall. She said she'd had enough of rookeries.'

'Did she ever mention the name Moonman to you?'

'Her joke?' He picked up a piece of sacking and blew his nose on it. ' "I'll be sunny till the Moonman gets me," she was always saying, and when I asked her her meaning, she said it were an old song and meant nothing. But perhaps it did, for once when I said it jokingly myself, she were scared out of her mind, till she realised I meant no harm. You think he was real, Mr Wasp? That he caught up with her? Murdered her?'

'Maybe, maybe not.'

'You find him out, Mr Wasp, and if I can help, I will. I can take my buckets anywhere you wish, and listen. I'd offer you my hand on it, only you might not like to take it. But there's a cold tap in the yard and I wash it regular.'

His eyes had tears in them, and seeing that, I took his hand.

And not just for Bessie.

Inch by inch up the chimney, wedge into the angles if it narrows too much, slowly does it, a careful clean with scraper and brush. So now I knew where Bessie was reared. St Giles, only a stone's throw from the grand houses and shops of New Oxford Street and Broad Street. But where to start looking? There lay my problem. Part of the St Giles Bessie would have known had gone now, and many of the people it displaced simply tucked themselves into what remained and made it worse. The rookeries housed a moving population, too, in their lodging houses. Every vagrant from the country fetched up in one, all looking for a better tomorrow, some prepared to work for it, some waiting for it to fall like the heavenly manna from the sky. No one could afford much to have their chimneys swept in St Giles, even if they boasted one, and it wasn't a place to take Ned to, so I set out alone next morning, hoping that inspiration might come. I took one of my pennies from the jar and bought a real newspaper that I might know what happened to Mr Drake. All wasted, because there was nothing in it save the bare announcement of his arrest.

I was not going to call on Sergeant Wiley to ask him what was happening, mindful of my promise only to go when I'd found the murderer. Wandering round St Giles made this seem a hopeless task. They were a different sort to the Nichol. There they are lost, crushed without hope; here they're like rats fighting over every crumb, defending their corner with sharp claws and eyes. Man, woman and child, all engaged in the same struggle for a few of the Queen's coins. I often wonder if she knows that the coins with her head on 'em are the cause of so much trouble.

I tried a few places, but they had never heard of Bessie. A pigman standing admiring St Giles from a safe distance laughed in my face at my talk of a friend who used to live there. And no wonder. Barton wasn't her name then, nor probably Watkins either, and I didn't even know if her Christian name was Bessie. I came across an old woman who looked as though she'd been born, lived and was about to die in St Giles, and asked her if she knew of a girl who ran away to be a flower seller. She didn't even take the pipe out of her mouth to spit at me. I can't blame her. What were flowers to her?

How did one run away from a rookery? It would be easy enough to run from these courts and alleys, along the narrow streets, and thus up to the big wide roads that skirted the darkness. But what then? For whether you went along New Oxford Street or Great Queen Street into Lincoln's Inn, you still carted the rookery with you in your heart. And it's my guess Bessie never could shake the fear of it off. Outside she had, but not inside. It felt strange to be here, without Ned, and without my soot bag. Fanciful ideas began to come into my head. Suppose I never got out into the fresh smoky air again? Suppose there was a wall I couldn't climb to stop my going back home again?

I asked a few more people. Some answered, some didn't, and I realised I was wasting my time. I could have been speaking to Bessie's family for all I—or they—knew.

There were chimneys requiring my attention for the next two days, and then followed the Lord's Day, so it was Monday evening before we could visit the Dragon music hall in Bermondsey. This time I took Ned, thinking not much harm could come to him there. It would be a bit of a holiday for him. We went to the trouble of paying for another bath before we went, not knowing the class of person we might meet. When I say we, I mean I did and Ned came to scrub my back. I didn't force him in himself. That's got to be his decision. As I took off my clothes, I was glad it was nearly spring now, and winter was passing. That made me think of Bessie, and I was colder at heart though warmer of body when I climbed out. A waste of three pence for it was no great palace, this music hall, when we got there. No airs and graces like they give themselves now. It was just a pub with a room built on. I was sorry we'd spent money on an omnibus, for we had no need to impress here.

By now I'd had by courtesy of the hand of Master Sweep Bolly Burke (everyone calls him that, though I don't know why), a photograph of Bessie, unearthed by Parsons, and now I flashed it before the publican, an unfriendly individual who showed more interest in entrance fees to the hall than our mission.

'You a pigman?' was all he growled, pushing two pints of ale towards us, unasked. I duly produced a penny.

'Do I look like it?' I was hurt. 'You ought to be more careful. I'm a sweep.'

He looked at my face and then at my bowed legs, and that was enough. Not that he exactly warmed to my company even then. 'We don't like blokes asking questions here.'

'If Bessie were a friend of yours and someone killed her, you'd ask them yourself.'

He considered this, and grudgingly said, 'Ask away, sweepie. She your doxy, was she?'

'A friend.' A doxy? My Bessie? I don't even think of my poor woman who died of the cholera that way.

He looked at the picture again. 'That's the one who's been murdered, ain't it?' There were posters all over London with a sketch of Bessie now Mr Drake's arrest had made it of interest.

'Yes.'

'What if she did work here?' He was a careful cove.

'All I want to know is when she left and why she left. And whether she seemed scared of anyone.'

'Wait here.'

He came back in a minute or two, and jerked his head for me to go into the taproom. I told Ned to stay where he was, having bought him a ginger beer. In the corner, studying an empty glass of mild and bitter as though it were the Holy Word itself, was an old gentleman with a white beard, smoking cap, dirty white waistcoat and rheumy eyes. 'Me father,' the publican's voice floated after me.

I saw the way the wind blew down this chimney, so I bought him a drink, sat down and kept it in my hand.

'Bessie,' I said, 'with the red hair. Worked here four or five years ago.'

'Did she?' He eyed that drink.

'Yes, if you want this,' I says, moving it away. His hand came out quicker than I moved mine though, and the contents sloshed over as he pulled it towards him.

'Maybe she did work here.' He sucked the beer in noisily, as though it were the first one he'd seen since Michaelmas.

'Singer, was she?' I asked.

'Serving girl. Took drinks round the hall.'

'Why did she leave?'

'Wouldn't oblige.'

'In what way oblige?' I asked dangerously.

'The customers. Not good for trade.' His eyes watered, as though in memory of some ancient time when a woman could be as important to him as beer. He leered. 'Wouldn't show what she 'ad or let 'em touch 'er.'

Good for you, Bessie, I thought.

'She left, and good riddance. Came to a bad end, I wouldn't be surprised. She had a sister worked here too. Now she *would* oblige. A nicer type altogether.'

'A sister? Still here?' Now I was getting payment for my pint.

'No. She went as well. Off to the streets probably. More money in it.'

'And that's all you know of either of them?'

'Yes.' He wiped his nose on the back of his sleeve most

elegantly. He pushed the now empty glass towards me.

I pushed it back. 'No, sir.'

He returned it again smartly. 'My memory freshens up well with a pint inside me.'

I took the hint, and when I hobbled back he snatched it from me. A trick, probably, but there, I was ashamed of my bad thoughts for he was willing to talk.

'Just before Bessie left . . .' He spat on the floor to emphasise his point, not bothering with the politeness of the spittoon. '. . . a geezer came here looking for her.'

A rising excitement inside me. 'What sort of geezer? What was his name?'

'How would I know? This was years ago. He wanted to know where she was.'

'Did you tell him?'

'Why not? He paid his three pence. I saw them talking in between turns. She didn't like him. I could see that. She was pale, very pale. Still, none of my business.'

'What was he like, this geezer?'

'He weren't a dook, that I could tell. What do you think he was?' he snarled. 'Big fellow, coster type, cap, jacket, dirty weskit, cracked boots, we get 'em in here all the time.' He looked in superior fashion down his own waistcoat, filthy with the spillage from beer and other tasty morsels from his mouth.

'Age?'

'He were a coster. How can you tell? Maybe twenty-five or fifty-five.'

'I'm much obliged,' I said, gritting my teeth and hoping to get out of there before I forgot that I was a good Christian and hit him.

'Tell you one thing,' his voice floated after me, 'his face was funny.'

I stopped. 'Funny?'

'He were a handsome bloke, round jolly face, only—'

'Only what?'

'One side was up, the other down.'

I stared at him, not taking his meaning at all, and believing I was being joked with.

'A scar it was,' he went on. 'It's what made him stick in my mind. It had faded, but it dragged one side down, as though he'd put his shutters up for the night.'

'Very poetic,' I said, though a chill ran through me like a damp November fog. I didn't say any more. They were ringing the bell for the show to begin and besides, I knew who it was. The Moonman. A moon has two faces and that was his dark one. The one with the hidden flue of black soot that sent him following in Bessie's footsteps, tracking her down little by little—until at last he found her.

'Now, Ned, where does a man start looking for one of the sisterhood?' I asks, not meaning a lad of his age to answer. But of course he did. I forget how quickly they grow.

The sisterhood in London is large, and it would be like searching for a particular grain of soot in an unswept chimney.

'The Haymarket.'

'No, lad. That's more for them that have fallen in the world. They started well and then temptation comes their way, and they trip right over it into the deep pit.'

Ned were unusually obstinate. 'You gets all sorts of judies there.'

I paid more attention to him this time. 'You may be right, Ned. If Bessie's sister left a music-hall for better pickings, she could well be up West, and the Haymarket would be the first place she'd think of, being born in St Giles. She's not likely to go straight to the Seamen's Rest in the old Highway, is she?'

That was the end of the long road for prostitution, and the Ratcliffe Highway ladies of the night guard their own territory too jealously to let strangers in. The good old Haymarket shelters all types of ladies, according to the time of day: those of high fashion, those of middle fashion, those that ply honest trades like hot chestnut and ginger beer sellers, those that ply dishonest ones like the dippers—and the prostitutes. They come in all shapes and sizes too, from those that just missed being acceptable at Kate Hamilton's night house in Leicester Square to those that have crawled out of St Giles to earn a penny if anyone will have them.

However, there was a delicate point. How was I, even with Ned with me to look respectable, to find one judy out of the thousands that flock round the theatres and cafés of Piccadilly and the Haymarket? True, the Haymarket Theatre was closed at the moment, for the new season would not begin until the Monday after Easter Day. That wouldn't stop the judies, but since Easter this year would be twenty-first of April, the Haymarket could not, I believed, be as crowded with theatregoers as usual. But even if I saw a judy with red-gold hair, my intentions could well be mistaken, and it could prove a very expensive business for my pot of pennies.

Then I started thinking straight, not aslant. This was a job for a patterer, or better, the regular sweep round this way, him whom I'd been obliging when I met Bessie here that day. I decided to track down Big Billy—this being a joke, for he's so tiny I reckon he could still get up a seven-inch flue like he did when he were a chummy. He's a miserable old cuss with it, and he still uses boys when he's half a chance. He does what a lot of them do. He has a machine and a boy with him, and if the customer asks no questions it's up the chimney with you, my lad, and never mind the law. There's a commission on at the moment, so I heard, to look into violations of the 1840 law. Gentlemen are coming round asking questions, though they ain't got as far as Rosemary Lane yet—and when they do they're more likely to get a soot bag in the face than a civil answer. Still, Big Billy owes me a favour for protecting his trade while he was down with the fever, and now was the time to remind him of it.

It took three days before he came to Hairbrine Court to tell me—and that was because he happened to be in the Lane, not because he thought so highly of me he'd traipse all the way out East.

'I found her.'

'Where is she?'

'Can't tell you. She don't want to know nothing about Bessie, murdered or not.' Good old Big Billy, I could see, was delighted I was getting nowhere but that he couldn't be blamed for it. 'Says she heard all about the murder but didn't know it was Bessie, because Barton wasn't the name she knew her sister by. Now she does know she don't want to know any more.'

I could see it was time for a little persuasion. I went to the jar of pennies, the best persuader I've ever known. 'Where is she, Billy?'

His eyes brightened. 'Haymarket. Outside the theatre.'

I knew her right away. She hadn't got Bessie's looks, nor her red-gold hair. She was mean faced where Bessie was open and generous, skinny where Bessie overflowed, but there was something about her I recognised. She had a way of holding her head, and the eyes were the same too. That's what must have fetched in the customers, I reckoned.

It was still crowded in the Haymarket, for there were gambling houses, coffee houses and restaurants, even if the big theatre was closed. Nevertheless, at six o'clock, when the gaslights were only just lit, Bessie's sister stood out by the gaudy dress and spangles. No silks, satins and laces for this end of the trade. More like cheap cotton or taffeta as bright as it comes, with a pork-pie hat. I had hesitated before bringing Ned with me, but remembering a lad can work wonders sometimes with a cussed woman, I let him come.

I ain't never seen a woman *scared* of a lad though! She took one look at me, heard what I wanted, and seeing my battered top hat from Rag Fair and the black marks of my trade, she seemed all set to give me a piece of her mind. Then her eyes fell on Ned, and she turned as if she were going to make for the nearest alleyway of escape.

'Wait a minute!' I bawled.

Not unnaturally, she took no notice, but in her haste she ran straight into a barrel of elder wine at the side of its proud seller and tripped over it.

Like a true gentleman, I hauled her to her feet, and she glared at me as I apologised to the indignant tradesman. 'Who's that?' she snarled, jerking a grimy finger at Ned. Perhaps her clients never stop to look at her fingers. For all my hands are black, I try to keep my fingernails decent with the end of my pipe-cleaner.

'My apprentice,' I says in some surprise.

'That true?' she shot at Ned.

'Yes, miss.' Ned takes the adult world and its eccentricities in his stride. Why get bothered, is his feeling. It's as it is. (Except, of course, when it trespasses on his past.)

She relaxed a little, but was still suspicious.

'I want to talk about your sister, miss,' I said quietly.

'Don't know anything about Bessie.' She hitched the dark spangled dress higher over her shoulders, her eyes looking out hopefully for a customer over my shoulder. Me being shorter than her, that wasn't difficult.

If I didn't know already, I did now. 'She was murdered, miss. Don't you want to find out who did it?'

'We all have to make our own way.'

'Even though she got you your job at the hall?'

She shrugged and seeing a toff passing, shouted, 'Hey, mister.'

Fortunately he preferred to take a cab than her offer, and she was forced to turn back to me.

Then Ned took a hand. 'Bessie knew a lot of rich people.'

Ned has a remarkable gift of summing matters up. She was suddenly all attention.

'They'd all be willing to pay those who can help find Bessie's murderer. Mr Drake certainly would,' I said quickly.

'If he's not topped first.' She shrieked with laughter at her wittiness.

'He won't be,' I said, full of confidence with no reason. 'I'm going to find out who really killed Bessie. This man she was scared of, for instance.'

She stopped laughing. She must have decided this was serious business. 'Scared of?' she repeated guardedly.

'Yes,' Ned answered for me.

She was frightened herself. 'I can't tell you anything. And I'm losing money.'

I couldn't see how, there being no one around save gentlemen looking much more like they were returning to their wives than looking for a judy.

'Bessie lost her life,' I wanted to point out sharply, but I didn't in the interests of our mission. Instead I said, 'Business is slack, I can see that, and I want to know *all* about Bessie.'

She wavered. 'Buy me a drink then.'

'A pie,' I said firmly, not wanting to waste money on liquor when it was needed for vittals. I remembered a nice café in Panton Street that produced a fair pie, and in my experience there's many a detail can get remembered on a full stomach, and many a one forgotten through a heavy head.

'And a port and lemon.'

Some women drive a hard bargain. 'Certainly,' I agreed. We

settled ourselves in the pie shop and I pretended to be surprised they didn't serve port and bought her a nice cup of tea instead. And this is what she told me:

'We was born Bunting,' she said, 'though I never knew if Ma had a right to the name. Dad was a butcher in Clare Market. George is his name. Sophie was the eldest, Bessie came next, then me, and then Polly. Ma died, and then three years later Sophie did. She was only eleven. A year later Bessie ran away. I hated Ma for dying, and don't mind who knows it, leaving me and Polly alone. Well,' she went on, rather hastily, 'the next thing I knows, I heard Bessie was a crossing sweeper on the New Oxford Street, and found out she shared a room up Titchfield Street somewhere, her and six other kids. They were all lucifer sellers. I told Dad and he went to get her, but she'd gone, tipped off. Then I started thinking that if she'd run away, I could go too, but I was caught. I was too useful to let go. Polly and I found Bessie a year or two later. She was selling flowers by then, and living with—' She stopped and pretended she wanted more tea, pushing the cup towards me. '—this cove.'

'He was older than her, and a big fellow. She wouldn't have a word said against him, though I knew she was scared of him. Told me she'd turned herself into a proper little cook. He took me and Polly in later, but I guessed it was just so as he could have me when her back was turned, and he did. Polly would have been next. Anyway, Bessie never fell, like I did. When Bessie found out about that, we ran away together. Bessie took Polly, and I went to the workhouse till the kid was born. Then we all lived together, Bessie, Polly and me. Bessie wanted us to keep the kid but I couldn't see no future in it, so I gave it away. Then Bessie went back to—' She hesitated. '—this cove. I didn't see her for a while. It must have been about the year of fifty-seven. I was eighteen then—a gentleman friend took me to the music hall. There Bessie was, serving the beer, large as life. Times were hard for me and she said she could get me a job there. There was a condition. I was to keep my mouth shut about her working there. Why not? Then one day a year or so later Bessie disappeared. Before she went, she told me Dad was released from stir.' She hesitated once more, pretending she was enjoying her tea greatly. 'This cove she'd been living with was after her and had found out where she was. She told me she'd got a respectable job again, modelling for artists. That was enough for me. I left too, but to go on the streets. I've done well for myself. I'm known here. The Haymarket's a respectable pitch.'

'It is indeed,' I agreed, wishing I could stop young Ned's ears from flapping. I meant it; after all, so it is compared with the Ratcliffe Highway. 'Tell me about this cove you and Bessie lived with early on.'

She looked out into the street as if he might even now be lurking there, then seeing I wasn't to be fobbed off, 'Joe.' She grabbed her cup as though she wanted to jump into it for safety.

'Joe what?'

'Nothing. Joe we called him.'

'Anything strange about the face?'

Real fear now. 'She called him Moonman.'

'Jealous sort, was he?' I asked softly.

'We was his. That's all that mattered.' She muttered it, as if ashamed. 'He wouldn't let no one leave him.'

'Where does he live now? And what trade does he have?'

'We ain't on calling terms,' she answered dryly. 'We lived in the Brill, but he's gone long since.'

The Brill. Of course he'd have gone long since. People did. Not only is it a select rookery that can rival St Giles, but being by the great railway terminus of St Pancras, it's even noisier too, though to my mind the roar of trains is sweeter than the noise of the brawls you get in the Brill. There was something she was keeping from me, I was sure of that, but you can't change the shape of a flue while you're in it.

'And young Polly?' I asked. That did it. She shut up tight as a button, announcing it was time she was back on her pitch. Scared of Moonman, I reasoned. If he did in Bessie, why not her?

Ned ran after her and took her hand, like in sympathy, as she went through the door, and sheer surprise stopped her.

'You're sure you're only his apprentice?' I heard her whisper.

'Yes.'

She looked round furtively, and whispered to him (so he told me when he returned to his pie), 'Tell your Governor Jenny says we had a brother. And it's no using asking me where. I don't know. He'll tell you about Moonman. I daren't.' She shivered then, Ned said, and for all her brave words, she didn't look happy as she stepped forth into the dark night.

The courts in the Nichol and around Rosemary Lane are dead ends, as you'd expect. Houses round two sides and at one end, and only a narrow arched alley, as thin as a flue sometimes, to get into it. All the dirt and muck, for those that cannot be bothered to reach the privy, pile up at one end, for the dustmen don't come in. There's a sort of gully down the middle meant to take the liquids away underground, where the worse nastinesses lurk. That's where I seemed to have come, to a dead end, and nastiness lurked everywhere. Where next to turn in the dark mass of this teaming city? It seemed to me I must tackle the other end now, at Chelsea, and leave the unanswered questions here dangling.

I felt I knew Bessie better now I knew more of her background, and it was as if she was telling me something. Think, Tom, think. So during my pie and baccy, I thought. To no result. All I could think of was that if my fate had been different, if I'd not been a chimney sweep, and met Bessie like regular folks do,

I might have dared to walk down the aisle of St George's with her on my arm, proud as a peacock. I'd be in a grey frock coat and trousers, with a grey wedding hat upon my head, and she in cream satin, a bunch of violets on her breast, and love in her eyes for me.

Instead that aisle had borne her coffin, and here was I alone, unable to find who put her there. But I would, I *would,* I vowed.

I often find if you stoke up the boiler in the evening, in the morning it bursts into flame all by itself. So it did today. I woke up to the cries outside of 'Pickled whelks. Penny a dram,' and it came to me. I'd been assuming we didn't know where Bessie lived, but we had a few clues. We dropped her as regular as clockwork in the Strand. She couldn't live towards the river, not unless she were lodging—or working—in the big hotel or the inns of court, and that didn't seem likely, so it had to be the other side. Wellington Street? No, too far away and too swell. It had to be somewhere where she thought she was safe, and Moonman would not find her, if he were still looking. It wasn't going to be a cheap lodging house, I reasoned. She was doing better than that. In my head I paced out the streets round the Strand, and then I had it. How about the maze of narrow streets on the northern side? One of those wooden gabled houses in Wych Street? Or even Holywell Street? In a street lined with booksellers, Moonman would never think of looking for her, even though it was mostly literature of a certain kind for those that have tastes that way.

The regular sweeps round Wych Street eyed me suspiciously, but because it was Tom Wasp and word had gone round, they let me be. Ned and I found a decent job at the Olympic Theatre to sweep four flues, but they didn't know Bessie, even when I showed them the picture. Money for a pint of porter was all I got out of that venture, besides my dosh.

Then Ned came rushing into the pub in Holywell Street to

take me to a lad he'd met outside, selling birds' nesties. A country lad, the lad tells us, and so he looked in his smockfrock and straw hat. At Ned's silent urging, I bought a nice water wagtail's with four eggs, for a penny, though how Ned's going to hatch 'em I don't know. A hedgehog would be more use (this young vendor having all sorts of snakes and creatures beside his nesties) to eat the black beetles that enjoy living in Hairbrine Court more than we do. But they're a shilling, a sum that has to be thought about much more careful.

'He knows a lady with red hair,' Ned pipes up eagerly.

'Have you seen her recently, lad?'

'No. She went, mister.'

'She lodged here?' We were on the corner of Holywell Street, though it was no more holy than the purefinder's job was pure. It was busy with old clothes shops and stalls besides the bookshops of questionable taste where gentlemen were reading as if they had no homes to go to.

'Over there.' He pointed to one of the small shops. 'She has a room over the bookshop. They let me shelter there when it's raining, if I can leave my nesties.'

'They, lad? You mean in the bookshop?'

'No sir, the lady and the boy.'

'Boy?' I was doubtful. Could this be Bessie? I showed him the picture. Well, he had trouble with that, photography not being so common in the country as it is here. But when I told him her name and then described her hair, he said yes, that was her. And the boy had red hair, just like hers, he said.

'What boy was this?' I asked sharply, now he'd mentioned him again.

He shrugged. 'Hers, of course.'

I leapt on this eagerly. *Did* Bessie have a son? Or could that be the brother Jenny talked of? Was that why Jenny had been nervous of Ned, thinking he might be Bessie's boy? 'How old was he, lad?'

My question puzzled him. 'Less than me,' he offered.

I guessed him to be about ten. 'About this high?' I asked, and gradually it came to it that this lad was about five or six, so a son was most likely. If Bessie had a son, she might even have been wed. Then a thought passed through my mind that wasn't so pleasant. Now Bessie had been murdered, what had happened to the boy? Could he be there in her rooms, lying dead of starvation, waiting for a mother who never came back?

I rushed into the shop to enquire, and the customers looked at me most suspiciously, as if I were their consciences coming home to roost. Then they smelled me and decided their nasty reading habits did not require further indulgence. The shopkeeper was so keen to see me leave, he didn't even take the time to be rude.

'The boy's gone,' I was told.

'Where? Who with?'

He shrugged. In London boys came, boys went.

I took off my hat as though I was prepared to wait a nice long time.

'A bloke came for him. That was the day before the woman disappeared. She was screaming and hollering, but there was nothing to be done. Most likely the kid's father.'

'What did he look like?'

'Big. Funny sort of face. Rough-looking.'

'Moonman,' I said sadly. 'That poor lad.'

'What was I to do?' The shopkeeper began to get pugnacious. What were any of us to do in this bitter struggle called life?

Chapter Four: In Which I Become a Swell

All that Sunday I worried about Bessie's lad, thinking of the struggle she must have had to support him as well as herself—and maybe young sister Polly and the brother. All the while she had been hiding from Moonman, who dogged her tracks wherever she went. For all we had his description, he remained a formless dark shape in my mind. Had he got hold of Bessie's son? Murdered her, then sold the lad—or worse? I took Ned to the Victoria Park pleasure garden in Bethnal Green to take our minds off things, but it didn't work. Families playing games, sweethearts strolling—there they were, all oblivious to Bessie. Ned enjoyed it, but I came home with a heavier heart, and was pleased when Monday morning arrived and it was time for Ned to collect Doshie. There was some delay, which was as well, for I had a rare visitor.

'One for you, Tom.'

I took the white envelope from the postie, an old acquaintance of mine from my apprentice days, by name of Charlie, and turned it over. Being the age I am, I can't rid myself of the habit of looking to see if there's a secret message on the back to save me counting out precious pennies to pay for it. Mr Rowland Hill obligingly changed all that, so now the sender pays the postage, and obtains a bonny envelope stamp for one penny with Her Majesty's bonny head on it, God bless her, but old ways die as hard as yesterday's bread. Letters are rare in Hairbrine Court, especially those with important red seals on them, and Charlie, feeling a proprietorial interest, likes to watch you read them.

He had his pennyworth that day. At first I thought it came from Buckingham Palace, it looked so grand. It was written in the best copperplate, which I learned when I was lettered, though I don't have much call to use it now. As for what it said, well, I had to read it twice, and then sit down to think about it as the beggar said when asked if he'd like an honest job.

The law is something I've not had much to do with. The pigmen at Wapping are part of living in our London, but the Law, meaning juries and judges, and all that goes with them, doesn't mean much in the East. A face is here or he's not here, meaning he's either been tapped on the shoulder by God (or, more likely, His opposite number), or in prison, or gone to the country, which is perhaps as bad as either. I have a proper respect for what happens to a villain from the time he's taken up to when he reaches prison, but I don't feel cosy with it. Over the Royal Courts of Justice, and the Old Bailey Court, I'm in agreement with Ned, though it's the chimneys he avoids. So I was dubious when I read that this solicitor, Mr Mudgwick of Mudgwick, Meekes and Tucker, wanted me to wait upon him at my convenience at Lincoln's Inn Fields in respect of his client Mr Valentine Drake.

'I don't know, Charlie,' I said. 'It's a big undertaking.'

'You go,' he said. 'A man's got to have an adventure once in a while.'

I always take Charlie's advice, but it put me in a quandary. Do I put my Number One on, being my Sunday best clothes? This would mean no chimneys for me today, and, as a regrettable consequence of that, no money. Or do I go in my working clothes? This vexing question was settled for me when Ned came back with Doshie, having called in at the bread shop to find a message left by a coster, that he had a message from

Sweet William (a jocular name for a regular coster on the Chelsea beat) that Mr Parsons would also be obliged if I'd call where I might hear some information that would interest me. No chimneys today then. I looked at the diminishing pile of pennies, and Ned read my expression.

'Don't worry, Gov.'

Now there's an awkward problem. He knows I'd never hire him out, so that means he'll dip a wallet or two to see us through. What was my conscience going to say about this? I had a brief word with our Lord, who pointed out to me that I was doing my Christian duty trying to help others today, so it was only right that others should lend a hand to me. 'But don't let it happen too often, Tom,' He advised me sternly. 'It's only because I know you got Rent Day coming up, that I'm turning a blind eye.'

'Dear Lord, I don't want a blind eye,' I replied. 'Just keep it open for me so I can walk tall.' (Inside me, is what I meant. Outside, the same old bowed legs carry me along each day.) So I decided to leave Ned behind me today, thanking the Lord for His understanding of the situation, and in quiet confidence in them both, I took tuppence for an omnibus.

It seemed queer to be in Lincoln's Inn and not working. When I have Doshie, the cart and my soot bags and brushes, I don't get a second glance, but done up in my Sunday best check trousers and hat, you'd have thought I was Dick Turpin himself, the stares I got.

There was a tradesman's door down in the area at Mudgwick, Meekes and Tucker, but being in my Sunday best and with that letter in my hand, I decided on the front door. It was a bright and shiny knocker, but I put out my old-gloved hand bold as the brass itself, counting myself entitled. Not if the gentleman clerk who opened the door had his way—*that* was clear. He looked me up and down as though he would clap me in irons sooner than let me in, until he saw the letter, and then I was with Mr Mudgwick as soon as he could scoot me up the stairs and stand aside for my smell to pass.

I'm glad to say Mr Mudgwick and I saw eye to eye at once, and not only because we were of a height. He was the kind of gentleman I like. A face as round as a plump cabbage, and a beam that warmed you like a ray of sun. He had a monocle in one eye, but the other was sharp, and that pleased me too. It's those blind to what's in front of them, who've made up their minds already, whom I can't abide. (The lady who had me lettered—which reminds me, I still haven't told you that story—will be glad to see that *whom.* It was a point of grammar that took a long while to appeal to me.)

'My dear sir.' Mr Mudgwick clasped his hands before him, having waved me to a seat. 'My unfortunate client has told me of your powers of perception in the matters of the world.'

'That's very gratifying,' I said, glad I'd put on the Number One when I saw the cream upholstery on the chairs, which, like the rest of this room, were fit for the Queen herself. I cast my professional eye on the marble chimneypiece, and from its likeness to others I have seen, saw that Mr Adam had been at work here. 'And how is Mr Drake?'

His face fell and his voice followed it, as though he were speaking of a gentleman nigh to death. That reminded me that Mr Drake *was.*

'Despairing, sir. Out of love with the world. Falsely accused. No doubt of that. But what's to be the end of it?'

I thought of Mr Drake, of how much he loved Bessie, of how kind he'd been to me, of his pictures, which, strange though they might be to me, I could see were a bright light in this gloomy world. 'Not the gallows,' I said firmly. 'I take it we're in accord?'

He sighed deeply. 'We are, Mr Wasp. We are.'

'Then let's get out the soot cloth, and to work, Mr Mudgwick.'

'A man of action. We shall immediately do so, Mr Wasp. Mr Drake has told me you were present during some of his acquaintance with Bessie Barton, and can vouch for that fact that he was truly fond of her.'

'I can, Mr Mudgwick, and to the fact that Bessie believed he wanted to marry her. But there's no use saying the chimney was clean once, if it's smoking now.'

'You are right, of course, Mr Wasp.' Mr Mudgwick took my meaning immediately. 'However, Mr Drake would not have suggested our meeting were that confirmation all he required of you. I hardly know how to put this—'

'Straight,' I suggested. 'I'm not one for slopes and slants. Too much muck can get hidden.'

'Since you are a working man, you might have an understanding of some parts of Bessie's life that would be more difficult for myself or for Mr Drake's artist friends to penetrate. He has been committed for trial at the Old Bailey Central Criminal Court, and is now in Newgate.'

I shuddered to hear this, for a more cruel place it is hard to imagine. It houses only those that are condemned to the gallows, and those who await trial in the Old Bailey court next door, no doubt so they be reminded of the grim fate that might lie in store for them. Even worse, the passageway through which they pass to their trial is the graveyard for those hung on the gallows outside. As their poor trembling feet walk along its flagstones, the prisoners know that underneath lie the remains of those that died for their crimes.

'Mr Drake has urged me to request that side by side with my investigations, you make your own enquiries.' Mr Mudgwick regarded me anxiously. 'Would you be averse to such an arrangement?'

I've worked alone all my life, and been the happier for it. But this needed thinking about. Suppose Mr Drake *were* guilty? It was something I could not yet completely rule out, despite my inclinations, and Bessie needed justice as much as Mr Drake his liberty.

'I'm not averse,' I answered carefully, 'but there's one thing I must know first. Why did the police arrest Mr Drake? If he was a *matelot* I could understand it, but the police are usually only too anxious to forget about a corpse out East rather than arrest a swell for murder.'

He nodded gravely. 'I see no reason not to tell you, Mr Wasp. It was difficult enough to get the police to reveal their information to me, now the Metropolitan Police have been brought into the matter. The Commissioner himself is taking a great interest in the case.'

This was news to me, but I nodded wisely. Now a swell was involved, and the newspapers following the story, even *The Thunderer,* as the patterer calls *The Times,* of course the detectives at Scotland Yard would want a look-in.

'The body had, as you may already know, been in the water about two weeks, in the police doctor's estimation. On Saturday evening, the twenty-second of February, several of Mr Drake's neighbours were aroused by the sounds of a disturbance outside. One of them, having heard a woman's voice, donned his hat and cape, and taking a pistol went out to investigate. He saw a gentleman under the trees by the riverbank paling fence arguing with a lady. By the light of the gas lamp, he could see the gleam on her hair, where it could be seen under her hat, and is certain it was red. Indeed, at first he took her for Mrs Rossetti, another of his neighbours, who by a curious and sad coincidence died that very night, and by her own hand, so rumour claims. The gentleman had his arms on the woman's shoulders and was shaking her violently, shouting at her, and he distinctly heard the words, "Bessie. How could you? Oh, how could you?" She was struggling to get away, and when the neighbour found to his embarrassment it was Mr Drake and the lady unknown to him, he bowed and retreated. Mr Drake called after him: "Miss Barton is my model, and we're practising for tomorrow's poses."

'The neighbour thought this strange, especially since the morrow was a Sunday, but since the lady made no appeal for help, and indeed seemed only too anxious for him to leave, he returned indoors, and when he asked his man to look out of the window, they had gone.'

'And what happened to Sergeant Wiley's theory it was a garrotter?'

'The injuries do not quite conform to those of the usual garrotting, where death may or may not occur according to the pressure used.' He hesitated. 'There were indications of great violence.'

'And what does Mr Drake say about this neighbour's story?' I did not want to dwell on the other unhappy point.

'He admits he was quarrelling with Miss Barton by the river, but his story remains that they were practising for a future picture, called "Love Betrayed." I naturally believe his word.'

'Yet you use the word "story," Mr Mudgwick.'

The sun on his face faded. 'I did, Mr Wasp. I have to admit I would prefer stronger evidence of his innocence.'

'It's a long step from a quarrel to murder, Mr Mudgwick.' But a short one to the gallows, I was thinking, and with Bessie now likened in the newspapers to Mr Dante Gabriel Rossetti's 'Death of Beatrice,' since her end was linked by date to that of its model, Lizzie Siddal Rossetti, the police could very well be set on it.

'He is my client, Mr Wasp.'

But he wasn't mine, and that story didn't sound likely to me. Mr Drake wasn't one for working in the street on cold chilly evenings. He liked a glass of wine, seed cake and a nice fire. It seemed all too probable to me that he had just found out about Moonman, or about Bessie's little boy. Would that drive Mr Drake to murder? It's a wise man who knows himself, let alone others.

'What do you say, Mr Wasp?' Mr Mudgwick asked almost pleadingly. 'I need hardly say that your expenses would be fully paid, and—er—' He coughed slightly. '—some compensation for loss of trade.'

I thought of golden sovereigns piled up before me. I thought of Ned out dipping. I thought of that empty jar, but I had no choice, not with our Lord breathing down my neck. He was telling me *this,* not Ned's method, was His way of providing. Unfortunately there was a difficulty. 'I say this, sir. I'll help you all I can, because I think and hope Mr Drake's innocent. If he isn't, then I can't conceal it, and I don't want to have to take his money. Now what do *you* say?'

'*I* say you are an honest man, Mr Wasp. I'll be content with what you propose.'

'Then I'll tell you what I found out so far.'

Mr Mudgwick listened intently, not interrupting, while I told him all, or nearly. 'Splendid, Mr Wasp, splendid. So we only have to find this Moonman.' Relief spread over his face, and the smile cautiously reappeared.

'Only's a big word when it takes in the whole of London at least, and ten years or more.'

'Try, Mr Wasp. Try.'

I didn't like the way this was going now, and I had to set him right. 'There's the Angels, too, sir. I've arrangements in hand to see what Bessie meant to them.' He frowned at that. 'All flues have to be swept, Mr Mudgwick,' I reminded him. 'No use cleaning one if the others catch fire.'

'You're right, of course,' he agreed reluctantly. 'But as to the

Angels . . . I shall be seeing each of them, but your views would be helpful. And yet—again, I hardly know how to put this—*how* will you inquire into their relationships with Bessie?'

'I don't know as yet, Mr Mudgwick, but if the Good Lord intends me to do it, He'll light the path. And if He don't, I'll ask Him to call on you.'

The beam returned in full force. 'Mr Wasp, it's a pleasure to do business with you.'

I walked away from Lincoln's Inn feeling like a king. Mr. Mudgwick had passed several gold sovereigns to me, for expenses only, and what's more, he had shaken me by my hand. I, Tom Wasp, flue faker, had become a swell.

The royal feeling vanished on the crowded omnibuses to Chelsea. Not that I grew gloomy. It was a fine spring day, and London was decked out in its Number Ones. There were trees in flower in the parks and gardens, and ladies and children were sprouting like daffodils, their dark winter cloaks given way to brightly coloured bonnets, dresses and shawls. Even the conductors didn't grimace as they took my fare on the three omnibuses I climbed on, perhaps because I was in my Number Ones too.

I remember that ride and what I was feeling, and the best way I can translate it is that as I was a swell, I was quite entitled to inquire into the doings of other swells, who, after all, are only God's creatures just like me. So I took a decision that otherwise I'd never be so presumptuous as to consider.

In thinking of them and what happened next, I'm going to call Mr Drake *Valentine,* and the others by their Christian names, too. Not to their faces, of course. But to think and write of them as God welcomed them into the world would help me see them as they are, not masked by their Misters or Sirs, which is how the world sees them. Furthermore, it will help you, my readers, to feel nearer to the Angels, and who could object to *that?*

In this way I may get closer to the truth, and I hope that poor Valentine will walk free. I trust you won't think this is too much of a liberty, but sometimes a liberty has to be taken so that you may see where your footsteps are intended to go.

Having been unable to let them know when I was coming, I found Mr Parsons in his shirt sleeves polishing the silver, for all there was no one to use it at present. Mrs Holly was roasting a nice joint on the spit for dinner, and Nelly and Ethel in their print gowns came flying into the kitchen, dustpans in hand, closely followed by Percy, my arrival having been announced by a bash on the gong. I must be royalty here too.

'It seems right to carry on,' Mr Parsons said when he saw me looking at his silver polish.

'It does, Mr Parsons,' I agreed, glad to know from Mr Mudgwick that Valentine was paying his wages. (Mr Parsons remains Mister to us of course, since in kitchens titles are more jealously guarded than by the gentlemen.)

They clustered round me at the kitchen table. A steaming mug of cocoa was before us all, and a muffin fresh from the oven.

'We've news to tell you, Mr Wasp.' Mr Parsons took the lead as befitted his rank. The cocoa left a fine moustache, which gave a venerable look to his face.

'I'll be glad to hear it, Mr Parsons.'

'First, I'll paint the scene,' he tells me. (Very artistic touch, I thought, but maintained a straight face.) 'There's four Angels altogether, and all four used that Bessie as a model sometime or other.'

'Did she model for them all at the same time, or one after the other?'

'That we don't know, but she began coming here about a year ago. That right?'

Five nods of agreement.

'In the spring,' Mrs Holly said. 'I remember thinking what a lovely bonnet, the colour of the daffodils.'

Ethel sniffed.

'She wasn't here every day,' Mr Parsons continued, ignoring this female preoccupation. 'She could have posed for the others. Or anyone.'

'Most astute of you, Mr Parsons,' said I. 'Before we talk pictures though, might I enquire a little more as to what happened that evening when Bessie came and was seen rushing out of the door, and Mr Drake shouting after her?'

Percy opened his mouth, but he was forestalled.

'In what way?' Mrs Holly looked as fierce as a goose determined on missing the spitjack.

'Did Mr Drake follow her out?'

'I don't know,' Ethel said regretfully. 'I went to bed.'

'Anyone see or hear him in the house after that?'

None of them could recall doing so, though Percy said he didn't see how they could, it being over a month ago now.

'Mr Parsons, when you came in from your evening off, was Mr Drake in?'

'Naturally. I bolted the front door as usual.' He looked offended, and I hastened to reassure him, whereupon he admitted he had assumed Mr Drake was in but had not seen him.

'When it comes to it,' I said, 'there's no evidence he was in the house.'

'Or that he wasn't,' Nelly added brightly.

I noticed Ethel was looking anywhere but at me.

'Tell me,' I said to her sternly. 'You do Mr Drake no good by hiding the truth. It'll be the law for you if you tell lies.'

'There's nothing to tell,' she shrieked, then seeing we didn't believe her, added, 'I don't know it was *that* day, anyway.'

'What is it, girl?' Authority took over.

'His bed wasn't slept in, Mrs Holly.'

'And you didn't tell me?' The jolly face grew a great deal less jolly. 'It's your job to tell me everything.'

'I forgot.'

'You mean I might have bolted the master out?' Mr Parsons' face was a study. 'And me thinking him in. He never said a word about it next day. You'd think he would. Anyone remember his coming back?'

No one did, and Percy pointed out it was church day.

'What's it matter, anyway?' Nelly asked curiously.

'It matters because another gentleman round these parts saw him arguing with Bessie by the riverside that evening. And if he didn't come home all night . . .' I left them to think it out for themselves.

'I might have bolted him out,' Mr Parsons said defensively, 'and he spent the night elsewhere.'

'Odd he didn't give you a wigging,' Percy said boldly.

'I'll give you one, lad,' Mr Parsons replied, fixing him with gimlet eyes.

I agreed with Percy that it was looking bad for Valentine. Then the Lord pointed out the way to me by a great shaft of light. 'But,' I continued, 'I've been talking to Mr Drake's solicitor.' That impressed them. 'Mr Valentine wants me to try to find out what happened to Bessie. Now why would he do that if he were guilty?'

'I know he isn't guilty. And if he was, she deserved it,' said Ethel helpfully.

'Don't talk that way,' Nelly said piously.

'Then let's hear what you've found out about the three Angels Bessie posed for.'

They were all relieved at my practical approach.

'I met the man of Mr Edward Harwood-Jones.' Mr Parsons, as befitted his status, spoke first. 'He spends much time in the public house, owing to the fact Mr Harwood-Jones does not approve of alcohol, except for beer, and his man is partial to a hot grog.'

He may not approve of it for servants, but he likes it well enough for himself, I thought, remembering him the night I came to tell Valentine of Bessie's death. There's a lot of gentlemen like that, though.

'That may,' Mr Parsons conceded, 'be because he lives with his mother. His father was a clergyman in Oxfordshire, and on his death his mother came to share Mr Harwood-Jones' Kensington home.'

'Does he have a trade?' I enquired.

'Not as you and I understand it, Mr Wasp. He's always been a painter, and the money to do so, that being an unreliable calling, came from his grandfather, a bishop, I understand. His mother is a vigorous old lady, and he is much in fear of her, although she has her own apartments. She resides on the first floor, he on the ground floor and top floors, with a studio in the roof.'

'Very handy to keep an eye on him.'

'Indeed, yes. He is, I gather, a very correct gentleman, as you would expect of a clergyman's son and bishop's grandson.'

'No naked ladies in his pictures then?'

'Mr Wasp!' Mrs Holly was outraged, as Ethel and Nelly giggled.

'I must apologise, Mrs Holly,' I said instantly. 'It's sometimes necessary to ask this unfortunate sort of question to gather the truth. No use sweeping rubbish under the carpet, is it?'

I could see I hit a bull's eye with my arrow as Ethel blushed, and Mrs Holly looked highly satisfied at my perspicacity.

'I asked,' I continued, 'because Mr Drake took me one day to the National Gallery, along with Bessie, to explain what it was the Angels liked and disliked about art and modern art in particular. There seemed many such pictures there.'

It had been a different chimney to 'Cast Out' and no mistake. It was a wonder to me that so many ladies needed to take their clothes off to have their pictures painted, and I told him so. Valentine explained to me that artists liked it that way for some pictures, so that, just as I told you about Christian names, nothing comes between them and what God gave us to start with. In that case, I asked him, why don't the men take their clothes off too? That, he said, rather shortly I couldn't help feeling, was not the same.

Valentine went on to explain that the Angels, since they mainly painted real scenes from modern life, didn't need models to take their clothes off as often, though they would if it were a very classical scene. And that I could understand. 'Cast Out' couldn't very well picture a lady being turned from her home by her husband without her clothes on, for even the most hard-hearted husband wouldn't grudge his wife a petticoat and cloak. Bessie had said Valentine had been planning to submit 'Cast Out' for the Royal Academy exhibition. I wondered what would happen now?

'Lady Godiva,' I had said knowledgeably to Valentine in the Gallery. 'There's a real story about a lady with no clothes.'

He had laughed at that and said I had caught him out. 'Oddly enough, Tom, we were just discussing that as a subject at the Angels' meeting recently, but Bessie wouldn't do it. I believe Mr Tait is trying to persuade her still.'

But I digress from my story.

'A very good gentleman is Mr Harwood-Jones,' Parsons continued approvingly, 'so his man says. He keeps the Angels in order, when they have a spot too much to drink.' I wondered if Parsons ever went round with the port decanter when the Angels met here, but then remembered the young gentlemen were eager enough to help themselves. 'He paints moral studies often based on Biblical stories translated into modern situations.'

'And what of Bessie, Mr Parsons?'

'His man doesn't remember Bessie posing, though he's only been with Mr Harwood-Jones about two years. He had a red-haired lady call in the evening once recently. She was alone, so if it wasn't Mr Harwood-Jones she was calling on, he would have taken her for a lady of the streets. He's certain there's been no red-haired model in his time.'

'Does Mr Drake sell his own pictures?' Meaning, does he sell them to a shop?

'Oh yes. Very sought after is Mr Drake. And he gets commissions. Not often,' Mr Parsons conceded, 'but that's his fault for painting like he does. Who wants to buy a picture with a sweep—oh, begging your pardon, Mr Wasp.' He seemed genuinely sorry, and I didn't take it amiss since I could very well see his point.

'I thought it on the queer side myself,' I said grandly, 'but there's no accounting for tastes.'

'I like a nice picture of Her Majesty's family,' Mrs Holly declared. 'Or a lady in a pretty hat. What's the point of painting rags? That's what I asked Mr Drake.'

'And Mr Fairfax?' I asked, when a silence fell.

'Not so grand as Mr Harwood-Jones,' Mrs Holly informed me, eager to take over the limelight, 'but lives comfortably enough. He has rooms in Wigmore Street. Now it so happens that our butcher's cousin does for Wigmore Street, also in the butchery line, and having an eye to retaining our custom—though his feather blade can be as tough as boots—Mr Sprig was glad to oblige by asking this cousin a few questions, and he in turn chatted to Mr Fairfax's landlady.'

'Mr Sprig no doubt wishes to spread our disgrace around his other customers,' Mr Parsons pointed out haughtily.

'The newspapers have spread it very well already.' Mrs Holly inclined to tartness.

'All the more reason they're interested.'

'Now—' I could see this discussion getting off the Dover Road and into the Dartford marshes if we weren't careful. 'About Mr Fairfax—'

'Such a nice young gentleman, his landlady says, though not so very young for he must be well over thirty. But he looks young, with his yellow hair and merry eye, and he has a courteous word for everyone, so she says. Especially ladies. I don't think he would have done it. He looks too nice.' Mrs Holly went pink.

'Someone did, Mrs Holly,' I pointed out quietly, 'and we don't want Mr Drake found guilty, if there's anything we can do about it.'

For a moment she seemed on the doubtful side, but then she came down—as housekeepers do—on the side of common sense. 'No, Mr Wasp. Mr Drake's a nice young man too.'

'So, Mr Fairfax, like Mr Harwood-Jones, is a bachelor, but unlike him he doesn't live with his mother. He has a studio in Wigmore Street and models posing, I take it?'

'The landlady objected at first, but he told her it was his trade, and he didn't think of them as young ladies. "You know the rules," she said. "Make new ones," he urged. (I had to smile at that.) "Let's say young ladies can come to my studio, or even my drawing room unaccompanied, but never—" Well, she shut him up short there naturally, and he laughed. Though I can see it's no joking matter. Mr Drake is very good. I will say that for him. He knows there are rules.'

'But you still don't know what went on in his studio during the day, Mrs Holly.' Ethel smirked.

'I'll thank you for no more dirty talk here, young lady.' Mrs Holly sniffed. 'Mr Wasp knows what went on in Mr Drake's studio was all to do with paint, wasn't it?'

'It was, Mrs Holly, it was.' *While I was there,* I added to myself, to keep an open mind. Young men are young men. If every baby in coster- and matelot-land had to be born after the wedding knot, there'd be precious few to carry on the trades.

Mrs Holly was gratified. 'Another piece of pie, Mr Wasp?'

'I would be much obliged, Mrs Holly. There's a touch of nutmeg about it that I rarely taste elsewhere. Does this landlady recall one model in particular? What about Bessie?'

'She remembers her well, because she stood out because of her hair. And her smile, though what that's to do with anything I don't know. All too free with them, if you ask me.'

This sad old world could do with as many smiles as folks would give, in my opinion, but I did not air it, it being more in Bessie's interests to keep on Mrs Holly's good side.

'How long was she a model, Mrs Holly?'

'Five years or so, she said. Only she didn't come very often, like some of his others. There was a whole long period when she thought she'd gone, then back she come.'

'And when might that have been?'

'That I don't know.' Her bosom swelled indignantly at my urging her to this confession. 'You got to remember I had all this through the butcher's cousin. I do remember he said it was when Mr Fairfax painted a picture called "Too Late." Gardens is what Mr Fairfax likes to paint.'

What few gardens there are in our part of London are more a matter of vegetables than flowers, and Victoria Park is more a pleasure garden than flowers, so I rely for my knowledge of the green and coloured things of life on St James Park when I can take a few minutes off to stroll into it to buy a pennyworth of milk straight from the cow. But the gardens in Frederick Fairfax's pictures aren't like any I've seen anywhere; they're more like a splattering of rainbows. The flowers look more alive—so far as I could judge from a picture in the National Gallery that Valentine pointed out to me—than the ladies and gentlemen. Hearing the title brought it back to me.

That picture I saw had been called 'Too Late,' because there was a drowned lady in the middle of the pond, and the reason I remember it is because it was Bessie, painted in an autumn scene, lying in the water, red hair streaming out all round her. *But when it happened to you in real life, Bessie, it wasn't beautiful like that.* Artists don't paint the fishes eating away at earthly beauty, and that's as it should be or the gloom of life would get the better of us. My memory jogged, I even remembered Bessie telling me of it, though I didn't take much notice at the time.

'Such a to-do,' says she. 'Buckets of water were being carried up all day. You'd think I was royalty, they were so anxious I couldn't catch pneumonia. Mr Fairfax tucked me up on the chaise longue on a waterproof after each sitting, or lying I should call it, with a nice hot water bottle and a blanket. I thought it ever so thoughtful of him.'

I could hear her saying it now, and the tears stung my eyes for the pity of it, for she was gone.

'Anything about Mr Tait?' I said gruffly to take the image of Bessie in this picture from my mind.

Nelly and Ethel exchanged looks. 'It was him done it,' Nelly said, with the air of a penny gaff conjuror who produces the rabbit out of the hat.

'And how do you know that, Miss Nelly?'

'He's the sort,' Ethel supplied darkly. 'We met his general.'

General maids of all work are much put upon in my opinion, but there's none better for an all-round view of what goes on in a house. Laurence Tait lives near the British Museum in Bury Street. I know it. There are some fine chimneys there, for all they don't flaunt themselves to the skies.

'He lives with his wife and family,' Ethel continued eagerly, 'and can't keep his hands off what he's no business to be touching. No wonder his wife's so jealous, though he sweet-talks her so she thinks he's good as Prince Albert himself. Then next day she's suspicious again. She's always popping in to try and catch him at it—but he's always too quick for her. She's a character, so the general says, and for all her tantrums better than her husband. The general said she'd leave, only there's nowhere to go, 'cos they wouldn't give her a character. She told him she'd tell his wife, but he just laughed at her. Mind you, he's all right some of the time. It's just when he's painting it seems to affect him. He paints like a demon, all hours of the day and night. Doesn't seem to need sleep then, all charged up as he is. She knows not to go near him at those times. Dark his paintings are, she said.'

'Black paint?'

'No.' Ethel looked at me scornfully. ' "The Beast Within Us" was one title. No one buys them, and he gets cross. She remembers going in there one day when Bessie was posing. And when he raged that no one would buy it anyway, Bessie asked: "Why not just paint happy things, Laurence?" "I have to paint what I have to paint," he growled back.' Ethel looked virtuous. 'Suppose I said I got to clean what I got to clean and then took against cleaning the stairs? Master would soon have something to say about that. "I wants and I gets" is a luxury in this world, Mr Wasp.'

'It is, Ethel,' agreed Mrs Holly, 'and you remember that on them stairs tomorrow.'

Ethel ignored this, continuing grandly, 'Bessie posed for Mr Tait like she did for Mr Fairfax. The servants' gossip is she posed for him when he, Mr Fairfax and Mr Harwood-Jones all shared a studio in the 'fifties, then she vanished when they gave up the studio, and began coming here again four or five years ago, though there was a break in the middle, from what they recall. It's their view,' Ethel said with hushed voice, 'she stopped coming because he had a go at her. Unless it were the other way round.' She sniggered, and Nelly seized the opportunity to step into the limelight.

'She's been there to model once or twice in the last year, and what's more—' She paused impressively, which was her mistake, for Ethel seized the limelight back again.

'She came round one *evening* back in February. And there was such a rumpus the general said that they'd all hoped Mr Tait was going to get what he deserved at last.'

'And did he?' This sounded interesting.

'No.' It was left to Miss Nelly to provide the anti-climax. 'The old goat sweet-talked her again.'

'Good. I'm much obliged to you all,' I said heartily. 'Most helpful you've been to Mr Drake, and I'll tell him so.'

'I told the general,' Ethel said importantly, 'that I knew a good sweep.'

'And I mentioned it to Mr Harwood-Jones' man,' put in Mr Parsons swiftly.

'And the butcher's cousin is willing.' Mrs Holly put in her pennyworth.

It was good progress. A lot of soot was beginning to loosen. Even so, were I to get myself a job cleaning all their chimneys, I said to Ned much later, I couldn't be sure of *meeting* all these gentlemen. It was a problem, and I might have to speak to Mr Mudgwick again, I told him.

'Why, Gov?'

'Because,' I said grandly, 'we've been assuming, you and I, that this young lad who lived with Bessie was Moonman's son, because he'd been seen taking him away. Maybe it was the muffins and the cocoa made my brain clearer, but suppose Moonman were not the father, thought I? Suppose it were one of the Angels? Even Mr Drake, though I don't like to think of that.'

'You got to, Gov.' Ned eyed me hesitantly, then diffidently drew out of his pocket a nice fat leather wallet. He put it on the table and we both stared at it. The Lord was peering down at it too. My conscience was heavy for having thought He was approving Ned's ways when all the time He was planning to provide through Mr Mudgwick. The least I could do, I decided, was take a proper interest when Ned opened the wallet.

Four golden guineas rolled out. That was going to brighten up the jar magnificently. He ferreted a bit further, pulling some cards out. I picked one up.

'What's this, Ned?' I roared, which is unusual for me, save when at our trade. I showed it to him accusingly. It was a calling card bearing the name Mr Laurence Tait.

'What about it, Gov?' Ned opened his eyes wide, but this time they didn't work their magic with me.

'Ned, Ned,' I said heavily, 'I don't suppose this came about by coincidence, did it?'

'No, Gov. I followed the cove,' he muttered.

'And why's that?'

'I didn't take to him at the cemetery, Gov.'

'That's a good enough reason, Ned.'

All the same, I was worried. Dipping at random is one thing, because the Lord makes His decision who's to be dipped. Dipping by plan is another. I didn't reprimand Ned too harshly, but decided those sovereigns would go under my bedding to join Mr Mudgwick's. 'We'll call it the Bessie Fund, Ned,' and rather wistfully he agreed. There was places we could change them so it wouldn't be noticed we were flashing gold sovereigns. I'd take them to a dolly shop where they ask no questions provided you take one whole shilling less than the twenty they're worth.

My evening engagement meant changing back into Number Two, but I didn't object. I'd be glad to get back to the world of chimneys (speaking metaphorically) where I'm not working in the dark all the time. I was groping through a fog in the world of swells, and I had a feeling the fog would grow thicker.

I don't ordinarily mix with the likes of Lizzie. It's not that I'm prejudiced against lady sweeps, but Lizzie was a special case. She'd been a climbing girl, survived it, and stayed in the trade. She was well known, for not many women become master sweeps. She covers Spitalfields, and besides sweeping she does a bit of brushing up, spinning a story so the women are sorry for her. Sorry for Lizzie? Don't bother. Be sorry for the half-starved children she pushes up the chimney when she thinks no one is looking. Be sorry for the customers she rooks out of their money for chimneys she can't be bothered to sweep clean.

Don't be sorry for Lizzie. She loves her life, and never misses a master sweeps' evening at the pub. Somewhere she may have a woman's heart, but it's so caked in soot it would never come clean. However, she'd sent word to let me know she had news for me. Lizzie's place wasn't hard to find when you got to the Nichol. You could follow your nose, for as well as the soot, Lizzie had a smell all her own. The best I can describe it is a touch of sewer mingled with bad meat and a bit of boiled cabbage.

'Come in, Waspie.'

There she was, grinning, only two teeth left on the top, squatting in sooty rags on a pile of sacks on the floor.

'Tom to you, Lizzie,' I said amiably, knowing she was trying to annoy.

She lives alone in this one room, save when she has male sweeps in and rents the one next door. How they stand it, I don't know. Never say we don't support our own trade in all respects. But I never forget Lizzie's more to be feared than the Walworth Terror if she takes against you.

'You put the word out about Bessie Barton.'

'Yes, though that isn't necessarily her true name, Lizzie.'

'Come from the St Giles? Bettered herself?'

'That she did.'

Lizzie nodded like she was an Old Bailey judge, very solemn.

'Heard something of her. How much is it worth?'

I thought of Mr Tait's kind, if involuntary, donation and of Lizzie's avaricious nature. The others do it for free. Lizzie does nothing for free.

'A joey.' (That being a four-penny piece.)

Lizzie was impressed. 'You're generous, Tom Wasp. I'll say that for you.'

'Though I can ill afford it,' I added hastily, in case she got ideas in her head about a session in the room next door.

'None of us can,' she cackled merrily. 'I met a certain gentleman.'

A gentleman? How would Lizzie know?

'Two or three of them was talking about the murder at a coffee stall in Rag Fair,' she continued. 'I was to one side and because my face is black they think my ears are plugged up with soot. "Didn't you say you had a sister called Bessie?" says one. "Once," this cove grunted. "Haven't seen her in years."

' "You said she'd done well, gone into the music hall, and you'd look her up."

' "Maybe I did," said he. "There's plenty go into the halls. I was born a Bunting, not a Barton though."

' "I reckon you should look into it. Might be money in it."

'He said nothing, finished his coffee quick and was off. Then the other two started talking. He were a rough one, they said. Kept himself to himself.'

'Anything odd about his face?' I asked eagerly, just in case this might be Moonman.

'Not that I could see. Handsome cove, jolly-looking. Wouldn't mind a roll in the soot with him.'

'Where did he go?' I asked, eager to know.

She shrugged. 'No idea.'

'How would I find him again, Lizzie?' I asked in anguish. 'His name?'

'They called him Slit,' was all she could offer.

It was something, and I clung on to it like a crab to his basket at Shadwell fish market. What was I getting so excited about? I asked myself. Even if he was Bessie's brother, he didn't have a moon face, and could well not have seen her since she was a child.

All the same, just like the feeling that sends me east or west when I wake up of a morning, I had a hunch I needed to find this brother, so find him I would.

That night I went to sleep quite peaceful. I was a swell. I might be sleeping on a straw mattress on the damp floor of a lodging house in Hairbrine Court, but I dreamed of a house where Ned and I could be set up nice by ourselves, sweeping only our own chimneys, and sleeping in a bed raised from the floor. Maybe even a privy of our own. Dream away, Tom Wasp.

Chapter Five: In Which I Reach for the Moon

This old London of ours is a strange lady. Like any woman, she has her moods. At times the shining side of her is hidden away, and the face you think you know is a stranger's. No more is this so than in the early mornings. In the half-light, folks haven't had time to put on their daytime masks, and nor has London. You see her without the blacklead the housemaids use up West to make the hearths and stoves clean from the soot and ashes of the evening before.

There's a mystery hovering in London's half-light, as though the day itself isn't sure where it's come from and is waiting to find out—trailing clouds of glory. I read that somewhere while I was being lettered years ago, and it stuck in my mind. Not that I see much glory around Rosemary Lane, but just now and then in the muck and grime you get a hint of Him up above smiling with relief at something well done. One day I saw a swag-barrow lad give a broken doll to an anybody's child, because she was crying. She couldn't have been more than five, probably one of the unfortunates cast out by baby farmers and the like, who take money from those with unwanted children to look after them 'for life.' When it comes to the need to pay for schooling and footwear, out on the street they go to scrabble alone for existence as best they can. There are good folks round here, too, who won't let them starve, but it's no wonder the Walworth Terrors of our town can find so many young slaves. Up chimneys they still go by day, and are often hired out as snakesmen by night to slip through small windows for cracksmen who prefer others to earn their money for them.

I digress from the glories of the London morning, which is to be appreciated—even at the gates of London Docks. At seven-thirty two or three thousand of those who cling to the bottom rung of the ladder of life seethe around each of the three entrances. The rung is called hope, and here it's the hope of attracting a foreman's attention for a casual day's work in the docks. There's no light work here. It's hard wheel or winch work, or the even harder truck work, which requires a man to walk about thirty miles a day, most of the time moving a hundredweight or more in goods. Hope is what they need, for outside these gates gather those who have descended a great distance down in the world, right down to the ruffians and scum, who hope by one day's honest work to hear of enough of the other sort never to tread a wheel here again. The London docks is one of the only places in London to get a job without a character, and it stands to reason that here in these mixing bowl assemblies, shabby office attire, labourers' wear, and even the rags of gentlefolk can be seen.

Helped by his new-found wealth, Ned had spent some time at the coffee stalls on Tuesday, and had returned proudly with two eel pies, a few oysters and the news that Slit used to be a ballast-getter at the docks, but had run foul of the publican at Paddy's Goose who arranged the contracts. I don't hold that against Slit because running foul of anybody at the most notorious pub in the East isn't hard, and since much of the regular dock work is run by such villains, he has to sup with the devil. I was less happy about Ned going to Paddy's Goose to make further enquiries, but he'd done it without asking me, and had been told the last the publican had heard Slit was a casual.

So here we were, surrounded by desperate men who'd either come down in the world or given up hope of climbing up.

Once when I was up West the old woman selling milk straight from the cows in St James Park offered me a half-pint, it being a bad day for her. I had to pay for it, not with dosh but by listening to her tale of woe.

'No money in it these days,' she'd grumbled, 'with only four cows.' One of them mooed in her stand as if in agreement that this was no life at all. 'It wasn't like this when I was young. The real quality came then, and I made 'em syllabubs with sugar, spices, wine and fresh milk. Those were the days, all right. But times change, sweepie, as you yourself may have noticed.'

I had, and so had these hungry eager hopefuls all around us now. We were at the Hermitage western entrance, having failed in our mission yesterday at the central Wapping gates. We reasoned that Slit was likely to be at one of the two since the western docks were larger than the eastern, thus putting up a man's chances. What's more, Shadwell, the eastern docks entrance, was the nearest to Paddy's Goose, and might hold unfortunate memories for Slit. So today we had joined the mob surging down Nightingale Lane towards the riverside.

'Anyone here by the name of Slit?' Ned and I shouted from where we were on the edge of the mob. Shouting was a vain task, but for Bessie's sake we tried. Even with our best calling voices, however, only a few heard or had the interest to turn.

'What's it worth, nipper?' one wit asked. 'This Slit come into a fortune, has he?'

'No, but you have,' Ned replied quick as a flash, before I could stop him. 'There's a sovereign in it.'

Everyone near enough to hear burst out laughing at that. As if a sweepie, let alone his chummy, could have a sovereign, or, having one, would part with it. Just then the mob began to surge forward. The gates were opening, the great rush began to claim a work ticket, and Ned and I were swept along with it. The old hands—as most were—made for their favourite calling foreman, where they'd had luck before and might again if they could attract his attention quick enough. This isn't the House of God. Not all who deserve entrance will be taken. Many will be consigned to the hell of hunger, lingering in the hope of even the miserly four pence an hour awarded to casuals taken on late in the day, or wandering the streets in search of some other miracle job, or more likely drinking any money they still possessed in order to enter the house of oblivion. The pubs after all are the places to be, for there one hears of opportunities, both honest and dishonest. The line between the two is perilously easy to cross, especially in winters as bad as we've been having, with sixteen degrees of frost by day. No work then at the docks, and bakers boarded their windows against hungry rioters.

'There's Slit for you,' shouted a slight man in battered stove hat and threadbare velvet jacket.

'And a sovereign for you.' A reluctant man of our word, I pressed it into his hand, and silent tears of gratitude crawled down his face. All his calling and jumping up and down was failing to attract the foreman's attention today.

He had pointed out a man whose brawny bulk had ensured him a place at the front of this particular crowd, who stood a good six inches above the heads of most of them and whose face turned towards us as he made his way off grinning in triumph towards the appointed station in the grand forty-foot tea warehouse. It was a broad face, balding on top, but heavy sidewhiskers, and with his height I would easily pick him out again.

There was nothing more to be done (save a few chimneys), but early that evening we were back, waiting at the gates till Slit came out. My plan was to follow Slit home. Here he could ignore me. On his own doorstep he could not, although Ned's presence, as he made clear to me himself, would be necessary to proclaim my status as an honest man, and not a bailiff dressed up in sweepie's clothes.

Being nearly April, it was still quite light, but you'd never know it, for round the docks with its narrow lanes and tall overhanging warehouses, the sun is a rare visitor, and walking down Nightingale Lane without the march of a thousand feet beside you is not salubrious. The lane runs between the London and St Katharine's Docks, and there are more murders committed here, so they say, than anywhere else in London, more than even the Ratcliffe Highway, which has the reputation for it. We had to cross the highway, as once we had to our relief spotted Slit, we had to follow him, though it was a struggle with my knapped knees.

We scurried past number twenty-nine, where poor Mr Marr and his family were butchered by a seaman, who later killed himself and was buried at the crossroads in Cable Street with a stake through his heart for his pains. Further along towards Wapping, the King's Arms, where his second victims, the publican and his family, were murdered, is no more, having been swept away by the need of the London Docks for more space. But to my mind, here and all along the Highway, the atmosphere still lingers, especially round number twenty-nine. Behind the doors of the music hall saloons, the gin palaces, and the sailors' pubs on the highway, throng the seamen of all nations in search of relief after docking, and outside I feel the menace of what would happen if they all burst forth together yelling, 'Tom Wasp, breathe your last.' Death is never far away here, even for those who try to live honestly, although against us hunger is its weapon.

Up by Wellclose Square went Slit, past Mr Wilton's music hall, and across Cable Street towards Commercial Road. He plunged into the narrow lanes, all but deserted at this time of night with the pubs still full. The light was almost gone by now, and we drew closer to him as he turned through an archway into a court. I plucked up courage as well as speed.

'Mr Slit,' I called as politely as I could from outside the archway, having no wish for a knife between my ribs or a fist in my face.

He turned round smartly, relaxing when he saw I was presenting no violence.

'Wotcher, sweepie.' He looked amiable enough, a huge grin splitting the round jovial face. 'You, too, chummy.'

'I heard tell you're Bessie Bunting's brother. She that was murdered. I'd ask a few words with you about it.'

That took the grin off his face. 'The police, are you?' he asked mockingly. 'Or was you one of Bessie's men? Fancy her ladyship turning to a sweep.' He peered closer at me and at Ned, and Bessie, in this cold, dark night, seemed very near.

'Your nipper?'

'Only as chummy.'

'He ain't got Bessie's hair. Too yellow. What's Bessie to you?'

'Our friend and a lady for whom we had a lot of respect. The police aren't going to find out who did her in because they think they've found him already. I want to be sure they're right, for Bessie's sake, and that it wasn't this Moonman she lived with for a time, so her sister says.'

'Which one of them?' Slit demanded. 'There was three besides Bessie, and only Sophie's dead, so far as I've heard.'

'Jenny.'

He whistled. 'You done well, sweepie. Where'd you find her? I ain't seen either of them since Dad come out of prison in fifty-eight. Nor Polly. Where's she?'

'Jenny's up west,' I answered evasively. 'She lived with this Moonman too.'

'What of him?' He came closer, and Ned's hand tightened in mine.

'She wouldn't name him, but she said you'd tell us of him. I reckon Bessie was scared of him too, for she spent a lot of time running. I need to find him.'

Slit looked at us without speaking for a while, then said: 'You need to take care, Sweepie, if you go looking for him.' The grin hadn't returned.

'You sure you don't know him?'

Slit didn't answer, and Ned's grip tightened on my hand. Then he said, 'You'd best come in. I'll tell you about Moon-man, sweepie, for my sister's sake. Best mind where you sit. My woman's particular about dirt and smell.'

You'd never have thought so; she had so much of her own. When we climbed up to their lodgings, two rooms on the second floor of one of the houses, a downtrodden pale wisp, who might once have been pretty in the days when she didn't know what life was about east of the Tower, jumped up nervously from a rickety basket chair. Then her eyes fell on Ned.

'Not—?'

'Shut your face, Maria. He ain't another anybody's kid for you to feed. It's not the women cost the dosh,' Slit added to us gloomily, 'it's all the stray dogs and kids they want to look after. Not that I mind. It makes for a bit of cheerfulness about the place.'

Maria didn't look as if she found much cheerfulness, but then few in this part of London do. They're too busy making ends meet.

Slit sat us down in two chairs, quite an honour for us, and Maria retreated to sit on a wooden soapbox in the corner of the room. 'I'm going to tell you a story about Bessie you won't like,' he said amiably. 'There were five of us, and a couple who died before they were named. I came first, then Sophie, Bessie, Jenny and Polly. I were named for William Hazlitt, you ever heard of him?'

'A man of letters,' I said.

'A cantankerous old cove who used to haunt the pub Pa went to afore he was lumbered with a wife. I was William, but I'm known as Slit. A good name to have in the rookery.' The grin returned. 'St Giles was worse than it is now, and with the seven of us and Ma and Pa in one room, it's surprising more of us didn't die, either from the cholera or the beatings. Boys, girls, it made no difference. Ma didn't care. She had a permanent appointment with the gin bottle,' Slit said bitterly. 'Then she died when I was around thirteen. What she do that for? It finished us. Sophie went to the bad and drowned herself, Bessie ran off. I was next to go, and then Jenny. Never heard when Polly went.

'Bessie went off on her own,' Slit continued. 'Didn't trust nobody, she said, and I heard nothing more of her for a couple of years. Then I ran into her when she was selling flowers somewhere, and she told me she and Jenny were living with this Moonman in the Brill, and that's the last I heard of either of them till I ran into Bessie at Wilton's.'

'She was a barmaid at the Dragon, Bermondsey way,' I said cautiously. 'Served drinks at Wilton's too, did she?'

'No, sweepie. I told you you weren't going to like this. Bessie were in the Poses Plastiques.'

'Not our Bessie!' I cried out before I could help myself. 'She wouldn't do a thing like that.' She wouldn't pose for the Angels as God made her, and so she wouldn't do so for the devils that snigger over the Poses Plastiques. Even if Mr Wilton, running a respectable hall like he does, had 'em all dressed in flesh-coloured tights and whatnot, those sailors up in the gallery with their doxies don't drool over the historical representations of Queen Elizabeth and Mary Queen of Scots. It's the imagining of what lies beneath they want. Bessie wouldn't have liked that.

'Bessie was having to fend for herself and her kid.'

Ned's eyes grew rounder. That made a difference, of course. When there were two to think of, you could be forgiven for resorting to desperate means. 'When was this, Mr Slit?' I asked.

'One, perhaps two years ago. The kid weren't with her, but she told me about him, how life was a struggle. You know what I said to her? I said, "Come and see me, Bess, if you need to. I'll see you're all right, you and the kid." She never did though. Proud, that's what she was.'

'Did she tell you who the father was?'

He shrugged. 'No. Moonman maybe.'

Poor Bessie. If her son was five or six as I guessed, she'd been living with Moonman till he was born. A man she'd been terrified of, yet something gave her the courage to leave him, and support the baby by herself. I had to remember that Jenny might not have seen her for four years or so, years when she was modelling for the Angels. But she might still have been living with Moonman to protect Polly. Bessie had lived in a dark chimney then, and I grieved for her.

Perhaps Mr Slit saw my distress, for he added, 'He never let her alone. "I'll track you down, Bess. I'll track through the alleyways, through the tunnels, through the green trees and the grey stone of London's streets. Wherever you go I'll find you." Reckon he did, and put her in the family way. "You're mine, and you remember that." That's what she said Moonman told her. And he would. He's that sort. All of them—*his.*'

'And how do I find this Moonman?' I asked bravely, feeling sick inside now.

'Ask Polly. He's after her, only he don't know where she is. He found Bessie again instead. Best take care, sweepie. Moonman's with the garrotters.' Slit sniggered, but Maria didn't.

This was odd. Polly had followed in Bessie and Jenny's footsteps to live with Moonman even when she must have known how scared her sisters were of him.

'But she still had her pa to protect her,' I said, puzzled.

Slit roared with laughter. 'Protect her, sweepie? Your brain's clogged up with soot. One, two, three, four in his bed. He never got over Ma's death. Her pa *is* Moonman.'

Oh Bessie, Bessie, what a life you were forced to lead, and you so cheerful and kind to others. The world wasn't kind to you, dear Bessie. I had a few questions to answer from Ned after we left Mr Slit's abode, mighty glad to be away in the fresh air, after what he told us.

I asked Valentine once why it was some artists liked painting the same old thing time and time again. It's the different light, he said, and that's what seemed to happen up there with Slit and Maria. After he told us about Moonman, I couldn't see things clear at all. It was like he were already casting his dark shadow over us, just by being identified, or maybe it was because I didn't want to know about Bessie's real life, only to treasure what I knew of her. But if I was here to help her, I must work in dirtier flues than that.

It's not as if Ned ain't acquainted with what goes on with families living in one room. What he found hard to understand, and rightly, as he knew Bessie, is *why* it should. After she'd left home to make a life of her own, how did she get sucked back into the sewer she'd tried so hard to escape from?

'I don't know, Ned, and that's a fact,' I answered him as best I could, 'but there was some reason, you can be sure of it. We have to trust what we think of folks, and we know what Bessie was like, don't we?'

'Yes, Gov.' Ned cheered up, and he grew even more cheerful when I made a sudden decision to spend some of our newfound wealth at Wilton's on the way home. Money was money, and there might be some corner we could squeeze in without putting folk off their food and drink. Besides, I visited the baths but two weeks ago, and, as for Ned, the Lord conveniently sent a day of heavy rain last week to wash him clean (in His eyes at least).

We found ourselves tucked at the end of one long arm of the gallery, sitting on a hard bench by one of the entrance doors, but overlooking the stage and next to two jolly tars and their even jollier judies. They smelled so strong themselves, there wouldn't be room in their nostrils for our soot and grime.

Wilton's might cater for sailors in the gallery, but down below in the supper room was a different story. Mr Wilton had started with the intention of providing a high moral tone, with opera and drama to improve his customers' minds. But most folks don't enjoy being improved, and of late Mr Wilton seems to have given up the attempt, which is why the Poses Plastiques have crept in alongside *The Bohemian Girl.*

Not that sailors don't appreciate fine sentiments as well as fine bodies. I could see tears in most eyes, as a tenor sang the gypsy lover's song, 'Then You'll Remember Me,' a popular song when I was first going up chimneys as a nipper. When another singer followed with 'Poor Tom Bowling,' there was more water in the beer from tears than added by the man serving at the old Mahogany Bar, next to the supper room. The supper room is a grand hall, with its mirrors and barley-shaped columns, and its five red curtains. You should go there and see it for yourself.

By the time the curtain dropped, Ned had been much improved, not only by song, but by an edifying drama about a farmer's girl who came to London to seek her fortune. Even though the tars seemed to see a lot in it that I didn't, it was better than the penny gaff, which is Ned's only other experience of theatre.

Mr Wilton was—not surprisingly—not available when I requested the pleasure of an interview, but the lady looking after the food who turned out to be Mrs Wilton was pleased to help, especially when I offered to sweep her chimneys free of charge when next required. She even gave Ned a stale sweetmeat.

'Bessie Barton?' She thought for a moment. 'No one of that name that I recall. Murdered, you say? Poor girl.'

'She had lovely red hair,' Ned volunteered.

'Ah.' Her interest was caught. 'Now I do remember a girl in the Poses Plastiques with red hair. Not a Bessie though. Janie she called herself, Janie Jones. She only stayed a year at the most, then said she'd got some modelling work up West. Pity. The customers liked her.'

And so did I, Bessie, I said sadly to myself. 'When was she with you, Mrs Wilton?'

She laughed. 'Lord bless you, sweepie, it would take forever and a day to answer that. It's in the records somewhere, but who has time to look? It was our first Poses Plastiques—so it would probably have been early in sixty she came.'

'Did she happen to mention why she came to you?' Why should Bessie have left her modeling work—which she seemed to have taken up again about fifty-seven or fifty-eight—to work in the Poses Plastiques?

'I learn not to ask too many questions here. And so,' she added, 'had you, Mr Wasp.'

I felt as though the dark shadow of Moonman had swallowed me up, and fight though I might, I could not be free of the horror. You may ask why I was so overcome, since in the rookeries with one bed to a family, it's often part of life. There was something about the cold-blooded plan of this, though, that was different, and chilling to me. 'When Ma died,' he'd said. That was when Moonman turned to each of the girls in turn, hunting them down when they ran away, using them as his slaves in bed and house.

Had Bessie gone back to him to bear her child? Or had she run in loathing from him to bear the babe alone? To the workhouse, maybe, or one of those homes for fallen women?

My Bessie—in one of those places? I could not bear to think of it. And where was that child now? He had been taken away by Moonman, but to what kind of life? Or death. That dark thought haunted me. Where were we to start looking? Slit couldn't even tell us if Polly was still living with her pa, or where that might be. To wander round the Brill asking questions would bring forth nothing. They are tighter than garrotter's hands when it comes to outsiders. And of garrotters themselves there are plenty in the Brill.

I could do nothing to ease Bessie's life now, but I could for her son. There was only one person I could turn to, and that was Jenny. Somehow I had to persuade her to speak. To tell me of Polly, who I realised she had barely mentioned, and of Moonman. Jenny had told us his name was Joe, but she could have been lying through fear.

Trade was good this Friday. The regular sweep being ill by lucky chance, we did ten straight flue chimbleys (as we call them) and three horizontal benders by the time sweeping hours were over. Closed offices and people at home who have tea and supper in mind, aren't looking for sweeps to make their Maids of Honour all sooty, so we finished quite early. We walked slowly up to the Haymarket. We watched the judies parade in their finery, and the old soldiers of the Crimea selling chestnuts or penny magazines. They had marched off to glory in the war in their scarlet marching frocks, but they came back sick and fit for nothing, counting themselves fortunate if they still had enough limbs to get by.

There was no sign of Jenny, and we began to think we were wasting our time, as the smell of the pie seller's wares grew ever more attractive. Our wealth mustn't be wasted on pies, so we held back, though it was hard seeing the wistful look in Ned's eye.

At last we spotted her, clad in her gaudy red satin. No mistaking that walk, like a bird ever watchful for enemies, with a few paces forward and a quick turn of the head.

When she came level with our hidey-hole in the theatre alleyway she espied us, and you'd have thought we were a big cat waiting to gobble her up, she looked so scared.

'I told you, I don't know nothing,' she shouted as we stepped out.

'Ah, but we do now, Jenny,' I said to reassure her. 'We know all you've had to suffer from your pa, and about him being Moonman.'

'Who told you?' She stared at us, as pale and jittery as the fake pearls round her neck.

'Your brother.'

'I don't want to know,' she shrieked at us, turning towards the roadway in the hope of finding a customer to take her away from all this.

I hobbled after her. 'For Polly's sake,' I pleaded. 'Tell me where I can find them, if she's still with him.'

'She's not. She's in a respectable job in millinery, but for pity's sake, sweepie, she'll be lost if he finds her. If he finds me, either. It would all start again, the—'

'Terror by night,' I supplied for her gravely, knowing my Bible.

'Sweepie,' says Jenny in a low voice, 'you don't know the half of it. I'll tell you this. It's my belief he's found someone else for his bed, but he won't forget us, oh no. Not me, not Polly. We're his, you see. Ma went and died so he reckons it's our job to look after him like she did.'

'Your brother would help you, Jenny. He offered to help Bessie, only she was too independent.'

She was white under her paint. 'No one can help, sweepie. Only oneself, with eyes to watch, and ears to hear. Say nothing, do nothing, and that goes for you too. That's what it is—terror by night.' Above us the gas lamps twinkled against the dark sky, and the Haymarket glittered with bright colours and living, laughing people. But turn those lamps out, shut the eyes in sleep, and then what dreams may come in the chimney of the night?

' "Thou shalt not be afraid for the terror by night nor for the arrow that flieth by day. nor for the pestilence that walketh in darkness—" '

She cut off my homily with a shriek of laughter, though her eyes weren't laughing. ' "Pestilence that walketh in darkness"—that's him, all right. There's no stopping him. Say nothing. Do nothing. And he may not notice you.'

'If you see Polly or Moonman, Jenny, you may not want to tell the police, but a message at Mrs Blunt's pie-shop in Rosemary Lane will find me.' I thought of Mr Mudgwick and his round, smiling face and cream upholstered chairs. 'Or there's a gentleman would like to know too.' I carefully wrote his address down with my pencil on an old theatre bill flying around the alley, and gave it to her. She looked at it blankly, and no wonder. Even if she could read, the Jennies and the Mr Mudgwicks of this world were even farther apart than Jennies and the police—who at least have the underworld in common.

Mr Mudgwick was on my mind, for all these enquiries into Moonman meant I was neglecting the other strand of my investigations, even though they were not so much in my line. I had an arrangement with Mr Mudgwick to see him every week to report on progress, and he was kind enough to suggest a hackney carriage there and back at his firm's expense. It was, he explained delicately, an arrangement that suited him, since he had not the time to visit Hairbrine Court, a sentiment I appreciated. On Monday I had an urgent summons, however, and so Tuesday, the first of April, found Ned cleaning our rooms (or so he said, but maybe it was a joke, being the day it was) and me in Lincoln's Inn. No sooner had I arrived than Mr Mudgwick ushered me into the firm's carriage. I had my best clothes on, and I was glad of it, for the cushions would not be improved by my working clothes.

'We are bound for Newgate, Mr Wasp,' he informed me gravely. 'The trial is set for June at the Central Criminal Court. Mr Drake still maintains his story is true, and I feel that you knowing Bessie might have better fortune than I in suggesting he—um—might have had a slip or two of memory.'

To see Valentine in such circumstances was most unhappy. The cells, Mr Mudgwick informed me, had been modernised a few years earlier and were now highly regarded. Not by me, and from the look of him, not by Valentine. In one corner was a rolled up mattress as bedding, in the other a bucket and water basin, a solitary hand chair and table by the door—though they were gracious enough to bring an extra chair for Mr Mudgwick and, at his frown of displeasure, one for me. It wobbled, but so do I, so we were well matched, that chair and I.

Valentine told us he had been photographed by the governor as was now sometimes done in prisons, and had taken much objection to it. To think of Valentine recorded forever with his present sunken look of despair was sad to think of, when I remembered his lively face as he exchanged banter with Bessie. His image had been registered forever as a criminal, although no one knew but himself and God how justified that was.

'They set me to pick oakum, Mr Mudgwick,' he said despondently, 'no matter how I pleaded for my hands.' He spread them out to display the hands that had once painted Bessie and were now red and raw from the tarred rope. 'They said it was the tread wheel, if oakum was not to my liking.'

Mr Mudgwick tut-tutted. Words, he suggested, would be spoken to the Governor. Valentine was not yet convicted.

Reassured, Val turned to me. 'Mr Mudgwick tells me you are

fast on the heels of this Moonman who is undoubtedly Bessie's murderer. What news, Tom? Pray be quick in your search.'

'Moonman is her father, Mr Drake, and not yet found. I am informing the police of his name.'

'Her father?' Valentine looked bewildered. 'But I had believed Moonman a lover, not a parent.'

'Both, it appears, sir.'

He stared at me as though he did not understand, and then at last he realised what I was telling him.

'Dear God,' he said. 'And I was to paint her as the Virgin Mary in "The Lowest Room." I took her for a virtuous girl. Fallen, perhaps, but not so low.'

It was all I could do not to walk out, and only Mr Mudgwick's hand on my arm stopped me. Instead I said, 'Up where you live, sir, I suppose you can't be expected to see life clear. Where I am, you can see how virtuous women can be forced, and how they come through it, either fallen or still virtuous. Virtue is a state of mind, sir.'

'You are right, Tom.' Val's eyes filled with tears as he leaned forward to clasp my hands. At which the warder swiftly changed his mind for him. 'How often have the Angels talked of this. Holman Hunt has painted this very theme in "The Awakening Conscience." I had thought Bessie a Beatrice but now I see she is an Annie Miller. If only I had not been blinded. If only I had seen the truth. And I call myself an artist.'

I tried to be patient. 'Bessie is not an Annie Miller, whoever that lady is. She was herself, sir, and we must find who killed her. For her sake—as well as yours,' I added meaningly, for Valentine, I saw, was apt to go off on his dreams as he used to, whereas to my mind the hangman's noose is a powerful argument for concentrating on facts.

Mr Mudgwick evidently agreed with me for he nodded vigorously. 'Mr Wasp finds your story of rehearsing for a picture with

Bessie on the river's edge less than convincing. As your solicitor, it is not for me to doubt your word—' He broke off, indicating it was time for me to start cleaning this chimney of its soot.

Val tried to look haughty. 'And why, Tom? I rehearsed with you if you recall.'

I did not reply this was in the studio. Instead I took a different tack. 'I do indeed, sir. "Cast Out" was the name of that picture and maybe that made you see Bessie as a fallen woman, but one much to be pitied. This new picture of yours, "Love Betrayed," doesn't sound the same thing at all, yet you say you were still thinking of her as the Virgin Mary.'

Val stared at me. 'That was "The Lowest Room." My inspiration vanished.' I've seen that mulish look on his face before.

'Truth is a powerful weapon, sir,' I said, getting tired of talk of art, 'and perhaps you owe it to Bessie to use it.'

'There are reasons I cannot—' he began.

'But your neck is a more powerful one,' I says brutally.

He fired up at once. 'A gentleman's honour, Tom. It must be thought of.'

'And Bessie's corpse stinking after days in the river. How about thinking of that?'

He burst into tears. 'I do, I do,' he wept, and I believed him at last.

'Tell us, sir,' I said gently.

He still hesitated, but seeing Mr Mudgwick nodding his agreement with me, he gave in.

'Bessie always refused to visit me in the evenings. She said she had her reputation to think of. She used to laugh—and I see why now,' Val added bitterly. 'She had little to lose. I was surprised therefore when Parsons said she was asking to see me that evening after ten o'clock. I naturally thought she'd—' He saw Mr Mudgwick looking disapproving and continued innocently, '—she'd come to discuss the picture we were to begin on the morrow, and asked Parsons to show her in to the drawing room, where I was tucked up with a brandy, fire and the latest instalment of Thackeray's *Adventures of Philip* in the *Cornhill.* She came in, looking distraught—most unlike Bessie—and bedraggled, as though she'd been walking through the rain all evening. I went to her, but she brushed me aside when I tried to kiss her. She needed my help, she said. Money? I asked sympathetically. Money was no use. She needed me to come with her immediately so violence wasn't used against her, and the police were to be brought in, too, with my help.

'I didn't like the sound of violence at all, being—as one might say—in my cups, and seeing my face—though I had not spoken a word—she burst into tears and fled from the house.

'I ran after her—I adored that woman, Tom, truly—and caught her up by the wooden rail near Cadogan Pier. I pleaded with her that I would protect her if only she would come to live with me. No one would dare threaten her again, I promised her.

'She looked at me with those dark eyes of hers. "I know you mean well towards me, Val, but what of my child? Will you take him too?"

'It was the first I'd heard of any child, and it came like a thunderbolt. I could not speak for some moments and then all I could ask was, "A love-child, Bessie?" It was idiotic. "Not a love-child," she replied, "but a boy I love. He's five now."

' "And you were going to marry me, Bessie," I cried, "without my knowing this?"

' "No, Val." Despite her desperation, she even managed to smile. "You said you'd marry me, I never said I would marry *you.* How could I?"

' "Who's the father, Bess?" I asked, stricken, and then I said, because I was wrestling with grief, having thought her pure, "or don't you know?" How could I be so cruel?

'Oh, the reproach in her eyes. I could not bear it, and stammered out my apologies. And then she told me. "There's this man I'm scared of. He wants me back, but I won't do it. I am never free of him. The only place I'm safe from him is modelling with the other Angels, and now with you."

'I couldn't help it. I screamed out, "One of them? How could you do it, Bessie? How could you?" And I shook her by the shoulders. She wouldn't sleep with me, pretending to be so pure, but here she was as good as telling me the father of her child was one of them. You know they all three shared a studio in the mid-fifties, and she modelled for them, don't you? She took time away to have the child, and then came back to them. It all fits. I could hardly listen as she tried to tell me this man she was scared of had stolen her boy to hold until she returned to him herself, and that the police would take no notice of her—'

'I took it Moonman was the father,' I interrupted gently.

'Perhaps, Tom, but I believe Bessie would not have come to me for help unless one of the Angels had fathered her child. I suspect she might have called on the others also, though they deny it. I would be the last, because Bessie was proud.'

Mr Mudgwick coughed. 'And what happened then, Mr Drake?'

'The neighbour came up, and after he'd gone, she said that now she knew there was only one man in the world who truly loved her. "I would to God he were here, Val." "Go to him," I screamed, though I am ashamed to think of it now. She said nothing and walked away. I watched her silhouetted against the grey river, walking towards Cadogan Pier. And, may God forgive me, I did not go after her.'

He raised his haggard face to look at me pleadingly. 'Which of them did she go to, Tom? Do you know?'

Chapter Six: In Which I Advance up the Chimney

'I must confess, Mr Wasp—' Mr Mudgwick turned a blind eye to the amount of sugar I was taking off the cone with his sugar-cutters for this cup of coffee—not a drink I am accustomed to. '—that I am at a loss.'

A gentleman of lesser breeding than Mr Mudgwick would have set a glass of beer before me. 'At a loss,' he repeated, in case by that method I might understand his drift without his saying more. He had summoned me to Lincoln's Inn a week after our last meeting, and knowing he had the intention of speaking to the Angels about Valentine's sad case, I was eager to hear his news. It was as clear as a dewdrop that if Valentine believed one of his fellow Angels guilty, if not of murder, then of being the father of Bessie's boy, he had a point. Would Bessie have given herself to any other than this man she believed truly loved her? Had she visited him on the night she was murdered?

I myself had something to report to Mr Mudgwick, having taken it upon myself to visit Sergeant Wiley in the last few days. This had been a move of which Mr Mudgwick had been doubtful, as Scotland Yard had put one of their eight detective policemen on the case, once they realised a touch of quality was involved. To my mind, however, they would have little inclination to seek for a villain to prove Mr Drake innocent, since it doesn't look well to arrest innocent gentlemen of Valentine's standing. Sergeant Wiley, on the other hand, had every reason to want to find the true murderer himself, because of his indignation at the way his case was taken from him, first by Chelsea's V Section, and then by Scotland Yard. It was not easy to converse with the sergeant, however, despite our common interest.

'Not you again, sweepie. I thought you said you was only coming back to bring me the murderer.' Loud guffaw. 'What yer want this time?' He held his nose delicately, an insult I ignored, as I explained what I'd come for. After he'd stopped laughing over my role as Mr Mudgwick's private investigator, he finally gave some thought to the interests of Sergeant Wiley. His nose was left to sniff what it chose, a good sign that the sergeant agreed these interests could very well coincide with those of poor Valentine Drake. He even became quite cordial.

'What sort of a bloke is this Moonman then?'

'Fiftyish, big man by all accounts, round face, pulled down at one side. Occupation butcher in the Clare. Last known address the Brill. Bunting by name, but may not be using it.'

Sergeant Wiley smirked. 'I'll find him by suppertime,' he says, using an ironical tone of voice.

'I've faith in you, sergeant.' So I had. He wouldn't want to fail in front of a chimney sweep. 'He's known all right,' I continued. 'The problem is no one will talk, owing to the fact they have an objection to being garrotted for their pains. But the police have powerful inducements at their disposal in the way of money. As well,' I added hastily, seeing him glower, 'as the intelligence our Lord has presented you with.'

Sergeant Wiley wholeheartedly concurred. 'He has, He has.' Then he glared at me again. 'I could have a word with K Division. But what's to be done when we find him? Can't bring him in. Case is closed.'

'You have your ways.' This wasn't meant as a compliment, since the ways of the crushers in the local K Division would bear no resemblance to the standards suggested by our Lord in

His Sermon on the Mount. The poor to them aren't blessed, only a blessed nuisance.

Sergeant Wiley looked gratified, however. 'I does indeed.'

That had been nearly a week ago, and I'd had no news since, not that I would expect to be the first to hear, but Mr Mudgwick had heard nothing either.

'At a loss,' that gentleman repeated mournfully yet again, his shiny white fingertips pressed together before him on the white blotter. No speck of soot would dare dirty those hands, though dirt is a strange thing. Grimy black is ingrained in my hands, but as I pen this, ink blobs fly everywhere, on the paper, on my hands, and on my clothes and cause me as much annoyance as soot would to the lawyers of this world.

'I was not satisfied,' he continued, 'with the outcome of my visit to Mr Tait, Mr Harwood-Jones and Mr Fairfax, although they have *all*—somewhat reluctantly, I must confess—agreed that Bessie did pay each of them a visit and that it might have been on the evening of the twenty-second of February, the night Mr Drake is accused of murdering her. This is cautious progress, but I fear I could hardly proceed to enquire whether any of them was the father of Bessie's child, owing to the fact that they were all at pains to deny to me anything other than the most correct professional relationship with her.'

The fingertips grew agitated as Mr Mudgwick gazed at me in what I might have called a helpless manner had he not been a representative of the law of our land. 'I am bound to admit, Mr Wasp,' he continued forlornly, 'that the unworthy suspicion crossed my mind that of course they would claim that. That, I gather, is what they told the police, and they could hardly say otherwise to me. You, however, could make further delicate enquiries.'

He bestowed on me such a sweet cherubic smile that it crossed my mind Mr Charles Dickens might have chosen him as his model for the Mr Cheeryble in the adventures of *Nicholas Nickleby*, which, so Joe the patterer tells me, took the world by storm in monthly instalments many years ago. It had been early days for his new calling, having not long been cast out of the printing trade, and thus he recalled it well.

How Mr Mudgwick thought a humble chimney sweep might chatter on such a subject to three artistic gentlemen put me at a loss, however. With Moonmen and magsmen, Tom Wasp had his methods, but with those who dwell in swell houses it's a different matter, which is why I had approached the gentlemen by the tradesmen's door. However, as I says to Ned, hair and hats are provided by our Lord to keep our brains warm. I have both, so I put some thought to it, having first explained my doubts to Mr Mudgwick.

'Suppose,' I suggested, 'you were to ask Mr Drake to pen a letter to each of the Angels asking as a personal favour to him if they could use Ned and me as models, me needing the money in order to help look for Bessie's boy?' They couldn't refuse such a plea from a fellow Angel to help in what their deceased model would most surely have wished.

I am pleased to say that Valentine was eager enough to agree to this plan, once convinced that the pledge of the Angels to remain loyal between themselves applied to art and not to matters that could result in a hanging. Thus it was that Ned and I set forth on Wednesday, April sixteenth, for an appointment with Mr Laurence Tait.

A dragsman once said to me that life is just one set of crossroads after another, and he should know since he haunts the highways by night to steal luggage from cabs and carriages. For all I know, that may be why in the old days gibbets were erected and suicides buried at crossroads, as if to point out the lesson that these folks had taken a wrong turning in life.

Now it seemed to me that with Bessie, too, we were at a

crossroads, only this was more like a fork. Should we search for Bessie's killer on the left or the right, among the dregs or among the swells? Whichever was right, I thought ruefully that Tom Wasp seemed to be doing his best to go up both paths at the same time.

'It don't matter, Gov,' Ned said, when I put this interesting point to him. 'I reckon they'll join up sooner or later.'

The reason? This is London, and no matter how you try to separate East and West, sooner or later they'll come together. The flow of a city is westwards. The ancient part of London is here, where the Tower of London stands. Then grand folk began moving west, and now London stretches even as far as Kensington. But never forget that the East is the solid heart of London, good or bad. So if our search for Moonman takes us west, or our enquiries of the Angels lead us back east, there should be no surprise. The face of the West is fairer than its feet, and the feet of the East sweeter than its face. Somewhere in the midst of the two, we'll find the killer of our beloved Bessie.

Having availed ourselves of the funds Mr Mudgwick had been good enough to bestow upon us, Ned and I took an omnibus to our appointment, and the sweet fresh breezes of the upper deck were pleasant indeed in April. Ned displayed such satisfaction at this adventure that I harboured an unworthy suspicion he accompanied me more for this than devotion to our cause. We presented ourselves upon the front steps of Laurence Tait's home in Bloomsbury's Museum Street at nine a.m., on the specified morning, knowing that though we should work for it, payment was already guaranteed. The learned of London were crowding past us on their way towards the British Museum and the less learned crowded the other way into the equally important (to my mind) institution of Mudie's Circulating Library at the far end of Museum Street.

I removed my best hat, as the manservant opened first the

door and then his mouth to shout *Trade!* and point down below to the area, as if despatching us to hell. The Day of Judgment will be a black time for chimney sweeps if St Peter ever trained as a butler.

Ned piped up for me. 'Tell your master his models have arrived.' I thought at first he would shout *Trade* again, but at that moment Laurence Tait himself came out of a door at the far end of the passage.

'Follow me,' he growled.

Accepting this gracious invitation, we clambered up several narrow staircases to the top of the house where was the studio. I gave several rooms a professional glance on the way up, and saw several fine fireplaces suggesting wide flues. The older the house, the bigger the flues, for as houses grew narrower and taller, so did the chimneys. I deduced this was an old house, by which I mean about the time of Good Queen Bess, who knew that good food came from good spits and fires, and that it had changed with the times. The rooms were small and there were a lot of them, though judging by the noise coming from some of them, this was not an altogether harmonious household.

Laurence's heavy jowls and beard were wobbling, little eyes glaring out over the full cheeks. He was not in good humour, I deduced, though whether this was our fault or Mrs Tait's, I could not determine. We were shown into the studio and told to stand on the platform so he could study us. The room was cluttered and untidy, though not cheerfully so like Valentine's, and one end of it was dark, despite it being at the top of the building. It seemed empty of character, as though Laurence purposely left himself behind when he came up here, put on his artist's smock and picked up his paints. There were several piles of paintings faced to the wall, jumbled anyhow, and what looked like several unfinished canvases on easels. All of them displayed ladies of a certain size and with a certain amount of their bodies revealing more than is common to see in public. In each, a gentleman to one side regarded them closely. One showed a trim ankle ascending the steps to a church, another a lady removing her stocking, and another a gentleman standing over a lady in a low-cut evening dress in a box at the theatre, although the drama on stage was not what was engaging his attention.

Valentine had explained to me that the Angels believed the brotherhood of Pre-Raphaelites had suffered through preoccupation with their 'Stunners,' who had become more important to them as women than as their models. How, Valentine had declared passionately to me, could one adequately portray the truly virtuous woman if she slept unwed at your side?

This was not a problem that had ever raised its head with me, but I tried to understand his point of view, even though I could not help remembering Valentine had done his best to persuade Bessie to stay with him out of working hours. Valentine had shown me two sketches by his neighbour, Dante Gabriel Rossetti, who was one of the Pre-Raphaelites. Both were of his wife, Lizzie Siddal, one the beautiful girl he had first met, the second the invalid she became, still beautiful but worn down with the cares of this world. She it was who had died on the same night as Bessie, though by her own hand, not another's. Lizzie Siddal had diverted Rossetti from displaying his true genius, in Valentine's view. Euphemia Gray had come between Millais and the critic Ruskin, Holman Hunt was obsessed with Annie Miller, Ned Burne-Jones and William Morris were diverted from their true paths by marriage. Again, I could not help remembering Valentine was only too anxious to divert himself by this means.

The Angels, however, had sworn an oath that married or not, art and their mission must come first.

From what I'd seen of the Angels so far, I hadn't taken them for such a collection of monks, despite Valentine's words.

I knew I had to tread delicately with Laurence Tait, and his first words confirmed it.

'Understand this, Wasp, or whatever your ridiculous name is, my models work for their money.'

'I've noticed that most money arrives that way, sir.' I'd also noticed Laurence seemed nervous, and dropped a paintbrush or two through fumbling fingers.

'I mean *hard* work,' he added. 'And the boy too.'

Ned, gazing at him all innocent-eyed, replied, 'Oh, I *will* work hard, sir,' but I knew what he was thinking: how glad he was he brought that wallet to a new home.

'Let me explain to you. I doubt if you've heard of Mrs Elizabeth Montagu. She died long before your time.'

'Most chimney sweeps have, sir,' I replied evenly. 'Just as I daresay you'll have heard of Michelangelo.'

'I don't pay you to teach me my job, sweep! Listen to me. The theme of my picture is "Gratitude," and it depicts one of Mrs Montagu's chimney sweeps' May-day dinners. Heard of those?' he barked ironically.

'From which sprang our sweeps' May first festival,' I said. 'Blue Stocking, they called her, didn't they? Famous for gathering all the cleverest men in London to Montagu House. Dr Johnson, wasn't it, sir? You'll know better than me.'

He ignored my own touch of irony. 'My picture will depict Mrs Montagu in her beneficent kindness handing an evil-looking sweep a new pair of boots and his accomplice—portrayed by this child here—busies himself emptying her reticule.'

'I see, sir.' And a nastier idea couldn't have occurred to him if he had deliberately been looking for it. As, of course, he might have been. I wondered what Mrs Montagu was going to reveal under his brush, and whether I, the evil sweep, would be doing the staring at it.

'I am prepared to spend up to two shillings each, drawing you. I shall not require you again.'

Then followed an hour or two while I endeavoured to look evil and Ned—with less effort—managed to look like an accomplished dipper. I pondered while I grimaced my way to my florin on how I could raise the question of Bessie.

'You'll have another lady then to model Mrs Montagu, now Bessie's gone,' I said brightly.

His head shot up. 'That woman was not my model.'

'Mrs Rossetti, perhaps. Lizzie Siddal as was,' says I to air my knowledge. Just to get him talking.

'Lizzie Siddal's dead,' Laurence replied casually. 'There seems no doubt Lizzie killed herself, and in any case, Valentine hardly knew her, so he would hardly be suspected of murdering her too.' He seemed rather sorry about this, despite his guffaw. 'Bessie of course was—'

'Foully murdered by someone unknown.'

'So you believe. I hope you're right. Val was besotted by the woman. The fool wanted to marry her. It looks black against him.'

'As it did against our Lord, sir,' I replied soberly. 'And He was falsely accused.'

'It seems Val himself is in the habit of making false accusations. According to his solicitor, he claims the unfortunate woman told him that she came here that evening and was turned away. I agree she called, though I had forgotten the precise date. She was hardly turned away. I gave her money—which is what she came for.'

His face darkened when I did not reply. 'I've no patience with Val,' he burst out. 'He sets the woman on a pedestal and then murders her when he finds out she was a whore.'

Then he seemed to recollect to whom he was speaking, for he snapped out, 'I'm only giving you the work for Val's sake.

The Angels vow to support each other.'

'Then you are doing it for Bessie's sake also. Owing to the fact the money will be used to find her son, and,' I added casually, 'whose son he was.'

Before he could reply, the door was thrust open and in burst a crinoline. Such are the ridiculous fashions of our day that a lady's skirt swings in several seconds in advance of the main body, especially when escaping from confinement while traversing a narrow staircase. A pair of black-shod feet with white frilly drawers-clad ankles made their appearance. Inside the crinoline was the lower half of a pink-bonneted and very angry Mrs Tait—or so I presumed—a most formidable lady judging by her jaw and flashing eyes.

'Whose? Whose *son?* I can tell you whose son. His!' The gloved finger trembled in indignation as it pointed at her husband.

'Be quiet, Adelaide,' Laurence yelled, but even the sight of her burly husband incoherent with rage failed to achieve this. 'I am At Work!'

'You're not. You're talking about that woman—you're always either talking of her or kissing her or pinching her. Like all the others. I know you.'

'Not here, Adelaide.' He advanced menacingly, and I believed he would lay hands on her, but she dodged him with a quick swirl of the crinoline to trip him and she sailed straight for Ned and me.

'Did he tell you that woman came here and that she asked to see *me?*'

'No.' I endeavoured to stop looking evil and look interested instead.

'She arrived about half past eight, *knowing,* I am sure, that I would be alone after supper. She told me a cock-and-bull story—as one mother to another, she said. How she was Laurence's model and her little boy had been stolen by a wicked man. Naturally I assumed she wanted money, but she said no, she wanted Laurence's help. He was to go with her, if you please, to the police to show she was a responsible woman. They would take notice of him. As if I believed anything that red-haired hussy said. You know what she meant, don't you?'

'Adelaide, this is only a sweep,' Laurence yelled at her, but she wasn't listening, fortunately.

'She was telling me the boy was Laurence's, of course. Why else would she come to me and not him? Then Laurence came in and found her. I only had to look at his face to see his guilt. *Again.*'

'Again, ma'am? You mean he has other love children?'

The look of rage on Laurence's face was ample reward for his insults to Ned and me.

'Probably. He's always pinching and poking his models. He thinks I don't know, don't you, Laurence? But I do. Even our housemaids prefer to leave without characters rather than stay with him.' Her voice began to wobble, and tears rolled down her face.

'He's a sweep, Adelaide, for God's sake.'

This time she did hear. She gave us a careful look. 'You mean he's a *real* sweep?' she cried, recoiling several paces. 'Not just a model?'

I made her a bow of assent, but she shrieked, 'I've been talking to a *sweep?* Get him out, Laurence, immediately.'

It was a pretty burlesque, I thought, as Laurence first escorted both crinoline and wife downstairs, although I reflected that burlesques grew from ugly stories.

Ned and I would be next on the downward path, so I took a quick opportunity to inspect the pictures both on the easels and by the wall. There was a darkness in his painting, so the housemaid had said, and surely a wild beast had painted this harlot, brassy, impudent, yet looking over her shoulder into the murkiness of the night, representing a dark future.

'Very powerful,' I said cheerily to Laurence as he returned.

'Get out,' was all the thanks I got for my compliment. 'But before you go, understand this, Wasp, I don't want you going to those police friends of yours with any fairy tales you've heard here. They're merely women's ravings. I'll tell you the truth. I may have touched Bessie now and then, purely professionally, which she mistook for more intimate approaches, but I never slept with her. Understand?'

'Or she wouldn't with you.'

'Out!' he yelled, face bulging with anger. 'If you want to know about Bessie, you go to Fairfax. He's the one who wanted to marry her, and then thought better of it.'

I stored this interesting tidbit quickly in my brain, and returned to present issues. 'And the money for Bessie's boy?' If we were going before he'd had his money's worth from us as models, Bessie's boy was not going to suffer for it. Nevertheless, after how he'd spoken of Bessie it seemed like taking thirty pieces of silver, instead of only half what we'd been promised, a shilling each.

Ned and I spent a long time making up our loss of earnings by sweeping our regulars, and I picked up an old tin that would do nicely to put our 'Bessie money' in, although most of the sovereigns still lived under the mattress. The following day we returned to Hairbrine Court, more than ready for a glass of ale and a pie. There's a song sung on the streets about 'Home, Sweet Home,' and though Hairbrine Court isn't sweet to most, it is to us. Not, it appeared, to Sergeant Wiley for rather than come to us, he sent a police van for us, one of those Black Mariahs as they're called in the villainous East. It was very civil of the sergeant, for in the kind of neighbourhood we live in to be carted off in a police van can do a lot to increase a man's good reputation. We walked past the usual water-booted and jersey-clad matelot-type Thames police waiting their calls, and found Sergeant Wiley in jovial mood.

'So you're here. Brought the judy's murderer, have you?'

I grinned politely. There are folk in all walks of life that have one joke per person, and have no qualms about repeating it. I got on with the business in hand. 'You've news of Moonman, sir?'

Sergeant Wiley seemed positively brimming over with goodwill towards us, but to my surprise he shook his head. 'Dead end, Waspie.' I took this latter familiarity as a compliment. 'George Bunting was last heard of in Queen's three or four years ago. No trace of him since, save that he was released. His debt was paid for him, but he'll be back. They always are.'

The Queen's is the new swell name for the old Fleet and Marshalsea prisons, but the new name hasn't changed much about it, and it's a marvel anyone gets out of there, for how's a man to pay his debt if he's locked up? George Bunting's was—and I know how, I reckon. By Bessie, to cancel all her 'obligations' to her father. Instead, poor girl, Moonman tracked her down for more.

'He's changed his name, I've no doubt,' I said. 'Jenny will know if only I can persuade her to talk.'

He looked strangely at me, but I thought nothing of it at the time, as I continued, 'I can see you found something though, Sergeant, if I read that smile of yours aright.'

'That's what I need you for. Look at this.'

He picked up a box from the table and dangled the remnants of a red silk scarf before my eyes, such as any girl might wear tucked round her neck. This one was different, for it had belonged to Bessie, and she'd bought it while she was posing with me for 'Cast-Out.' I would know it anywhere even if she hadn't embroidered her name upon it, so proud she was of it. Real silk, and now I know where she lived, I understand how she could have come by it, for there's a shop in Holywell Street called the Golden Ball that sells silk remnants. She'd embroidered her name on it too—Bessie Barton. I had wondered why she'd needed to display her name and now I knew. This scarf was Bessie Barton's, and nothing to do with Janie Jones, Lizzie Watkins or Eliza Bunting. This was part of her new life—and it had been taken from her. The gaslight was on the white thread, as bright as the tears that made streaks on my cheeks.

'It's hers,' said I. 'Where did you find it?'

The sergeant was only too eager to tell me. 'I got talking to one of the steamboat captains at Waterloo Bridge pier, you having told me this Bessie lived nearby. They know the river, and his view is she went in the river near where we were standing, not Chelsea. I didn't have much hope, there being precious little to find once the mudlarks have been at work, but F Division told me I could go ahead and search all I like. So I did.' He looked mighty pleased with himself—and so he might.

'I found it under a pile of muck on the back by Milford Lane. Know it?'

I did indeed. Milford Lane leads from St Clement's in the Strand down to the muddy riverbank, past the big printing houses, and it's just the sort of place Moonman might choose to garrotte our Bessie at night, when all's silent save the hum of machinery to drown any screams. It's not far from Temple Stairs, where there are always boats moored, so that's where people gather, not in the darkness of the lanes.

'You know what this tells us, Waspie?' The sergeant was very chummy now.

'That Mr Drake isn't likely to have met her in Milford Lane.'

'It's true he could have followed her there, since she lived round these parts. He's got no evidence to show where he was after he was seen with Bessie by the river.'

'He might, but he wouldn't know the river like Moonman did.'

'If that fellow of yours is still alive,' Sergeant Wiley said glumly. 'Can't find no trace of him.'

'Oh, he's alive all right. Some Moonmen are just bogeys in our minds, but Bessie's was real, just as Jenny told us.'

'You may be right, Wasp. Jenny too.' The sergeant looked uneasy. 'While I was at F Division I saw this, circulated from C Division in Little Vine Street.'

I had no interest in divisions. I was staring at the face provided by this newfangled police photography. It was dead, very dead, but to me it looked a lot like Jenny, her bulging eyes gazing out at me in reproach.

'Garrotted,' Sergeant Wiley informed me lugubriously.

Chapter Seven: In Which an Angel Falls

It was fortunate that Sergeant Wiley was feeling well disposed towards me, for even as I said to him, 'The poor soul could be Jenny,' it occurred to me that it could go badly for me, having seen Jenny so recently. The sergeant didn't seem disposed to point this out to me, and, as for me, I was busy trying to get my own thoughts straight.

Have you ever tried to find your way through a London particular? Maybe you call it something else where you come from, but here in old foggy London we live in clouds much of the time, and not like the angels' white and fluffy residences. Our clouds are smoky, thick and yellow-black. They reach out to clutch you by the throat and choke you to death, almost as bad as the soot that killed so many climbing boys in the bad old days and even now claims its young victims. A learned gentleman once told me we have ninety days a year of particulars, but I wouldn't know the truth of that. My old master, a good man as master sweeps went for those times, used to say we should thank the Lord for the belching chimneys, for otherwise we sweeps would have no job. There's two points of view on that, as to my mind it's the evil smoke from those chimneys that causes the particulars.

Being April, the worst of the particulars are behind us, and the fog I speak of now is in my mind. Out of it loom sudden and unexpected shapes, sinister and menacing, but then they disappear like the phantasmagoria show I once saw at a fair years ago. There above our heads came the shape of a fearful spectre in a great circle of light growing ever larger as it sped towards us, only to vanish just as you thought it was the Devil himself come to claim you. The spectre in my mind now is Moonman, indistinct and formless, reaching down the chimney to grasp me. With Jenny's death I felt he was coming closer, and one day I would reach upwards and *touch* his claw-like hand.

The pigmen at St James's Division in Vine Street were of the opinion, according to Sergeant Wiley, that Jenny had been murdered by one of her clients. She had been identified by one of the other streetwalkers. It happens often enough, poor souls, but garrotting shouted out Moonman to me. I was sure somehow he had heard of my enquiries and caught up with Jenny at last. Who knows? He might have followed me to the Haymarket when I last met her, and killed her to stop her telling me more. Maybe he wanted her back for his bed, or a share of her money.

Perhaps he was not ahead of me in the fog, but a short step or two behind me. Now that was an unwelcome thought, for it made me responsible for Jenny's death, as well as having me thinking I should be walking with one eye forward, one eye back. Sergeant Wiley seemed to agree with me as to how Jenny died, for he was willing enough to talk, obviously pleased that his little hunch had proved right.

Sergeant Wiley surprised me by being sympathetic when I told him how I felt. 'Can't look at it like that, Waspie. You're not God.'

'No, but He gave me brains to think with. And what I'm thinking now is that I have to find Polly, Jenny and Bessie's little sister.'

'Take care, Waspie, or she'll be the next.'

I'd thought of this for myself. 'If I don't,' I pointed out, 'we'll never find Bessie's child, and there'll be another death.'

Wiley shrugged. 'Ten to one he's dead cargo'—that meaning Moonman, being balked of his prime reason for taking the boy, would be getting rid of him too, if he hadn't already done so.

'If it was his own child, he'll let the boy live.' I wasn't too sure.

'But if he was sired by one of those Angels—' Wiley didn't finish; there was no need.

'I'll find Polly,' I said bravely, 'and what's more, Moonman won't be following me.'

All I knew about Polly was that Jenny had said she was in millinery. Now that was a hat that covered a lot of possibilities. It could mean a respectable young lady working in a swell establishment, or, more likely, that she was working at the back of a Haymarket sweatshop where money was so poor many of the girls had to walk the streets by night. 'Start with them, Wasp,' the Sergeant advised me, and accordingly, six o'clock on Saturday evening found me at the Haymarket.

I spotted a judy who looked kinder than most, and approached her, doffing my hat. This surprised her greatly. Her red spangles glittered as her body shook with mirth. 'Not your lucky night, sir. I don't take sweeps as clients.'

'Information, ma'am, about poor Jenny found dead near here last week.'

She wasn't smiling any longer. 'What do you want to know about her for?' She was backing away as though I were the murderer himself. As, indeed, I suppose she might have thought I was. The girl shivered. 'I guessed it was Jenny when she didn't turn up any more. She was scared of someone. You?' She peered at me, white under the paint.

'I'm a sweep, miss. How could I afford a lady like you or Jenny?'

'You might have been the one she was afeared of,' she persisted.

'It was her father. She called him Moonman. Did she ever say anything to you about him? George Bunting was his name once. Did he ever come here for her? Big man, side of his face pulled down.'

'Jenny said nothing. She wasn't the sort.'

'What about her sister, Polly? Did she ever come here?'

'Not that I know of. She did mention a sister who made hats.'

'Do you know where?' The bright lights of Piccadilly blind you to the black holes all round it, and Polly could be anywhere.

She didn't like being questioned. 'I wouldn't tell you, even if I did know, see? But I don't. Round here we learn to keep our mouths shut. Why was Jenny killed, you answer me that?'

I didn't know the answer to her question. The fog was no clearer in my mind, but being at the Haymarket standing surrounded by the bright lights and swell carriages of those who ride upon the crests of the waves of filth of London life, put me in mind of the carriage that had picked Bessie up that day. I was no nearer to finding its owner, nor Polly, nor Moonman, and I went home despondent, feeling Ned was right. I was only a sweep, and although God had picked me out to do justice for Bessie, He wasn't giving much help.

I found Ned curled up in his bed already peacefully sleeping. Well, sleeping anyway. It had been a hard day, for we'd done all our regular Shadwell chimneys, and after his morning at the Ragged School I made him attend, he said he had somewhere to go. I suspected the worst, but he said no more and nor did I. Looking at him, sleeping under a soot bag, his skin healthy even if grimy with soot, I was filled with new resolution. Ned was my home, and I hoped that Bessie's boy would fare as well. Thinking of Ned and the Ragged School put me in mind of my own lettering days, and suddenly I had an idea about how I might be able to find Polly.

A sweep couldn't go into milliners' establishments. They wouldn't let me over the threshold, whether it was a respectable shop or a sweatshop. I needed a lady of quality to help me and I knew who that would have to be since I only knew one: Lady Beezer.

I made you a promise early on in my tale that I'd tell you how I was lettered. As I mentioned, my climbing days began when I was not yet five years old, but my master was not as bad as some—and he frequently told me of my good fortune. I was quick, agile and highly prized, and he had a number of grand houses on his regular list out in the country, one of which was at Hanwell, to which we travelled by cart.

These old houses were confusing to a youngster, even though I'd been in the trade three years by the time I got lost in Hanwell Place. 'All up!' I remember crying from the roof, meaning the brushes were through and the chimney clean, and there remained the task of finding my way back down again. This is a skill for a climbing boy, and none too easy when there are several flues, some branching.

On this particular day I slipped as I was wriggling downwards with my feet braced against the flue walls, and on recovering myself, couldn't tell in the blackness whether my feet should go to the left or right flue, having turned round in my fall. The smell of soot is at its scariest then. It chokes you in the silence of being confined so closely. I took the wrong flue, and emerged not in the grand dining room where my master awaited me, but in an entirely different room, which I'd not seen before. There was no wallpaper on the wall, or if there were, I couldn't see it, for the entire room was lined with books. Books were something new to me then. I'd seen one or two, but not like this, lined up in battalions, neat leather covers. Every book in the world must be gathered here, I thought.

I was scared, even though as a courtesy the fire was not lit, and even more scared when someone rose up from a large leather armchair. She was a tall woman, and a large one. Skirts in those days were not like those of today with big crinolines and tight sleeves. They were as big on top as below, large full sleeves being very popular. The lady was dressed in cream, and seemed enormous, as fat as she was tall, though that may have been her dress.

'Who are you?' she demanded.

I wailed, already aware that this appeal to the lady might avoid a scolding.

'Poor child.' She walked towards me and I stood my ground, though I'd dearly have loved to shin up the chimney again. She had a plate of biscuits before her and normally my eyes would be hopefully feasting on them, but today I couldn't take my eyes off those books.

'If you please, ma'am,' I asked, 'what are these all for?'

'It's a library, child. Haven't you seen books before?'

'Not like this,' I piped.

'Can you read?'

'I don't know,' I answered doubtfully.

She produced what I now know to be a Holy Bible and opened it before me. Black squiggles danced before my eyes. She pointed out a row of them. 'That reads "Suffer little children to come unto me." Do you understand?'

'No, ma'am.'

'It means be kind to little chimney sweeps for the sake of our Lord.'

'Is that your husband, ma'am?'

She looked shocked, till she saw it wasn't my fault.

'No, Tom,' she said gently, having asked my name. 'Our Lord is Lord of all, and you shall be taught about Him.'

That was the first time I met Lady Beezer, but far from the

last. Her husband, I learned, was in parliament and a member of the Society for Superseding the Necessity for Climbing Boys. She tried to explain what that meant, but it sounded frightening to me. Lady Beezer told me the society had our good in mind, and they were trying to get laws through parliament to help boys like me.

My master wasn't very enthusiastic after she summoned him, but seeing who she was, he reluctantly agreed I could go to a Ragged School one day a week, that being a charity school, and her ladyship said that I could spend Sundays at Hanwell Place. When my master triumphantly pointed out I could not walk that far, she said a cart would be sent for me every other Sunday, and I was to attend the Hanwell Church Sunday School. I spent my day in the kitchens, but her ladyship took a great interest in me, and when I could read she let me go to her library to look at the books, always being careful to wash my hands first—which is how I got in the habit of washing once a week at the Model Whitechapel baths, though sometimes for the adventure of it I try St Martin's or even Marylebone.

I was thirteen when Lord Beezer told me an act had gone through Parliament forbidding the use of climbing boys under ten, but however much Lord Ashley, now Lord Shaftesbury, fought with Lord Beezer's help, the House of Lords watered the terms down so much it didn't make much difference on the streets. I was grown by then, and past lettering, but Lady Beezer made me promise to go to see her once a year, not to sweep her chimneys, but just to tell her how I was. She offered to set me up in a different trade. I thought about it but told her no. Chimney sweeping was what I knew, and seeing the law wasn't working, I could do more for climbing boys by becoming a master sweep myself and treating them properly by spreading the good practices than by starting a new venture. My choice hasn't won me many friends amongst the master sweeps, but it's won me respect. Lord Beezer died some years ago, but her ladyship lives on, through growing older, as we all do. I still visit her once a year in December. This year, I decided, I would go in April as well. Straightaway in fact, for all it was Easter Day.

'Call at the front door, Tom,' she always says, but I won't for it would cause her ladyship's servants to look on her with disrespect. Besides, I enjoy the progression upwards through the house. I feel like Jacob on his ladder to heaven. I call at the trades entrance in the basement, where I have an understanding with the housekeeper Mrs Tiggle, and then I am led out of the basement to the ground floor, then up richly carpeted stairs to the library. Her ladyship always receives me there, for she guesses rightly that I'm eager to see those books.

This Sunday afternoon, having taken her by surprise, Lady Beezer was in her drawing room, but saw me straight away. She always wears black now, but the kindness of her face beams out over the dark beneath.

'What is it, Tom?'

I don't recall my mother, but I imagine her like Her Ladyship. When I get to heaven and the dirt has fallen off me, there she'll be, waiting for me arms outstretched, and looking just like Lady Beezer.

I explained to her about Bessie and Bessie's boy, and about how she and her poor sister Jenny had both been done to death, most likely by Moonman, and her ladyship listened very attentively.

'I've heard about the arrest of Mr Drake, of course, and thought of you, for you told me last December that you were posing for him. I am truly sorry, Tom, for he sounded a nice young man.'

'And an innocent one, I believe,' I declared stoutly.

'And are you sure this Moonman isn't one of the other Angels?'

Now this was something that hadn't occurred to me, but I dismissed it, seeing that Bessie was on modelling terms with at least three of the Angels.

'The boy may belong to one of them,' I concluded, 'but not Moonman himself. He comes from her past life, and few of us can shake that off.'

'But perhaps you are mistaken in thinking Moonman murdered her. That could have been an Angel too.' Seeing the doubt on my face, her ladyship added, 'Even if they would not do it themselves, these Angels might have hired someone to kill her. Had you thought of that?'

I admitted I had not, though why I could not tell. I thought of an argument against it, however. 'She visited them all the evening she was killed. There would be little time to hire a killer to murder her.'

'*If* she died that evening. Surely the police cannot be sure, Tom, even though it looks that way.' She hesitated. 'Why have you come to me? I am delighted you have done so, but I am an old woman. Did you require assistance—of the financial kind?'

She asked so kindly I did not take it amiss, and explained about Mr Mudgwick. Then I explained the reason for my coming, finishing with, 'I use a hat, your ladyship, the same as anyone, but I can't ask around in milliners' shops.'

'Nor I,' she replied sadly. 'I rarely leave this house, but I can help you.' She summoned her maid, who looked down her nose at me as she always does, thinking the less of her mistress for knowing a chimney sweep on social terms. 'Watkins,' her ladyship said, 'my friend Tom here' (I grew two inches round my chest) 'has a task for you.'

'Indeed, madam.' The ice on St James's lake during the Great Frost wasn't as thick as that in her voice.

'Will you explain to Watkins, Tom?'

I told Miss Watkins about Bessie and Jenny, and all the while

I could see what she was thinking. Two women of the night, no surprise they were killed. 'I can see you have a kind heart, Miss Watkins,' I continued persuasively. 'And bear in mind I only ask this in order to save a noble gentleman from the gallows.' She looked interested in that. 'No doubt he'll want to thank you personally for your help when he's free. Even paint your portrait.' I pushed it a bit further.

And further still. 'There's a little boy lost too, motherless.' From the slight smile on her ladyship's face I was going too far, but I meant what I said. I kept thinking of that lad growing up without the loving Bessie, and shut up with Moonman.

I described to Miss Watkins—having gained her interest—what I knew about Polly. 'Someone somewhere, whether it's a shop or sweat factory, will have heard of Polly Bunting. She was the youngest so she'll be about twenty. Or,' I added, thinking of what I would do if I were Polly, 'Polly something else.'

After tea with Mrs Tiggle (which pleased her, since she was preferred over tea with her ladyship) I left Bayswater for Hairbrine Court.

'Hallo, Gov. I've got supper going.' I *was* doing well, and Ned was so proud. The fish cooked, on the communal stove downstairs, smelled out the entire house. I hated herrings, but I looked at the love in Ned's eyes, and they tasted like a king's feast.

On Tuesday came our second Angelic modelling assignment. To tell the truth, I wished we were out sweeping chimneys. The swell world—apart from Lady Beezer's—seemed to shrink behind the scenes as much as our world did on top. I assisted Ned into his second jacket, which was not quite so threadbare, for I noticed that even Valentine didn't like painting holes and rents, and always smartened us up on his canvas. Valentine once read me an essay by a Mr Lamb about chimney sweeps, and much as this gentleman assured us he liked chimney sweeps, you could tell that in his mind the holes, the hunger and the cankers had been pushed under the carpet.

Frederick Fairfax lived in Wigmore Street, and two omnibuses suited us well. A book I once looked at in her ladyship's library informed me there were 3,000 omnibuses running each day in London, employing 30,000 horses. It's strange, therefore, that whenever I can afford one there's never one in sight. Ned and I waited half an hour before we could sail in princely style to Mr Fairfax's studio.

I retrieved from my brain Laurence's interesting information that Frederick had once wanted to marry Bessie, but that was odd, because there'd never been any sign or word of it before. I wondered if Valentine knew of this.

Frederick lived in superior rooms, and was looked after by his landlady, her cook and her general. If you ask me, he was the sort who like to keep themselves to themselves, but this must be hard with a landlady who, I saw immediately, preferred to live her life through her lodger's doings rather than her own. Her face lit up eagerly when she opened the door herself. She spied chatting material, which outweighed the risk of odd specks of soot on her carpet. 'You're the sweep for Mr Fairfax's picture,' she said. 'I'll show you up.'

Frederick didn't give her that pleasure, as he was bounding down the stairs to meet us. Such eagerness was most gratifying, whatever the cause, and Mrs Pringle went away, disappointed that her role was over. 'What does he want to paint a sweep for?' I heard her mutter crossly to her general.

Shown into the studio, I was minded to ask the same question, for whoever told us Frederick liked painting gardens was correct. Every canvas displayed a garden, which was odd for a studio from which all you could see was a forest of chimneys and rooftops, although many plants in pots were adorning the studio. It was hard to understand how gardens fitted the uplifting theme that Valentine explained was the trademark of the Angels. Were all these pictures portraying paradise or Eden? They all differed, for there were trim and perfect gardens which made you wonder why someone had apparently gone to so much trouble to take the personality out of them; riotous and sensuous gardens that had little to do with spiritual values to my eye; gardens full of things to eat and gardens full of statues with even fewer clothes than Laurence's buxom living ladies. There was even one of a pleasure garden—and I think it was Cremorne, near to where Valentine lived. The more I looked at them though, I saw these weren't pleasure gardens at all—they all had some nasty serpent or other evil lurking within them. I presumed I was the evil element for his present work.

'It's good of you to employ me, sir,' I said deferentially, nudging Ned to look the same.

'It's the least I could do for Val, a small request.' Frederick smiled. 'Handing in day is past, so I am free to plan future work.'

'Handing in day, sir?'

'For the Royal Academy. It's the last day we can hand them in for the exhibition that opens on the first of May. Not that we shall receive much publicity this year since the International Exhibition opens the same day. I expect you have heard of that.'

It would be difficult even for a sweep as far away as America not to have heard of it. The huge building on the Cromwell Road was finished at last, and Joe the patterer had been bawling his head off about the great excitements to be unveiled within it in May. That included pictures, but I gathered from Valentine that this would be a very insignificant display (from which I also gathered the Angels had not been asked to contribute).

'I'm sure Mr Drake must have told you of the exhibition in the National Gallery.'

He had indeed. This Royal Society of Arts with its headquarters in Trafalgar Square took rooms in the National Gallery for its display of pictures, and that's where Valentine was submitting 'Cast Out,' Bessie's and my picture. I hoped he still was. Valentine had explained that this was a yearly event, highly valued by artists. It mattered just where you were hung, I could hear Valentine explaining earnestly to me. Poor Val, those words had a different meaning now.

'Your coming,' Frederick continued, his golden hair flying around in his enthusiasm, 'has given me an excellent chance to begin a work I have had in mind for some time called "Cleansed of Sin." In a garden of confusion of many paths, there is a pond at which you, the black sweep, will be standing, looking hopelessly for the bubbling stream of redemption. Young Ned here has found it more easily, being a lad, and is already bathing in the stream.'

Ned's eyes grew wide, and he clutched my hand. 'Does that mean I'm having a bath, Gov?' He was terror-stricken, and I had to hold on to him to prevent his rushing for the door. I explained to Frederick the little difficulty about Ned and water, and I thought the great artist was going to cry, he looked so disappointed. I realised if we were to get anywhere in our Bessie enquiries I had to think up something to replace the idea of Ned frolicking in water. 'How would it be, sir, if there were a fountain and Ned, in his chimney sweeps' rags, was climbing up to it, as though towards heaven?'

Frederick, looking sulky, unwillingly agreed. He left us alone for a few minutes while he went to see his landlady to arrange the water, and I soothed Ned down, explaining that all artists were a little strange and had their funny ways, just like master sweeps. When Frederick returned, he looked happier, and he positioned me on the dais looking soulfully down into an imaginary pond, and told Ned to wait in the chair by the door until he reached the need to sketch the fountain.

'It's good of you to agree to my modelling, sir,' I began cheerily, 'it being all for Bessie's son.'

He looked up sharply and I glimpsed another Frederick, one that hadn't had time to arrange for an angelic smile on his face. 'Val said nothing about that.'

'No, sir, it was my idea. The lad has disappeared, you see, and I thought these pennies Ned and I are earning could go towards the hunt for the boy. Bessie would have liked that.'

'Yes.' Frederick appeared to be very busy sketching.

'And seeing that Mr Tait said you were to marry Bessie at one time, you'll—'

'Damnation to the man.' Not a very pious remark for an Angel. 'What does he mean? It's nonsense.'

'It's untrue, sir? I thought it might be so, as Mr Valentine never mentioned it. It might explain why she came to you for help the night she died, however.'

'She came on the twenty-second,' he whipped back instantly. 'How can the police be sure that was the night she died?' Frederick then pretended he was concentrating on sketching my boots, but I could almost hear his brains ticking like a long-case clock. 'I was,' he said airily at long last, 'considering marriage when Bessie first modelled for us. That was about seven years ago, when I was still a youth, and over-impressionable. I may well have said I wished to marry her, but I later discovered I had been mistaken in her character, and thought no more of it.'

Poor Bessie. I kept my temper though. 'You said "modelled for *us*," sir.'

'Mr Harwood-Jones, Mr Tait and I shared a studio in Pimlico in our first days as Angels. The arrangement only lasted about eighteen months, and by fifty-seven we were all established in our homes. Mr Tait was already married, I took over these rooms, and Mr Harwood-Jones set up a studio in his own home in order to be closer to his mother, who was moving there in her widowhood. They were splendid, exciting days.'

He smiled at us engagingly, but somehow I wasn't engaged. 'We all thought Bessie the most beautiful—and, I regret to say, virtuous—woman we had ever seen,' he continued, 'and in my immaturity I naturally considered marrying her, as all unwed artists consider marrying their inspiration. Naturally I wanted a virtuous woman and when I discovered that Bessie was hardly that, I considered marriage no longer.'

'Because she was going to have a baby?'

'Yes.' Frederick spoke most curtly.

'Yours?'

He flung down his brush. 'You are impudent, sir.'

'Concerned to find Bessie's murderer, as you must be too, having been so fond of her.'

He bit his lip, obviously not liking being fenced into a corner by a sweep. 'The baby was not mine.'

'Yet she came to you on the night she probably died.' My heart bled for Bessie, that she had fallen in love with this handsome face, as shallow as a drained pond, and then had been rebuffed. And that was through no fault of her own, of that I was sure. 'What time did she arrive, sir, on that evening?'

'It was quite late. About half past nine or so.' It was almost a snarl.

'Why did she come, sir?'

'For old times' sake,' Frederick yelled angrily. He seemed on the verge of adding something else, when the door burst open and the stalwart figure of Mrs Pringle and a burly gentleman in shabby black rushed in.

'Now we have you, nipper!' roared the man.

With a scream of terror, Ned was bundled into a blanket to stop his struggles and scooped off before I could reach him to stop the outrage. The door was slammed behind them, and I heard the sound of a lock being turned, then poor Ned's screams all the way down the stairs. Frederick was grinning his head off and it was clear this was some terrible plan.

'Let me get to him, sir,' I shouted, rattling at the door. 'What are they doing to do? Will they murder the lad?'

'No. Strip him and throw him in a bath so that I can go down and sketch him.'

I howled in despair. 'You've no idea what you've done, sir. Let me go to him, I beg of you.'

'Nonsense, man. Earn your money and forget about the boy.'

I was beating on the door, and without manhandling me too, he could do no more painting. 'For pity's sake, sir, unlock it,' I moaned. He ordered me back on the dais, but I would not budge. So he amused himself, arranging his paint pots for a few minutes, and I amused myself by enlarging on my views of those who were cruel to children.

'Very well,' Frederick laughed after an agonising wait. 'We can go now. He should be ready to work for his money.'

'He'll not do that, sir.' I could still hear Ned's screams although muffled by the two floors below us, and waited in anguish while Frederick gathered his paints and pad. At last he condescended to open the door, and I hobbled down as quickly as I could to the source of the yells. There in the kitchen I saw poor Ned held down naked and forcibly by the man, while Mrs Pringle held his clothes, laughing her head off.

Ned was still shrieking in terror as I went straight to him.

'His clothes,' I demanded grimly of Mrs Pringle.

'Not till I've drawn him,' Frederick smirked.

'Let him be!' I roared so loud that in sheer surprise the man let go. In a trice Ned was out of that bath, had ducked under restraining arms and was out of the room, still yelling.

'I'll be reporting this to the Royal Academy,' I told Frederick. I would too. I'd give Mr Mudgwick one of his own sovereigns to write for me.

'Are you threatening me, sweep?'

'Yes,' I roared. 'Tell your landlady to give me his clothes, Mr Fairfax.'

'Hand them over,' Frederick told Mrs Pringle sullenly, and she threw them at me, catching me in the face. I went after Ned. He couldn't have gone far in his state, and I found him shivering in an under-stairs cupboard.

'Here you are, lad.' I gave him his clothes. Ned seized them, hiccupping with relief, as he clambered back into his dignity.

Frederick had followed me, and so I made our position clear to him. 'We'll not be modelling any more for you, sir, and you can keep your shilling.' Stained money, I thought, reminded of Bessie. Had Frederick been the disembodied voice in that hansom in the Haymarket, the only man she believed who had ever truly loved her, the man who turned her from his door to send her to her death?

He tried charm then. 'Look, Ned, I'm sorry—just a lark.'

His boyish grin and golden curls didn't work on Ned, nor on me. I didn't trust a word he said. We'd seen what lay behind.

Chapter Eight: In Which I Gather More Soot

'There's no need for you to come, Ned,' I said gently next day. 'How about you sweeping the Jack Tar on your own?' We're known there and he'd have no difficulty managing.

'No, Gov, I'm a-coming with you.'

He's a gallant little fellow, and I was curious what made him willing to come to Edward Harwood-Jones' studio after the ordeal he'd been through at Frederick's.

He wouldn't tell me at first, but then he said: 'I don't want Bessie's kid to climb no chimneys.'

'The law is supposed to prevent that, Ned, not you. It's taking time, but it's working now.'

'Not for Bessie's kid.'

I understood now. Ned was remembering his young days as an anybody's child.

'Why do you think that, Ned?'

'He'll end up a chummy or a dipper. Don't want that—all right for me. Not Bessie's son. But it'll happen now Moonman's got him.'

This worried me. I was getting used to the looming shape behind and around me, but I didn't want Ned haunted. 'Moonman's my worry, not yours,' I told him, but he set his mouth obstinately.

It was a long time since I'd been to Kensington. In my youth it was a village. Now it's a town and like to be swallowed up by the greedy westward march of London. As the four-wheeler bowled us along in grand style, I saw to my regret the old Halfway Inn near the old turnpike had disappeared, and not long ago judging by the wood and rubble still lying around. That inn must have seen many monarchs riding by in its time, and I daresay they often paused for a pint of porter, as I did, for the landlord had an easy hand with the beer, after my sweeping work was done.

The inn had an old Toll charge board outside, as it stood halfway between London and Hammersmith, and I often wondered what lay at Hammersmith that took the fancy of so many carriages. It occurred to me the publican might have a brother who ran an establishment there, and this was by way of an advertisement for it. The old Kensington Bedlam still stood, however, and I doffed my hat for the poor inmates, as a reminder that Ned and I needed to use our wits, lest they turn against us.

There had been a great fire in the heart of Kensington by the church, so the patterer had roared out a week or two ago, when the vast mansion of Campden House had been burned to the ground. As the growler approached the High Street, I could see the ruins of Campden House's theatre near to the road, exposing for all to see the gardens within. The smell of smoke still seemed to linger in the air, as the growler turned towards Kensington Square. It made me sad to see the sight of such splendour reduced to ruins. It reminded me that all the grandeur of Mr Harwood-Jones and his like was no more than the poverty of Tom Wasp when old Master Fate was pointing his long finger.

Kensington Square was full of grand houses, one of which was a school, judging by the serious young gentlemen to be seen outside it, and in another corner a convent, so a nameboard proclaimed, making this a most respectable area for a clerical gentleman's son, as I gathered Mr Harwood-Jones to be. The builders didn't have much thought for the chimney sweeps though, when they built the chimneys narrow. I remembered climbing up one or two of these, when I was small, and a time when I was stuck and had to be rescued through the register plate. I began to shiver, feeling back there again, but fortunately the door to Edward Harwood-Jones' house was opened at that moment, by a frosty individual whose red nose bore out Mr Parsons' comments.

'Mr Harwood-Jones, if you please. By appointment.'

He'd obviously been told of our coming, for though he looked as though otherwise he would dearly have loved to kick our black figures right down the lily white steps, instead he told us to come in and *wipe our feet most particular.* We wiped away, half expecting to be handed angelic lily-white smocks to don, in case we bumped against something with brushes and rods (no machines required for artists' representations). We were escorted behind a stiff black-clad bottom up several flights of stairs. It was obvious this was a God-fearing house, which boded well for our good treatment. There were samplers and texts reminding all those who toiled upwards that the Lord had His eye on them, and that toil was good for the immortal soul. I'm not in agreement with this. The housemaid who toils up the stairs at seven o'clock each morning and six o'clock each night with jug after jug of warm water, or hauls in the daily coals, might take more convincing of the value of toil than Mr Harwood-Jones, who works away at his painting. Not that I'm denying painting is work—I've seen the anguish Valentine goes through when a painting doesn't go right, and, contrarily, when it does work right, he's toiling so hard the sweat pours from his face.

Edward's studio was on the top floor, if you don't count the servants' attics, and a fine light room it was. He must be about the same age as myself, and though he must be wearing better inside, you wouldn't have thought so to look at his face. It was long, anxious, and severe, which is perhaps what comes of being a clergyman's son and always trying to do right. Though that is strange, since he has the privilege of living with his mother. He must dearly love her, for many are not so lucky. I must have had a mother once, but I don't recall her. I had a father, I suppose, for I recall a big voice, a black shape, and a wide belt that descended on my naked body. There were women, too, that came and went, but none were what I now understand a mother to be.

'Come in,' says Edward, pointing to the dais impatiently, as if to show he hadn't time to waste on chimney sweeps.

'Certainly, sir. I can see you're in a hurry to begin, though I understand Handing-in day has passed.'

He looked at me in surprise, then nodded reluctantly. 'Clearly you've been sitting for Mr Fairfax or Mr Tait. Mr Drake is fortunate to have such good friends.'

I wondered what Valentine was doing in Newgate if he had such good friends. They hadn't proved good friends to Bessie. Even Valentine had let her run off. Frederick must have turned her away too, and so had Laurence Tait. However, I answered him brightly:

'He is indeed, sir, and Bessie too.'

'Bessie?' He looked at me suspiciously, and Ned piped up:

'Our modelling money is going to help us search for Bessie's son.'

'I would prefer it spent to help free Mr Drake—if he's innocent.'

'Oh, he is, sir.' I was convinced of that now. 'And maybe when we find Moonman, we shall find both the boy and Bessie's murderer.'

He stared at me with a most strange expression on his face, which I could have thought was relief if I were more acquainted with how the gentry feel. 'Then you should begin your work here,' said Edward with a sarcastic note in his voice. 'Let me explain what I'm seeking to do.'

'Do you paint gardens like Mr Fairfax?' I enquired, deliberately innocent.

'I do not. We each have our own interpretation of the Angels' objectives. Valentine uses stories as his medium. Frederick chooses gardens to portray the evils of mankind. I portray them through the double-sided nature of night, usually with a biblical theme in mind, Laurence through the relationships of men and women.'

I looked around me. Full of evil they might be, but all the pictures I could see were full of colour and pleasure-loving folk enjoying themselves, night or not. To my eye, however, they were flat compared with the paintings of his friends. Whether I liked them or not, there was a lot of fire about Laurence Tait's work and even in Frederick's, although I'm not knowledgeable about gardens.

'Which sin are we, sir?'

'Envy. On the one hand, there will be richly dressed patrons of a theatre descending the steps to their carriages, and at one side yourself and Ned picturing yourselves amongst them. I will show you the pose I have in mind.'

'Thank you, sir.'

We waited deferentially as he joined us on the dais and demonstrated attitudes of envy, chiefly involving clasped hands, and a foot out behind so we could lean back and envy upwards at the great folk. I caught a grin on Ned's face, a rare thing, and so I warmed to Edward Harwood-Jones for his ridiculous notions of how he believed we chimney sweeps live. There's no point spending energy envying other people when it takes all your efforts to stay alive.

'I've decided Ned should be the centrepiece, the focus of the eye.'

'I'm not having no baths.' Ned believes in warning shots.

I hushed him. 'A bad experience, sir. I know you won't force a bath upon him, seeing as how you want us dirty.'

Edward looked as though he had no intention of wasting more time than was strictly necessary.

As I posed in the way he showed us, I faced a different part of the room. My eye fell on a pile of canvases turned against the wall, backs to me, but one had been placed the wrong way and was half staring out at me. Even from here, I could tell it wasn't like the pictures Edward had shown us. It was a night scene in what looked very much to me like the Haymarket, and with a woman all dressed up as—well, as Jenny was, her face and hair lit up by the gaslight, blotting out the moonlight above them. What caught my attention was that the model without a doubt was Bessie. Ned followed my gaze and piped out, 'That's Bessie.'

Edward turned, and a look of annoyance crossed his face. 'Observant of you, child. It's an old canvas. I've passed on from that stage now, which is the reason it is stacked on one side.'

I cleared my throat as he began to sketch us. It was time to start wriggling farther up the chimney. 'Very understandable, sir, in the circumstances.'

'What circumstances?' His crayon was passing rapidly over his paper, and he wasn't paying much attention to what I said. That soon changed.

'That explains,' I said, 'why, when Bessie came here that night for your help, you turned her away, not realising what a desperate situation she was in.'

He flung down his brush irritably. 'You know nothing about artists and painting, Wasp. How can I paint you sympathetically as envy, when you persist in raising a subject you must realise is painful for me? Bessie was no longer modelling for me, and I considered it an imposition for her to appeal to me and to visit me in the evening. I gave her some money. She was here a mere five minutes, and left quite contentedly.'

'And what time would that have been, sir?'

'I really cannot recall, and it cannot be of importance, since she visited Mr Drake after me. My mother and I were about to dine, and I suppose, therefore, it was about half-past seven. It was highly inconvenient. Nor, in case you ask, did I leave the house after she had left, as my mother can testify.'

'What puzzles me, sir, is that she appears to have come to you first, rather than Mr Valentine, who wanted to marry her. Mind you, I understand you were old friends, and that she modelled for you in the studio you shared with Mr Fairfax and Mr Tait in Pimlico.'

Edward gave a short laugh. 'I imagine that is why she came to me first. She did not wish to sully her chance of marriage by revealing to Mr Drake she had a son.'

'He didn't know?' I asked this to draw him out.

'I hardly think he would have contemplated marriage with the girl if he knew she had a bastard.'

I don't know whether Ned was acquainted with this word, but from the look on his face, he followed its meaning. Ned and I are in accord that babies arrive in this world free of sin, and that the bastard tag should more justly be applied to the father. I intervened quickly before Ned could speak.

'Perhaps she came to you first since you're a clergyman's son, and she knew you had a kind heart.' Buried deep, if it was, I thought privately.

'You may be right.' He looked pleased. 'I have in fact taken holy orders myself, Wasp, and Bessie knew it. When the Angels were first formed, poor Frederick was desperately in love with her, and even Laurence was attracted. I myself was still undecided between the church as a future and my painting, and marriage was not a possibility then, although Bessie modelled for me.'

'Here, sir, or just in Pimlico?'

'Only in Pimlico. I am afraid I could not consider Bessie as a model after she revealed she was to have an illegitimate child, and it was not long after that before we gave up sharing a studio. Just as,' he added sternly, 'I cannot paint you as envy while you persist in talking about Bessie Barton. Pray hold still, Mr Wasp.'

In my agitation I had lost the pose, and could see Ned's cheeks bulging out with indignation, though he restrained himself from speech most admirably. He was helped in this by the door opening, and a servant appearing to inform Edward that Mrs Harwood-Jones wished to meet the chimney sweep in her morning room.

Now this was an interesting turn of the chimney, although Edward apparently did not agree. He turned a shade of purple that would have enhanced any of his pictures. He snarled a 'Wait here' at us, and hurried down, no doubt to tell his mother that despite her kindly thought, he did not wish her to entertain chimney sweeps, however Christian the household might be. His absence suited me very well, for the moment he and the butler had gone, I hurried over to that stack of paintings with Ned hard on my heels. Here was a find.

'Look at these, Ned. Here are your deadly sins.' I lifted the pictures upright one by one. Although the pictures on display were meant to represent sin, they were empty compared with these, which *breathed* it. They were all dark night-time scenes, several of the Haymarket, displaying the carriages and women of the night in the gaslight, and the hint of blackness behind which only the moon knew about. Others were of pleasure gardens by night, perhaps Cremorne again—I could not tell—and most had Bessie as model. It was a Bessie I did not know, beautiful but sensuous and lustful. She must have been an actress, for I cannot believe that of her. There was even one of her in the moonlight by the river, about to throw herself in, her red gold hair lit by moonlight, and that set me shivering again.

Another showed a cab with a woman climbing into it, with the figure of a man inside. It was all part of a nightwalker's trade, but not Bessie's, even though I'd seen her get into such a cab with my own eyes. Something else bothered me about one of these pictures, and at last I realised what it was.

It was the red scarf round the model's neck. A scarf Bessie had bought herself only last autumn—and yet Edward said she hadn't modelled for him for some years.

We were only just back in our positions, clasping our hands upwards in envy, when Edward returned. 'My mother wishes to meet you,' he informed us sourly.

'Very civil of her ladyship,' I said heartily, amused that he had been over-ruled.

'*Mrs* Harwood-Jones.'

'I can tell your mother is a lady, sir.'

Indeed, I fully expected to find a Lady Beezer awaiting us, but I was in for a surprise. This woman sat like an empress in a high-backed leather chair, her claw-like lace-gloved hands on the arms, a lace cap on her head, and clad in deep purple, still mourning for her late husband presumably. As she slowly turned her head, I saw a beak-like face with sharp eyes and no motherliness, as I imagined it. I wondered if Mr Dickens had met her before he wrote of Miss Havisham. As part of my lettering, Lady Beezer had allowed me to read some of Mr Dickens' works, and my knowledge of the human nature and condition is the greater for it.

'I asked to see you, sweep, since I understand you are employed by Mr Mudgwick to make enquiries about the woman Valentine Drake murdered.'

'Employed?' Edward asked sharply, as shocked as I was by the way this was said. 'What do you mean, Mother? Have you been making enquiries? Is this true, Wasp?'

I was taken aback, but telling myself that anyone who can lift up his face to God can deal with anything, I did my best, with two pairs of stony eyes on me.

'Hardly employed, ma'am, sir. Just trying to do my best to help Mr Drake, since he has been kind to us. Knowing Mr Harwood-Jones here and his friends all have sworn to help each other, I saw no harm in asking questions that might assist poor Mr Valentine. What's more, Bessie was a friend of mine, and Ned and I want to help her by finding her son.'

'Is this boy her son?' the empress thundered, making Ned, who ain't scared of drunken matelots at Paddy's Goose, creep behind me for protection.

'No, Mother, this is a climbing boy,' Edward said dismissively.

Now that I won't have. 'My chummy apprentice, if you please. Climbing boys, thanks to Lord Shaftesbury, are illegal.'

My hosts weren't interested in this most virtuous and charitable man or his works.

'What is this about finding Bessie's son?' Edward asked.

'Did she accuse you of being the father, sir? You'd have told the police if you were, of course.'

It was the empress's turn to grow purple in the face. 'How dare you, sweep? My son is an unmarried man, and the wages of sin are death,' she reminded us.

'Who defines sin, ma'am? Only St Peter has that job, to my mind.'

'Levity concerning religion is not permitted in this house.'

Nor was much laughter at all; that was clear, although God gave man the gift of laughter. No other animals have that privilege.

'Bessie's son has disappeared. That's what Bessie was upset about when she called here that Saturday evening. It was probably that night she died.' It occurred to me Edward might not have told his mother about this, but there was no reason for delicacy that I could see. 'He'd been stolen away. That's why she was asking for your help, Mr Harwood-Jones.'

The empress answered for him. 'The woman interrupted our dinner about seven-thirty, demanded money, and that my son accompany her to the police. Naturally we refused, and she left.'

'You saw her too, ma'am?'

'Of course. If my son is to be importuned by every model he has ever employed, he needs my assistance.'

It was then I realised Edward was as scared of his mother as poor Ned, and if there were any more to be learned about Bessie and her boy, we wouldn't be hearing it tonight. One thing Ned and I did agree on as we left after an hour's more posing: if all mothers were like that, we hadn't missed anything at all in life.

Valentine had, so Mr Mudgwick's letter informed me, requested the pleasure of my company again to hear of my progress, and after a brief discussion with him, we set off. The cell at Newgate was just as bare as before. I thought of the elegant painted bathroom and water closet at Cheyne Walk and pitied Valentine the bucket and bowl he was now reduced to. He had been given a pencil and pad on which to draw, but he had done little, and was looking haggard. June would be here all too soon, and I appeared to be his only hope.

'What news, Tom?' he cried.

'The brush is up the chimney, but it ain't reached the top yet.'

'Then hurry it up, man,' he said, agonised. 'Are you no nearer finding this Moonman?'

Mr Mudgwick looked saddened on my behalf. 'Enquiries are continuing, Mr Drake.'

'Unfortunately, I may not be doing the same,' Valentine attempted to jest, 'if you are not quick.'

'Mr Wasp and I feel we are labouring under a difficulty, Mr

Drake.' Mr. Mudgwick spoke quite sternly.

'Why?' Valentine looked guarded.

'We realise that there is a pact between the members of the Angels group to help each other—although so far, I regret to say, neither Mr Wasp nor myself has found much evidence of it. Your three colleagues all admit to seeing Bessie that night, but each of them claims to have remained at home the entire evening thereafter, as verified by Mr Tait's wife, Mr Fairfax's fiancée and her parents' (this was new to me) 'and Mr Harwood-Jones' mother. They maintain that as Bessie came to see you last, Mr Drake, they can have had nothing to do with her death, nor does any of them admit to being the father of her child. However, it transpires that at least one is dallying with the truth, according to Mr Wasp.'

Valentine answered immediately. 'That cannot be, sir.'

I took a hand in the talk. 'Now, look, there are long corridors in Newgate, and one of them leads to the gallows. If we don't forget about delicacy, Mr Drake, you'll be walking along it very soon.' I thought of that grim path, and silently wept for him.

Valentine's face went very white. 'Who do you believe is lying?' he asked sharply.

'They all could be, but Mr Harwood-Jones certainly is. He says Bessie wasn't his model recently, yet there's a painting of her with a new red scarf round her neck, the same she was wearing when she was killed.'

'It doesn't seem much.' He relapsed into gloom, and I hastened to cheer him.

'It's like a coster's pile of fruit, sir. You put your good apples on top, and all the rotten stuff underneath. If you look carefully though, the merest sign of a bruise on top is a hint that there's a heap of crawling worms underneath. Mr Fairfax's fiancée, her parents and Mr Harwood-Jones' mother can only provide evidence, I presume, up to the time they retired for the night. If

Mr Tait does not share the same room as his wife, the same would apply to him. There's something we're not being told, sir.'

'I know these gentlemen, Tom. We are sworn brothers.' Valentine made an attempt at dignity.

'Will they be there to watch you hang, sir?'

Valentine cried out. 'For pity's sake, Tom. What shall I do?'

'Tell us the real truth, sir.'

'I have,' he moaned.

'Then tell us more of it, sir. You're leaving something out too, I know. You didn't sleep at home that night after you'd seen Bessie by Cadogan Pier. Where were you?'

He looked at me as though I was the Spanish Inquisition trying to force a confession from him. 'I was walking the streets,' he finally admitted, defeated.

'Who saw you?'

'No one. And that *is* the truth, Tom. Very late, about three perhaps, I went to Hummums Hotel in Covent Garden. I know they are famous for giving you a room any time of night. I thought I'd try it.' He made a pathetic attempt at bravado. 'The chamberlain met me at the wicket to give me my candle, and show me to the room. He might recall me. What I haven't told you, however,' he continued, 'is what happened after Bessie left me.'

Now we were getting that stuck brush up to the light. 'What's that, sir?' I asked encouragingly.

'You knew Bessie told me her boy had been kidnapped by this man she was scared of, the one you call Moonman.'

'We *think* it was Moonman, sir.'

'The man wanted her to go back to live with him, and had taken the boy as hostage. She was terrified of him and refused to do so, which is why she came to the Angels. She had asked the man to meet her at midnight, bringing the boy so she could see he was safe. If one of us accompanied her with a policeman she believed she would get the child back safely, and Moonman would be frightened off for long enough for her to establish herself somewhere new. She had, you recall, told me she would never have married me, because of the boy.'

That's the Bessie I loved.

'She was to meet this man near her home,' Valentine added.

'Holywell Street,' I said.

'I did not know it,' he said, too quickly.

'Come, sir,' Mr Mudgwick intervened vigorously. 'Even I am aware that with Wych Street, it is the greatest seller of indecent literature in London.'

Valentine flushed defiantly. 'I had never been there, although she did mention her lodgings were there. She'd never let me know before. Anyway, immediately she had run away from me, I felt ashamed, so knowing where she was going I followed her in a cab. She was walking quickly, but somehow I lost her. I went to Holywell Street and hung around until the time of her appointment. Suddenly I saw her, about five minutes to twelve, standing on the corner. I was pondering on whether to approach her when a cab arrived, and a man in evening dress got out. She walked up to him, and they walked away together. I was surprised, but as she showed no fear of him, I was not concerned for her safety, particularly as the last thing she had said to me was there was only one man who truly loved her. I presumed this must be he, and in my jealousy I followed them.'

'No sign of the boy?' I asked hopefully.

'No.'

'Did you recognise the man?'

'I was too far away to see.'

'You're not lying again, sir? Was it one of the Angels?'

'If it was, Tom, I *would* tell you. Truly. I have no desire to hang. Just think. It will be Hanging Day soon at the Academy. I thought it would be "Cast Out" hung. Instead, it will be me.' He began to laugh hysterically, and only Mr Mudgwick's sombre face made him pull himself together. 'I saw Bessie and this man crossing the Strand towards the river. I believed she was safe, so I went no farther. I could not bear to see them together in my jealousy. The thought of Bessie with another man made me wander the streets, as I told you. The hotel would recall me perhaps, but for the hours between twelve and three no one would remember me.'

'You were in evening dress, sir. You'd be memorable.'

Valentine shook his head. 'There are many such staggering round London by night. I went to the Cave of Harmony in Leicester Square intending to get drunk, but the noise sickened me and I left. I did go to a coffee stall somewhere near, but who would remember?'

'Why didn't you tell us earlier, Mr Drake?' Mr Mudgwick moaned. 'It looks bad.'

'That's why,' Valentine said glumly.

'And that's all you saw of Bessie, sir?' I asked, determined to shake him like a chimney brush for every bit of information.

He hesitated. 'All I saw for certain.'

'Tell us what you *fancied* you saw, then.'

'It was foggy—this was February, remember. But I thought—a mere fancy, perhaps—as they walked out of the range of the gas lamp on the Strand down Milford Lane, that someone was following them. It could just have been a shape in the fog.'

Which could have been Moonman.

Ned was very quiet the rest of the day, more than usual, that is, and when we'd finished our regulars I asked him why. He'd gone out about six, clutching tuppence from the jar to buy himself a new jacket. When I say new, I mean new to him. Any jacket from Rag Fair would have made its appearance in this world many a year ago, and furthermore would have found survival hard. And when I say buy—that's what I hope, but knowing Ned I doubt it. He came back with one three sizes too big for him but no holes, which shows what a sensible lad he is. He hadn't said anything else—and a trip to Rosemary Lane not being a pleasure, I thought little of it.

At last, unexpectedly, he did say something. 'I had a pot of whitebait, Gov.'

So that was it. He was worried I'd be annoyed at this extravagance. Crisp battered whitebait is a delicacy and costs a penny, whereas you can get two herrings to cook for a half-penny. But it turned out that wasn't what was in his mind.

'At a stall, Gov. And Mr Slit was there—he recognised me and asked how we were doing with Moonman.'

I frowned. 'Why didn't you tell me you were going, Ned?'

'Dunno.'

I'd made an error. Ned would shut up like a mussel shell now I'd tapped him. It took half an hour for him to speak. He came to find me down in Mrs Parsnip's yard, washing a few clothes in a tub of water from the communal tap. It was at such times I thought wistfully of Miss Burdett-Coutts' model lodging houses in Columbia Square, Bethnal Green, which shared a laundry room (so I heard) on the top floor. Water *inside* the house? It was a far cry from Hairbrine Court, home though it was.

Ned planted his feet in front of me, and crossed his arms truculently. 'He's something to do with dogs.' It all came out in a rush. 'So Mr Slit says.'

'Who?' I was lost.

'He told me to tell you he'd heard some buzz about Moon-man. And he's calling himself George Clare.'

'And what else, Ned? What sort of dog work?'

'Dunno.'

And that was that. I could see by his eyes there was nothing more, and that's probably what he was worried about. Working with dogs could mean a lot of things. It could mean breeding them for ladies of high society, it could mean handling their dead meat at Clare Market, it could mean kidnapping ladies' dogs for ransom (a highly fashionable trade at present), it could mean working in a menagerie—or it could mean collecting up their muck for sale.

Which brought us back to Daniel Truebottom.

Chapter Nine: In Which I Glimpse the Light Above

To my mind, it is sad that those who work the hardest and most honestly get the least. Truly it is said our reward is in heaven, for men such as Daniel Truebottom have had little on earth, and justice must lie somewhere. Nevertheless, next evening Ned and I found Daniel looking cheerful enough over a glass of porter in the Stag and Fox, a salubrious tavern in Rosemary Lane. He was on his own, which is not unusual with purefinders.

'Life,' he observed, after we had exchanged greetings, 'goes up and it goes down. Today it is up. I collected two stable bucketsful and took them to my regular, Leomont and Roberts, who paid me at the generous rate of one shilling and four pence per bucket. I make sure I present them with a high quality product, for they prefer the dry sort of pure, and not that from kennels, though I might earn more that way. I have my reputation to think of, Mr Wasp, and the street is where you find the quality dung. Some I know would drop old mortar in it to swell the bucket, but they know from me they may expect the best, and they are very particular, being in the bookbinding and kid glove business. I often wonder,' he added, just as I was about to mention my purpose in coming, 'if those fine gentlemen who are so proud of their books and their ladies who don their kid gloves know the leather is purified with dogs' dung rubbed by hand into them.'

'Society is like circus tumblers,' I agreed. 'We folk at the bottom of the pile support those at the top waving at the angels.' I changed the subject, reminded of the reason for my presence. 'Your job takes you around the town then, Mr Truebottom?'

'As far as Bermondsey to deliver my product,' he said, pleased at my interest.

'I was wondering if you ever came across a cove—' and I described Moonman as best I could '—not that you would have to do with this gentlemen with his dark, evil ways.'

Daniel listened attentively, but shook his head. 'Purefinding's a small trade. There's not above three hundred of us. I never saw a fellow such as you describe. New to the trade, is he?'

'That I can't say,' I replied. 'He works with dogs, and that's all I know.' It wasn't tactful to add that George Bunting, now Clare, might have come down in the world, for today Daniel Truebottom was as happy as a king at his good work. St Peter judges the purefinder and the factory owner by the same standards.

'I knows the dog trade,' said Daniel helpfully. 'There's many branches to it.'

'Street sellers?'

'I'm acquainted with most, though fancy dogs don't have the quality pure as street dogs. Still, we have a fellow feeling, and I don't know one such as this Moonman. Mind you, there's villainy tied up with this business.'

'Theft?'

'Yes, and not just the dog stealers,' Daniel said darkly. 'There's them that take them, them that receive them, and them that give them back. I heard of one lady as lost her dog and paid handsomely for its return, so it was promptly pinched again and she was charged more for the second time. What's more, they told her its throat would be cut if their demands weren't met. After that she left the country with the dog, so they say, in case they came back again for the poor animal. It isn't a right way of dealing, and I don't want to know about it. I work an honest trade.'

'Could this Moonman be one of them?'

'That might well be. There's many ways a man can work with dogs, from pure to dog shows. I'll keep my ears open. And my throat—' He held out his empty glass, with the first grin I'd ever seen on his face.

I obliged, thinking this a rightful use of Mr Mudgwick's money. 'Bessie would be grateful, Mr Truebottom. Every step nearer Moonman is a step nearer to finding her boy, whom he stole away.'

Daniel's face darkened. 'A son? I never knew she had one. And you say he was taken away? Some men are born evil, Mr Wasp.'

'It seems to me, Mr Truebottom, that our trades are much the same. Your pure depends on the type of dog it comes from, just as the smoke released into the air from chimneys depends on what's burned on the fire beneath.'

'Like man himself, Mr Wasp.' Daniel grasped the point instantly, being an intelligent man. 'What we are is written on our faces.'

'And never lost, Mr Truebottom. We'll track Moonman down for Bessie's sake.'

We shook hands again, and parted.

There was good news when Ned and I returned. A letter from Lady Beezer was delivered *by hand,* for fear the postman didn't bother to deliver to the more insalubrious streets of London. Her ladyship didn't deliver it herself, naturally. Letters delivered by private carriage are not common in Hairbrine Court, and it caused quite an audience to gather. They were merely curious, but her ladyship's coachman decided not to risk descending from his seat. Instead he blew his horn like the Archangel

Gabriel's trumpet to attract our attention. Ned, being spryer than myself, leapt up to receive the letter.

When I unsealed it in the privacy of our rooms, I read that Miss Watkins had at last come across someone who admitted to being our Polly. She was working at a large millinery establishment just off Bond Street. I once read in a book that London had well over 40,000 workers involved in the millinery trade. I knew not all of them were tying pink ribbons under the gentry's chins, however. Most of them were sweated labour in back rooms, earning a pittance and working from early morning until late into the evening. This Polly, now Polly Pinkerton apparently, was probably one of them.

Having been told I was a friend of Bessie, she had reluctantly agreed to meet me outside her place of work early one morning, having refused—quite rightly—to reveal where she lived. In the evenings she went straight from work after eight o'clock to another job, and thus it was I was standing in Maddox Street at six-thirty on the morning of Monday, the twenty-eighth of April, with my cart, brushes and faithful Ned. We had to turn down three offers of work which was a sadness, for pleasant though it is to see Mr Mudgwick's riches under the mattress, it is pleasanter still to know they've been earned by honest toil.

Chimney sweeps gazing into a high-class milliner's window are bound to attract attention at any other time of day, but the only folk around then were too busy scurrying into their working burrows to care about us.

Bonnets nowadays seemed to be little more than narrow bands covered with silk, bows, lace and flowers, not affording the substantial protection of those I saw in my youth. These were pretty, though not much use in the rain. Each had its own personality, however. One was called Japanese, another Scotch, one looked like Ned's favourite meat pie, but made of velvet and feathers. I thought of Jenny and her kind in the Haymarket, where for all they aped fine apparel, their gaudiness had not the quality of what I saw before me. It was another world, and the door to it was locked against them.

'Excuse me, sir, would you be Mr Wasp?'

A neat and modest-looking young lady of perhaps twenty was addressing me, as unlike Jenny as I could imagine.

'Miss Polly Pinkerton?' I asked doubtfully, since she bore little resemblance to Bessie.

'Yes.' She looked around anxiously, and I saw she was worried lest her employer arrive. We moved to a doorway a little farther up the street, and Ned perched in the cart with Doshie, in case a large delivery wagon demanded he move it.

'And you're Bessie's sister, miss? Bessie Bunting.'

She looked scared at that. 'We don't use that name now, not since—'

'Moonman came?'

'Yes.' It was whispered so low, I hardly heard it.

'I think it was he killed your sister Bessie, and Jenny too. And he's taken Bessie's young 'un, who may be dead already, or soon will be if we don't reach him. I'm concerned for you, miss.'

'He won't find me, not here—unless—' she looked round fearfully, then said quickly, 'I can't help. I don't know where he is. I haven't seen him since I was sixteen.'

'You lived with him too?'

'We all did. Then Bessie told Jenny and me we were going to run away, and she'd look after us all. I was only about ten then. But he found us a year or two later, and told us we had to go back. Bessie saved me and Jenny though. She would go, if he left us alone, she told him.'

Polly would not look at me, but I knew what she meant, and slow rage built up in me, so I was shaking at the thought of our Bessie's goodness and her sacrifice.

'Then after a year or so, Bessie came and told us we were all going to run away together again, and she'd look after us. She had this job modelling for artists, and one way and another she'd support us. Jenny went off on her own, 'cos she was nearly sixteen, but she was soon back with us. Bessie did well at modelling. This gentleman, she said, was going to marry her, but then when she found she was expecting he wouldn't. She couldn't model then either, so I looked after her. Bessie had got me a job making hats, which helped, and I've been doing it ever since.

'After Oliver was born—she joked about calling him that because she'd been cast out, just like in this book called *Oliver* something.'

'*Twist,*' I said sadly. Of all Mr Dickens' stories, I know this one best, for it struck to the heart of life here east of London's city. I could picture Bessie, the babe in her arms, and laughing despite all that had happened to her. And still I did not know the full story.

'She went to work at a music hall after that, and Jenny with her, but Jenny didn't stay long. Bessie had already gone—' she stopped.

'Because Moonman found out where she was.'

'Yes.' She glanced to left and right as though expecting the grey morn to darken any moment. 'She went back to modelling to escape him, but she never did, not entirely. Nor will I. I never went to him, but he's after me. Always.'

'What is it about him, miss? Why does he track you down time after time?' I thought she might have no answer to this, but she did.

'We're his, he says. Always, forever, he'll find us wherever we try to hide. Sometimes I think—' She hesitated, and I waited. 'I think that he wants us because of Ma. She died, and he couldn't stand that. He wanted her back, because we were—'

'Made in her image.'

'Yes,' she whispered. 'Bessie and Jenny said—when he was doing it, he'd not be talking to them, but to Ma. Terrible, terrible things. That's why no one else will do. First there was Sophie—and she killed herself because of it. So Bessie came next.'

I couldn't ask her more. I could not bear it.

'Tell me about him, where I can find him,' I said. 'Then he'll not trouble you any longer.'

'I—' she seemed uncertain, then said, 'Not here. I have a new job in the evenings at Cremorne starting when they open for the season on Thursday.'

Everybody knows Cremorne, the pleasure gardens in Chelsea by the river. Even in the far off East End there are folk who have visited the gardens, for they cater not only for the swells with grand restaurant and supper boxes, but for thousands of ordinary folk who can afford the shilling entrance fee and to enjoy a day's entertainment at marionettes, sports and theatre, or just strolling in the gardens with the comfort of a hot pie. I'd been hearing about all its new attractions this season from the patterers.

The owners of Cremorne try to keep its good reputation, but for all this hard work they can't prevent tragic accidents like that of fifty-five, when a spectacle of an attack at Sebastopol resulted in twenty-five 'soldiers' being carried off to hospital. Nor can the lamps and flares reach every dark corner of the gardens. While couples dance, watched by those enjoying their food in the supper boxes, others creep to the darkness to continue with more private intimacies.

'I'm working with the ballet dancers at the big theatre,' says Miss Polly proudly.

Ballet is something I've heard of, from which I gather the chief attraction is the young ladies' legs, and it grieved me to know Miss Polly was a performer. But then Bessie was a model, and she displayed many an ankle for art lovers to admire.

'It's a *Harlequinade* on opening night,' Polly told me. 'I'm helping them behind the scenes with costumes. There are all sorts of other shows on at Cremorne too.'

I was relieved she was not a dancer, for all I knew *Harlequinade* to be a most respectable dance. I had the honour of meeting the butcher who supplies the sausages to Clown in the Harlequinade at Covent Garden. It was then that a terrible thought came to me. Other shows? I remembered hearing that this season it was offering a *dog* show.

Was that the kind of work with dogs Moonman had? Had he heard about her new job, and was planning to find her there? He'd already killed Jenny—either because she would not return to him, or because he feared she would inform on him for Bessie's murder. Was he now on Polly's trail?

'Take care, miss! When the lights are dim at Cremorne, and the ways unfrequented late at night, Moonman could strike.'

To my surprise, she just smiled. 'Oh no. I shall be safe there.'

'Miss!' A large purple crinoline gown surmounted by an equally broad purple cloak, topped by a bonnet as tall as a chimneypot over a dragon-like face, bore down on us. 'To work, if you please.'

Polly dropped a scared curtsey. 'I'm sorry, Madame Mantua. I'll come immediately. I thought you might need a sweep today.'

The dragon opened its mouth and out roared flames. 'Not this calibre of sweep.' She waddled away, and Polly prepared to scuttle off in her wake. Before she did so, she said to me hurriedly, 'If you could come to Cremorne on Thursday, I can tell you more about Moonman.'

I saw my chance. 'And the police too?'

She hesitated, then to my relief said, 'Very well. Ten o'clock. The show's over by then. In one of the outdoor cafés by the supper boxes and dancing area.'

I watched her walk away, highly pleased. If I was right about Moonman and the dog show, Polly need fear no more.

Mr Mudgwick looked at me gravely. I had gone straight to him with my news. To my mind, Moonman was as good as caught. 'It seems to me, Mr Wasp, that the police should most certainly be present if you're right, and George Bunting will be working at Cremorne. I realise there is no evidence to prove your guess, but even if it is wrong, Polly can still provide useful information about her father. A plan to trap him might even be arranged.'

'If Sergeant Wiley were there, he would.'

'We shall have to approach the Chelsea Police at Wandsworth, though we may make a case for Sergeant Wiley's presence also. You may leave this to me, Mr Wasp.' He did not look very happy at the prospect.

'There's another flue to sweep in this chimney, sir.'

'And that is?'

'The three Angels should also be present. It's unlikely after what Miss Polly said that any of them is Moonman, but on the other hand we don't *know* that Moonman murdered Bessie. Suppose it were one of them? If he were young Oliver's father—and what other reason would one of the Angels have for murdering Bessie?—Polly might well know which it was.'

I was proud of this plan, and Mr Mudgwick seemed to approve also, although he stipulated that Valentine must be consulted, and despatched a boy to the telegraph office. It turned out that the Newgate governor was not of the same opinion, but Mr Mudgwick sent a sterner telegraph about upholding justice, adding a postscript indicating it would not look well for the governor to have obstructed an innocent *gentleman's* attempts to avoid the gallows.

A hasty message came back that we might see Mr Drake at

ten o'clock on the morrow morning, and Mr Mudgwick promptly sent word by telegraph to Hairbrine Court. By this time even the dulled eyes of my neighbours had been opened to the fact that something odd was going on. Letters from carriages, telegraphs, police vans—Mrs Parsnip was emboldened to ask if I was one of those Fenian revolutionaries, but I was able to assure her I had no dynamite stacked beneath our bedding.

I did not recognise in Valentine the bouncy young artist of my first acquaintance. He made no attempt to appear his old self. Instead he showed us the sketch he was working on—of a hanged man.

'Now, sir,' I said reproachfully. 'Don't despair. We have good news.'

'Oh, I have it already, Tom. My comrades joined the queue at the Academy door last week for the privilege of hearing the porter inform them whether or not our works are to be hung. The *porter*—what indignity is heaped upon us by these wretched academicians, drowned in the slime of mediocrity, dragged down by the weight of their own traditions.'

'That's more like it, sir,' I said encouragingly.

'Do you know, Tom, when I first submitted a *masterpiece*, and there is no doubt that is what it was, I had to endure that terrible porter shouting out "Nay" for all the world to hear? Edward, Frederick and Laurence were more fortunate. As a newcomer, I was dismissed, despite my recognition by the Society of British Artists, by the Watercolourists—'

Mr Mudgwick coughed to indicate time was passing.

'This year,' Valentine said, relapsing into gloom, 'both "Cast Out" and its painter are to be hung.'

'Not if you'll listen to us for a moment, sir.'

He would not. 'Do you know what tomorrow is, Tom?'

'Wednesday, sir.'

'Varnishing Day. Tomorrow we humble artists are permitted

to add the last finishing touches to our works, and to see where we have been hung. It's so important, this question of hanging, although I already know my destination.' He laughed hysterically. 'Outside the walls of Newgate. I hardly think that the Governor will allow me to attend the Varnishing as well.'

'I can go, sir.' I saw an unexpected opportunity.

Despite himself, the corners of Valentine's mouth began to twitch. 'I hardly think—'

Mr Mudgwick intervened on my behalf. 'I think that would be most suitable, sir, if you would scribble a note that Mr Wasp is your representative. You see, Mr Wasp has an appointment to meet Bessie's sister in Cremorne Gardens tomorrow evening, and fully expects Moonman to appear. The police will be present, but Mr Wasp wishes all the Angels to be present too, in order that we may establish with Miss Bunting's help the parentage of Bessie's child.'

Mr Valentine's face turned mulish. 'How could my friends help? This Moonman is obviously the father.'

'We can't be sure of that. All we know is that he came to Bessie's lodgings to take him away, and that's no proof of parentage in this case.'

Valentine stared at his sketchpad, and perhaps the drawing made some impression on him at last.

'Come sir,' I said, 'there's a time to consider yourself alone.'

'I don't know who it is,' Valentine cried with anguish. 'I merely suspect—'

'Perhaps it would help, sir, if I told you Mr Fairfax wished to marry her years ago, and then refused to do so when she was expecting, although knowing Bessie to be virtuous, he must have been the father.'

Valentine gazed at me as if I'd said that the late Prince Albert had got her with child. 'Marry her?' he shouted. 'I was never told!' He leapt up and paced around his cell, struggling to control his shock and justify Frederick's harshness. Eventually he spoke, in what can only be said to be somewhat complacent tone. 'We artists are a strange lot, Tom. We worship beauty, and if we find that beauty has been tarnished, it changes our image of the model and, thus, the picture itself. Mr Tait is very outspoken on the subject. He is submitting something new for him, to the Academy, "The Conquered Beast," though I doubt it will keep that title. It is somewhat after the style of Mr Holman Hunt's controversial "Scapegoat" and displays the capture of a wild beast by a saint, symbolic of the struggle within us all to conquer the lusts of the flesh. The saint was Bessie, but alas, he has no doubt had to alter his plans. The same thing must have happened to Mr Fairfax.'

I was outraged, despite Valentine's plight. 'Soot and rubbish, Mr Drake! Bessie deserves more than that of you, and well you know it. Bessie did nothing but good in her life. Can you and your Angels claim that? Were you good Samaritans to her when she came to you for help? No. You all passed by on the other side.'

Valentine burst into tears. 'You're right, Tom. You were a true friend to her. We weren't, for all our claims to love her. We failed her. I'll do what you want. The truth must be told.'

'Excellent,' Mr Mudgwick said briskly, indicating it was time to get down to business. 'If you would pen a short note both to the Academy and to your artist colleagues, we can proceed with our efforts on your behalf.'

I detected a dryness in his voice as he emphasised his last three words, as though he, too, were he not a solicitor, would have been shocked at his client's attitude.

My view is Valentine doesn't mean half of what he says, and that he's been bamboozled by the stars in his eyes about the Angels, lapping up what they have to say like a spaniel. He means no harm—but as to what the Angels wish him, I am not at all certain.

Valentine scribbled the required notes with a bravado that I could not but admire. As he handed over his letters, he remarked with studied casualness, 'I admit that Frederick might possibly have been the father of Bessie's child.'

'And possibly her murderer also? Or one of the other two gentlemen? Was one of them the gentleman in the carriage whom you saw the night she died?'

'No,' Valentine cried, getting upset again. 'I have worked and dined with the Angels for two years. I *know* them, Tom. A murderer amongst them? Never.'

I sighed. 'I believe her murderer to be Moonman, sir, but whoever that man in the hansom was, he would have something to tell us about Bessie and what happened that night.'

'Might I point out, Mr Wasp,' Mr Mudgwick added, 'that there is a *possibility* that the gentleman in the hansom was—um—a casual customer? Perhaps he already knew Bessie. Perhaps he knew Jenny too?'

'Bessie was no streetwalker, sir. You never met her, but Mr Drake will tell you. Won't you, sir?'

For a moment I thought he would not answer, but he did. 'Tom's right, Mr Mudgwick. Bessie might have sacrificed her virtue, but she wouldn't walk the streets.'

'I'm not sure sacrificed is the right word, sir.' I was determined not to see Bessie done down, for unless we saw her as she was, we wouldn't find her killer, and a terrible suspicion came to me as I saw a slow flush creeping up Valentine's cheeks.

'Sacrificed, sir? Is that true?' I asked again.

'No,' he admitted—unwillingly and no wonder. 'She told me that last evening she had been taken by force and had the child as a result. Oh Tom, I believed her.'

Not many sweeps present themselves for admittance to the

Academy Rooms in the National Gallery, and especially not on Varnishing Day for the summer exhibition. For all my letter of authority, I wished Mr Mudgwick were with me, but he was busy with other clients. Once past the gatekeeper, it proved easier than I expected, for the rooms were abuzz with business, and smells with which I was familiar filled the air: turpentine, varnish, paint. Some work was being carried out, but most of the gentlemen—and indeed several ladies—were in little groups, talking, gesticulating, complaining loudly about where their work was hung. A few were displaying smug satisfaction.

'The Line' figured prominently in the conversation, this being the ideal hanging place for well-esteemed pictures, level with a man's eyes, unless he happens to be a bow-legged chimney sweep like Tom Wasp.

I found all the Angels in the North Room, engaged in discussion over their respective positions. My eye was taken by a picture of a young lady with a title-plate 'Kate Nickleby,' and I was pleased that Mr Dickens was so represented.

'It is too bad, Edward,' Frederick was sympathising, 'that your "St James' Park at Night" is hung so high.'

We all looked up at it. To my mind it was an insipid piece. Not like those pictures of London by night stacked against his wall that breathed out passion and turmoil.

Frederick's 'Too Late,' on the other hand, was hung just above the line, which he seemed pleased with. There was no sign of Mr Tait's 'The Conquered Beast' by that or any other name, but tucked in the lower corner of the wall I saw the lady walking up the church steps.

Frederick was bemoaning the precedence being given to another picture of water, this one being a woman ducked in the water as a test for witchcraft, called 'Ordeal by Water.' I saw also a picture of an old soldier with his grandson on his knee, and several scenes of our parliament, all dull material to my mind, though their artists stood proudly by. I could sympathise with the Angels' desire to give mankind a message, even if the message and the means weren't always portrayed to my liking.

Edward was intent on decrying a new work by Mr Frith, which he said was on display in a gallery next to the Haymarket Theatre.

'What kind of noble theme can a railway station present?' Frederick agreed.

'To my mind, a very good theme,' was Laurence's view, 'for all human life can be found there. Partings, meetings, sweethearts, families, the rich and the poor, all meeting together bound by a common cause: the railway journey.'

'And dippers too,' I volunteered, so that at last they noticed me. All respect for these gentlemen Angels had vanished after Valentine's admission.

'I see our chimney sweep is with us once more.' Frederick tried to laugh, his boyish locks tumbling over his face. It was obvious none of them were pleased to see me, but then that was hardly the reason for my presence. 'Sweeps seem to be in fashion, Wasp.' He pointed to a small painting in which two children were curiously watching while a sweep disappeared under the black tuggy cloth across the chimney's mouth. For all the song and dance these artists make about painting from real life, their idea of it is always inside out, not outside in. The eye of the viewer would be on the children emerging from their nursery to see this strange beast, a chimney sweep. Even to Valentine we were only symbols, not real.

Today, I *was* real. I had an important task.

'I'm here to give you these,' I handed out Valentine's letters, 'and to crave your help on behalf of our mutual friend, Mr Drake.'

They immediately all endeavoured to look concerned, as they opened their letters.

'Tell him his picture is hung well,' Laurence said to me. 'There it is. Do you see?' 'Cast Out' was on the Line, and I wondered that I had not seen it before, so beautiful it looked. 'Of course, the position is merely because its attraction of being painted by a supposed murderer will be irresistible—much as I admire it,' he added casually.

'The reason Mr Drake wishes you to listen to me,' I explained, 'is that his solicitor and the police are coming to Cremorne Gardens tomorrow evening to meet Polly, Bessie's sister, and we hope to track down Moonman. Mr Drake feels you should be present too, seeing that he may try to put the blame on one of you about being the father of Bessie's son.'

All three of them went as stiff as a brush with clogged wet soot.

'I am not in the habit of visiting places such as Cremorne,' said Edward, as though that settled the matter.

'Come, sir, was that not Cremorne I recognised in one of the pictures by your studio wall?'

A smirk from Laurence Tait, as Edward added even more stiffly, 'I should have said, save for professional purposes.'

'I don't recall a Cremorne Gardens in your work, Edward,' Frederick said quickly.

'An experiment. It failed, for it is more your field than mine.' Edward smiled gravely. 'Gardens hold a great attraction for you, Frederick, do they not?'

'Pleasure gardens are a good setting for the sins of mankind,' was Laurence's offering. 'I'm interested to know what purpose we shall serve Valentine if we go. Your explanation seems hardly credible so far, Wasp.'

'It will be. Mr Valentine believes that as Bessie could find no help from you the night she died, you would naturally wish to help her son and her sister. Bessie and Jenny have already fallen to Moonman. Will you see the third sister die also? If you go, you will lend support to Polly and convince her she is safe if she leads us to him.'

'Put like that,' Laurence said soberly, 'we should go. Would it suit you if we all took supper together in the restaurant at Cremorne House?' Frederick and Edward remained silent.

'I should prefer the supper boxes, if you please, by the dancing area,' I said firmly. 'That is near where I shall meet Polly.'

'Is the food as good?' Frederick laughed, though I could see his other self was furious.

'I believe,' Edward said sarcastically, 'Mr Wasp will assure us it is. He is quite determined we shall spend a cold and pointless evening in the interests of providing poor Val with false hopes.'

Chapter Ten: The darkness of Cremorne

You might think we were on our way to Paradise, as we chugged on our three-penny boat ride west along the River Thames to the pleasure gardens of Cremorne. When I say 'we,' I mean of course Ned, who insisted he was coming with me. I was honoured, I told him, seeing as how he seemed to have taken an aversion to my company ever since last Thursday, when he was off on his jaunts with his fellow apprentices for the May Day festivities.

These aren't what they used to be in Mrs Montagu's day, or even Mr Charles Lamb's, who wrote so jauntily about the life of 'unpennied sweeps' and the dinners held by Mr Jem White for sweeps' chummies at the fair of St Bartholomew. Ned enjoys dressing up in the green for May Day though, and parading through such streets as they are allowed—fewer each year. This was his third year at it, and he comes back more pleased with himself each time.

This year I sensed there was something more that he wasn't telling me. I've learned not to press him though. Ned is his own man, and if I have to do my own hollering and brush cleaning once in a while when he's about his own concerns, it is no great hardship. Nevertheless, I was suspicious at his enthusiasm for this evening outing, for there's plenty of dipping and buzzing to be done in the dark corners of Cremorne.

'You ain't thinking of anything but Bessie, are you, Ned?'

His jaw jutted out and his mouth grew mutinous. 'Have to

keep my hand in, Gov.'

'Not in other people's pockets, Ned.'

There are rich pickings to be had at Cremorne when the Lord takes his golden eye the sun away, and relies on man's lighting systems. It's then that Paradise breeds its serpents. Mothers and children fade away, and in swarm the dwellers of the night. Not all of them are serpents of evil, for the majority are honest folk come to enjoy themselves after a day's toil. Girls on their sweethearts' arms, come to dance, stroll along the gas-lit paths amid the flower beds, and steal away to quiet corners. Married folk come to watch the many spectacles, the circus, the ballet, the marionettes, to visit the sideshows or the gypsy's tent, and in the summer sup at one of the many outdoor tables. I've not visited the gardens in recent years, but once I knew them well, for the old Cremorne Farmhouse first opened as Cremorne Stadium in the early thirties. I was a nipper then, and my master was called in to assist in the sweeping at Cremorne House. I don't remember that first occasion, but they kept us on for several years and, seeing I showed an interest in the place when he mentioned it, Valentine had told me about the Cremorne Pleasure Gardens of the present.

'It is splendid, Tom.' His dark eyes were alive with enthusiasm, his hands waved energetically in the air, with the usual result that a spatter of paint from his brush came to join the soot on my number-two clothes. 'As Dr Johnson said of London, so it is with Cremorne. When a man is tired of Cremorne, he is tired of life. It is fertile ground for the Angels, Tom.'

Where there are Angels, devils lurk also, was my view, and there are plenty of places in these leafy grounds where souls are lost to evil.

Not that many chimney sweeps visit Cremorne to pay their shilling entrance fee. In the East End we have our own pleasure gardens; as well as Victoria Park, some taverns like the Eagle offer such attractions. It was at the Eagle that we master sweeps celebrated May Day, and to us it seemed as fine as Cremorne. However, the Eagle is a tidy step from Hairbrine Court, and even those pubs that keep a garden are far removed from us, so despite the gravity of our mission, I felt like a king in my royal three-penny barge arriving at the waterside entrance to Cremorne.

It had been arranged that I should talk to Polly first to persuade her to accompany us to seek out Moonman, and then send Ned for the Angels. Mr Mudgwick would be meeting the police at the King's Road entrance and accompanying them to the pagoda.

All I knew about Cremorne did not prepare me for what I found after we handed over our shillings to the gentlemen in the pay box by the ornately carved iron gates. In the east of London, pleasure, violence and menace are mixed up together at the penny gaffs, in the public houses, the gin palaces and the music and dancing saloons, which has the virtue that you see the enemy. Here in Cremorne the gas jets were burning so yellow bright that the sight of couples enjoying themselves, dancing, and squealing with laughter was such a spectacle that one could believe that was all there was, and that darkness had been banished.

We strolled over to the pagoda where the band was playing and couples dancing on what they call the crystal floor surrounding it on which it was said four thousand people could tread a measure. It was nearly ten o'clock now, but no sign of Polly as we selected a table at a refreshment stall and sat down to be waited on like lords. Behind us and to our right were the supper boxes, the building enclosed but the boxes open to the air to give the diners full view of the merrymaking beneath them. High-class gentlemen normally dined at Cremorne House, for in the boxes there were only standard half-crown suppers. Two shillings and sixpence being nearly half a week's earnings to us, this seemed grand enough.

In the dark our black skins did not cause so much attention, and when our Cremorne sherry was brought to us—an innovation this year, so the billboard declared—and one of which the owners seemed mighty proud, I began to look around more confidently. Ned fidgeted and people around us murmured at a child being up at such an hour.

'Our Polly's late, Ned.' Having no watch, I have a sixth sense of passing time.

'It's ten past ten, Gov.'

'Ned,' I hissed. 'I told you to be on your best behaviour. I looked closer. Dancing from his fingers was a fine Albert chain and watch.

'Yes, Gov.' He grinned as he put his new acquisition away, confident it was his by right. He would be down to a dolly shop tomorrow with his trophy unless I can impress him otherwise, which is sometimes possible. 'We'll give it to the needy,' I said.

'We *are* the needy, Gov.'

Ned had a point, but so did I. I informed him we were lucky compared with the Spitalfields weaver and his wife who just starved to death for lack of food, although they worked fifteen hours a day and every day for the grand sum of four shillings and sixpence a week. The patterer had given out the inquest report, and it shook me badly.

As the minutes passed, I grew ever more uneasy. Had Polly changed her mind? The theatre ballet must be over, and it was hard to believe she would take this long to reach us. In front of us, the pagoda dancing floor was crowded, and the band playing most joyfully. Each one of these dancers had his or her own story, but there was only one I was interested in and that was Polly's.

'Ned,' I commanded, 'you stay here to wait for Mr Mudgwick. I'll be back as quick as a brush up a clean chimney.' I walked up to the theatre in the centre of the grounds, but every door was closed, and no lights showed. Cremorne, anxious to keep on friendly terms with its neighbours, did its best to close at eleven, but intentions aren't always enough. There would be a grand firework display beginning shortly, which meant that tonight at least, being the first of the season, the shows closed in good time.

Which path would Polly have taken? I turned round. Before me was the grand illuminated avenue of trees leading to the fireworks, and the King's Road entrance in one direction, and the supper boxes, circus and pagoda in the other. On my left I could see the American bowling saloon I had passed on my way here. Behind me was the lawn where balloon ascents and other marvels take place. Polly could only have gone one way—to the avenue leading to the pagoda, which would take her past the circus.

Where Moonman must surely work, if Tom Wasp had a brain in his head.

I walked over to the grand semi-circular columned building, where the evening performance had finished for crowds were already thronging the trellised avenue.

The new owner of Cremorne had laid on many new attractions for this season. Such wonders were advertised outside the circus. Bell's Performing Elephants, Signor Quagliani's Sardinian Troupe of Equestrians—and Cooke's Dogs and Monkeys. That was the item that interested me, convinced as I was that Moonman was in charge of the dogs, having discovered that Polly was to work at the theatre.

Was he with her even now? The circus might be closed, but the animals must still be here. I could hear them, trumpeting and squealing, and walked round the far side of the circus building to find some pens by the side screen of trees, hidden from public view. It was here that the animals were clearly confined. It was dark, and none too warm, and with the eerie sound of strange animals around, I decided not to linger. There was no sign of human life.

Sudden fear of the dark seized me, as though I were a child again. I prayed to God that He would lead me into the light again, that this nightmare taking hold of my waking brain would vanish as I returned to Ned. By now I would find Polly there, with Mr Mudgwick and the police and the Angels. I was certain of it, and broke into as much of a run as my legs and boots allow.

I hurried past the circus again, jostling through crowds that were still flocking in the opposite direction for the fireworks. As I reached the end of the building, however, I noticed a narrow alley between it and the beginning of the long supper box building, and saw that there seemed to be a light in the circus. What made me go down to investigate, I'll never know. I reached the light to find it was an illusion, cast by the one lamp in the alley at the far end. I turned to hurry back, but then something caught my eye.

It was hidden in the dark hidden places of the night, protruding from a gap between the back of the supper boxes and the row of tall trees that encloses the whole of Cremorne from the gaze of the curious. In the distance I could still hear the band playing, the squeals of laughter, and the roar of animals, but they were far off as I looked at the outstretched hand, small and gloved in cheap cotton gloves.

From where I stood, I could see nothing more. I had to go in to that gap and see to whom they had belonged. It was a body, bonneted head towards me. I could not see the face, but in my guts I knew. I hardly needed to drag the girl out and turn her over to see that it was Polly.

I was sick at heart, and though I told myself that Polly was in our Lord's loving arms, it did not help the pain. He could have left her longer. She had been garrotted.

I knelt down at her side, seeing her poor staring eyes and blue face and hoping for a gasp of her sweet breath to tell me there was life yet. None came. No rise and fall of her bosom, no pulse in the delicate wrist. Polly had joined her sisters, poor lass, and she but twenty years old. Moonman the Monster had murdered all three daughters who tried to escape his terrible clutches, and maybe Sophie too.

I had to leave Polly there, alone in the dark, as I hurried back to where I left Ned, and found to my relief that Mr Mudgwick and the police were there with him.

'Wasp,' Sergeant Wiley roared, as he saw me coming. 'Where's the girl?' Then he saw my face. 'What's up?'

'The girl's with her Maker, let her rest in peace,' I replied soberly. 'Dead.' I choked, as I never did on soot.

The other two policemen were looking at me strangely, and so were Mr Mudgwick and Ned. It meant nothing. All I could think of was my Bessie and now Polly, and how I hadn't protected them when they needed it. The dancers—fewer of them—were still circling round the pagoda, the band was playing 'Sweet Lass of Richmond Hill,' but my sweet lassies would never dance again. The monster had tracked them down and swept them away forever.

'Dead where?' Wiley asked.

'I'll show you. Ned, you stay here.' But he didn't, either from curiosity or because he thought I needed help. Mr Mudgwick came too, though there was no sign of the Angels.

Polly was still there, as I'd left her. No other fellow human had come this way, and now I had to surrender her, like Bessie, to those who had no feeling for her, to whom she was another body in a day's work.

Not to Mr Mudgwick though. He looked very shaken. 'Poor

girl. You're sure it's Polly, Tom?'

'Oh, yes.'

'A judy. Killed during the course of business,' I overheard one of the policemen saying to the other.

'No. A respectable girl,' I said. 'Killed by her father, because she wouldn't give in to him. George Clare, once Bunting, who looks after the dogs at the circus.'

All three pigmen conversed, their swallowtail coats wobbling as they argued amongst themselves. This being May, they'd donned their summer uniforms, with the white trousers, and it seemed all wrong when Polly had never known her summer.

Then one of them turned to me. 'Just happened to find her, did you? The body's still warm. Sweeps have strong hands. Brought her down here for a spot of wapping and when she wouldn't you—'

The words meant nothing at first, and when I understood, Ned did the answering for me.

'No.' Ned started pummelling the pigman. 'He's good, is the Governor.'

'Maybe you were with him, lad.'

Fortunately, Mr Mudgwick took a hand, highly indignant. 'Mr Wasp, as I explained to you, is here at my request to assist my efforts to prove Mr Drake's innocent of the murder of Bessie Barton. This poor girl was her sister, and Mr Wasp was determined to find this George Clare through her. She too feared her father. Mr Wasp would hardly murder our chief witness.'

'Chimney sweeps are crafty.'

'Then consider this,' Mr Mudgwick retorted, crossly for him. 'Mr Wasp stands to make money if we are successful, and needs Miss Polly alive to do so.'

This was news to me, and not welcome, but it was a good argument, for they saw the sense of such talk. Money, for once, had proved good, not evil.

'We're wasting time,' I said. 'This George Clare, Moonman, is getting away again.'

Sergeant Wiley saw the point immediately. His promotion would be vanishing with it, and he quickly conferred with the Chelsea police. The three pigmen then disappeared into the night in different directions to check the exit gates, instructing Mr Mudgwick to keep an eye on me. As an afterthought, they sent Wiley back to join us and to summon help. It was only then I realised Ned had disappeared, although almost as soon as I'd noted the fact he reappeared.

'You'll find him in the American bowling saloon,' he said importantly.

'Who?'

'Moonman, Gov. I found out the circus mob always go there after the show.'

'Good lad.' Wiley beamed at Ned, and I reflected, not for the first time, that young wits are quicker than old.

The bowling saloon was in the middle of the grounds and contained, so Valentine had told me, not only the game of bowling, which sounded to me like skittles, but served American drinks! I am not impressed with America, which seems to have taken a sad turn since they chose to be independent. They are in the midst of a Civil War, so the patterer says, with great cruelties and hardships involved, and so for them to be sending their games and drinks over here seems an insult to our Queen.

Sergeant Wiley did not share my concerns, judging by the way he led the charge to the saloon. He burst in with the full authority of the law, roaring out, 'George Clare. Where is he?'—an approach that to my mind lacked subtlety.

'Who wants him?' A short plump gentleman, deeply interested in a glass of what looked like green milk, looked up at Sergeant Wiley's announcement.

'Police, on account of his daughter Polly.'

We weren't quick enough. I just had a chance to glimpse a tall burly man, middle-aged, glaring at us from the back of the hall. I even saw the up and down of the inimical-looking face before he disappeared, and I realised there must be another entrance.

'Gone,' said the short plump gentleman, with what appeared satisfaction. 'You'll not catch him now.'

Ned thought otherwise. He was out of the door like a Thames eel who's caught sight of Shadwell fish market. Sergeant Wiley and the other pigmen rushed after him, and I was left in the rear, though not for lack of trying.

'The gates,' I heard a pigman snarl, as I caught a brief glimpse of Ned squirming his way through the crowds, massing over the lawns, and ahead of him the crowd parting for a tall burly man.

I could hear the faint sound of police whistles, and then lost sight of Ned, so I made my way straight north to the King's Road entrance, which I found blocked off, with pigmen already checking all leavers. To my left was the firework gallery surrounded by a huge crowd. If I were Moonman, where would I go? Into the crowd to be lost among thousands, or over to the right, the less frequented part of the grounds where I might stand a chance of climbing the bordering trees to leap into the adjoining road, or find a way into the picture gallery, which had its own entrance from the roadway, and which the police would not think to check? There was no sign of Ned, so I plunged ahead on my own. It was quiet here, ill-lit, save for one or two paths, and in the gloom I lost my way. I thought these trees to be the hedge surrounding the gallery, but instead I found myself in a narrow alleyway with tall hedges either side. It twisted round, and seeing it had no ending, I turned on to a cross path, and then another, only to find myself against another hedge.

It was then I realised. I was in the maze, and when I turned,

I knew not which way to go. I stood there, helpless. If Moonman had come this way, he might be near me now, waiting in the dark, for I was away from nearly all light now, thanks to these hedges. The silence was heavy around me. In the distance I could hear the fireworks, and saw one shooting up into the sky. I could hear the crowds shouting, but here I was alone and all was quiet.

I was in a green chimney with no way to the light, the walls closing in around me. Suppose that clutching hand should come now? Suppose Moonman was inching his way towards me? I felt as though that hand gripped itself around my heart, for it beat and fluttered in panic. I had to move, but which of these green flues should I choose?

Grown man that I was, I wept for loneliness and fear, as I stumbled to right and left, each time to come up against a wall of green soot, and not the blessed light.

'Ned, Ned,' I croaked.

I thought the merciful Lord had answered my prayer, as I heard a faint sound, and cried out again.

'Gov.'

I couldn't see him, only hear the sound of his voice. Or was it crying only in my mind? I stood there, calling feebly, so he could track me down, and at last he did, his cap peak appearing round a corner, and then his welcome self. No phantom of the imagination this, for Ned was real.

'Where's Moonman?' I whispered bravely, so he wouldn't guess how scared I'd been.

'Gone, Gov. Scarpered.'

'You're sure?' We were still trapped in the green nightmare that might contain Moonman.

'Yes, Gov.'

It was my duty to look after Ned, not the other way around, but this evening I let him lead me like a child back to the King's

Road entrance, where we found Sergeant Wiley, the Chelsea policemen and Mr Mudgwick.

'I regret to say your Moonman appears to have gone, Tom,' Mr Mudgwick told me, looking very grave.

'If he ever existed,' muttered one of the Chelsea policemen. His eyes lingered on me lovingly, and had not Mr Mudgwick pointed out no evidence existed against me save that I found the poor lass, I would have been sitting next to Valentine in a trice. Such is the justice of this world. The Lord had saved me through Mr Mudgwick.

'Of course, it is by no means certain that Moonman was the murderer.' Mr Mudgwick had his eye on me, seeming to want something of me, though my wits were still befuddled, and I could not guess what this might be.

'He ran when asked for,' I pointed out.

'Many men run when they hear policemen asking for them, especially those who have experienced detention.'

Sergeant Wiley guffawed at Mr Mudgwick's comment, and suddenly I grasped what he was trying to hint to me. The supper boxes where the Angels had dined at were very close to where Polly's poor body had been found. They were not above suspicion—far from it. One of them could easily have been the gentleman Valentine saw Bessie walking with that night she met her death. He only *thought* he saw someone following them. In my distress over Polly, I had forgotten their presence. It was time to remedy that.

Gentlemen at table cannot be rushed, and although the local residents strongly object, Valentine had told me the gates remain open until far into the night. I made my way back down the main avenue, leaving Ned with Mr Mudgwick. Even though I had my Number One suit on, people fell aside as I majestically made my steady path along it.

As I reached the circus building, I could see a policeman

guarding the entrance to the alleyway, and the shapes of men moving about with lanterns. The dancing floor was cleared now, and the band departed, although a few intrepid souls still lingered at the outside tables and in the supper boxes, for they were open to the outside air. They were built in two storeys, and I walked up the steps to the higher tier where I could see the three Angels in silhouette against the oil lamp on the table, engaged in earnest discussion.

Did they know about Polly? Was it her terrible end they were discussing? I stood in the doorway to their box, but not any of them noticed me for their backs were to me, and they were engaged in heated debate—or rather argument—about the splendid opportunity the Government had missed to display a wide range of modern painting (especially their own) at the International Exhibition.

' "The Light of the World," ' Mr Harwood-Jones was saying, 'is a fine enough painting for its time, but it speaks of the fifties. Why not today's best, not the past?'

'Hear, hear,' Frederick hiccupped.

'We are too strong for them. We look to the future, the Exhibition is too cautious.' Laurence banged his fist on the table.

'Millais—' Frederick began and howls of agreement interrupted him.

'A traitor to the brotherhood he founded,' Laurence shouted.

'A Judas,' Edward agreed. ' "The Black Brunswicker" defies nature and art also. The puppy is a disgrace, a blatant appeal to sentimentality.'

'Mr Drake thought the use of Mr Dickens' daughter as a model rather fine.' I could not resist putting my ironical hap-porth of soot into the discussion. My heart was heavy with anger for hearing them discuss such trivialities as Polly lay dead.

For a moment I thought they hadn't heard me, then one by one they turned to look at me. Perhaps they read my thoughts through the grime on my face, for they instantly grew quiet.

'There's been murder done,' I told them.

'By Jove, not again,' said Frederick cheerfully. 'Can you think of no other entrance line, Wasp?'

Laurence's red face glared at me. 'Any one of ten thousand men could have killed Bessie *and* her sister. Why does Valentine still continue to command his sweep to ruin our days *and* our evenings?'

'It's not Bessie, or Jenny I've come to tell you about. It's Polly, the youngest sister you came here to meet, who never arrived for our meeting. She's been found garrotted behind this building.'

Frederick spoke first. 'Poor girl. I'm sorry for her, but it's one of the risks of finding custom in the pleasure gardens.'

Rage consumed me. 'She was a respectable girl, sir. A milliner.'

'A milliner!' Laurence snorted in disgust. 'It's well known that many find extra work on the streets.'

It nearly choked me to be so disloyal to Polly, but I had to ignore his words if I were to find the truth. 'A death is a death, sir. No doubt the police will be asking you questions.'

A split second for this good news to sink in, then Edward said quietly: 'This is your doing, Wasp. Some plot of Valentine's. You get us here under false pretences, murder the girl, and we are implicated.'

'No, sir,' I replied quietly. 'Drink is making your wits drowsy, perhaps. You're all three feeling guilty about Bessie still, so it's natural enough to blame me.'

'Why should *we* feel guilty?' shouted Frederick, not meaning, I am sure, for me to answer. But I did—for I had their attention. Fear made them forget I was but a chimney sweep, and anger let me step aside from my sooty clothes.

'You Angels are proud of the way you stand together, so

together you must be judged. How did the Angels treat Bessie? You forced her against her will and left her with child. You rejected her after promising to marry her; you pestered her for attentions no model should have to endure. For all this, poor Bessie was convinced that one of you truly loved her, yet though she came to you all that evening, you all sent her away to her death, even Mr Drake. I tell you, gentlemen, if you ever listen to anything but the sound of your own voices, you'll hear the cock crow thrice.'

I was ready to cry, having spoken my mind, but what effect my words had, if any, was difficult to guess at. I was past caring about the need to watch them, to be on my guard, for all I could think of was Polly's body lying there, and how I'd let Bessie down by not preventing it.

'Gentlemen.' It was Laurence spoke first, addressing his fellow Angels only. 'This fellow is right. It is time to speak. We have, after all, an even higher aim than brotherhood amongst ourselves.'

Justice, I thought? The Lord's way?

'Art,' he continued. 'If we are to be true to our sworn purpose for forming the Angels, sacrifice of our private emotions may have to be made, even though we have nothing to hide. I am prepared to speak—'

'I will do so,' Frederick said instantly. There was a very long silence then, ending in reluctant nods.

I hoped I might do better than Pilate in recognising truth, for I had little experience of it from the Angels.

'Bessie,' Frederick said, 'came to us, as you know, shortly after we set up our joint studio in Doughty Street and formed the Angelic Band, as we termed it, though we quickly became known as the Angels. This was in early fifty-five.'

'Who found Bessie as a model?' I asked.

'I did,' Laurence admitted readily, though he was glaring at

Frederick, and I wondered why. 'I visited a music hall one evening, and as soon as I saw Bessie's wonderful red-gold hair, it was clear to me that here was our inspiration. She was not eager at first, doubtless mistaking my motives, but after seeing our most respectable studio, she agreed. Edward and Frederick were in full agreement as soon as they saw her.'

'We were.' Frederick was eager to take over. 'I have already told you I mentioned marriage to Bessie, until she broke my heart by telling me she was with child by another man. That would be in fifty-six, and the child was due in spring fifty-seven. The idea that one of us raped her, however, is quite ridiculous. Edward is a God-fearing man, Laurence is married, and I worshipped the ground she trod on. No, you must look elsewhere for her assailant, Mr Wasp, as we could no longer employ her as a model, and we saw no more of her until Valentine joined us. He had been greatly impressed by some of our early works, and particularly those for which Bessie had modelled. Nothing would stop him from tracking her down.'

'You tried to stop him then? Why would that be?' I picked up the slight stumble in his words as though he had thought better of them.

'That would *be,*' Laurence growled, 'because we wish to preserve peace at our homes. Introducing a harlot as model in our home studios could cause offence to our families.'

'Bessie was no harlot,' I said, too weary to be angry now, 'and well you know it. Mr Drake told his solicitor that he followed Bessie to Holywell Street and watched her walk away with a gentleman who had descended from a hansom cab. What gentlemen did Bessie know other than you?'

'Who knows?' Frederick said lightly.

'God does,' I replied. '*He* knows she came to see you that evening because she believed she had the right to ask you all for help on account of the way you treated her—and that's why she went to Mr Drake last. He wasn't the boy's father, and had always behaved well towards her.'

I'd sooner walk into Paddy's Goose at midnight with a bag of gold sovereigns than deal with these so-called gentlemen again.

'You're not quite accurate, Mr Wasp.' Edward decided to play his part in the 'truth' proceedings. 'Bessie saw us as opportunity for blackmail.'

'Edward!' Laurence cried sharply.

Edward ignored him. 'Bessie came to me first on that Saturday because she knew my mother has strong principles of moral conduct, as indeed I have myself. When I refused her ridiculous request to face this Moonman at midnight, she informed me she would tell my mother that I was the father of her child. My mother would never have believed such a ridiculous notion, but I did not wish her upset. I offered Bessie money. It was refused. I threatened to summon the police and have her ejected, but she left of her own accord.'

'But that's almost the same as happened to me that evening,' Laurence exclaimed. 'She asked, you will recall, Wasp, to see my wife and hinted to her that I was the father of her child. It was nonsense of course.'

'Bessie appealed to me on other grounds,' Frederick informed me sadly. 'That I had wanted to marry her, and must therefore hold some fondness for her. When I said this fondness did not extend to involvement in her sordid intrigues, she lost her temper.'

The Angels all looked at me expectantly as if to see what I'd thought of all this. I did not give them the satisfaction of telling them that Truth was another lady whom the Angels had treated as badly as they had Bessie, and now was the time to tell them so.

'So it's not true,' I said slowly, 'that in that studio of yours a terrible deed took place, when one of you left alone with Bessie took advantage of her against her will.'

Relief spread across their conspiring faces, and they relaxed. Laurence poured out more wine.

'Far from it,' he said complacently. 'That studio was dedicated to harmony and art.'

I interrupted. 'Would that be the studio in Pimlico or the one in Doughty Street you mentioned?'

A terrible silence. 'Damn you, Frederick,' Laurence yelled.

'An error,' Edward said smoothly. 'Doughty Street was Frederick's studio after we left Pimlico and before he moved in here.'

'That is right,' Frederick said, smiling brightly.

'No,' Laurence thundered. 'By God, you'll have us all in prison, Frederick, with these damned lies. There's nothing to be ashamed of. Why not tell him?'

Brotherly accord vanished, judging by the looks on their faces, but Edward did his best.

'You are right, Laurence. Let me explain the confusion, Wasp. We shared a studio in Pimlico, where Bessie first modelled for us, and left it early in fifty-seven to move into our independent studios. However, such is our intimacy that after a while, eighteen months or so, we missed the closeness that we shared in Pimlico, and our art was suffering as a result. Frederick had a large studio in Doughty Street and kindly said we could share it. Although we each kept our studios in our homes, Doughty Street was admirable when we had projects that would benefit from joint discussion.'

'And from Bessie,' I added for him.

He flushed. 'Bessie, Frederick discovered, was working in a music hall in Bermondsey, and persuaded her to rejoin us. She did so, for about eighteen months and then grew bored and left us until Mr Drake found her once more.'

'Boredom and Bessie don't fit together,' I commented. 'Who

was it made her leave Doughty Street with his nasty ways? And who was it followed Bessie to Holywell Street in a hansom cab that evening? Was it you, Mr Harwood-Jones? You, Mr Tait? Or you, Mr Fairfax?'

Again fell the silence amongst them that I likened once to that of the Last Supper. A band of brothers—and one traitor. Two of the Angels, I believed, had no idea that Bessie had not given herself freely to the third, and that that same person had driven her away by attacking her again in Doughty Street. They knew now though.

'I'll be outside Beezer House, Sussex Square, tomorrow morning at ten,' I told them. 'It's me or the police.'

I left them there and walked back through the gardens, full of grief.

Chapter Eleven: Tom Wasp's Cleaning Machine

Which Angel would visit me today? I had my own ideas, but liking to size up the chimney before I clean it, I haven't mentioned all my thoughts to you in case the brush became stuck. There was a plan years ago for a miraculous machine for cleaning chimneys that climbs its own way up the chimney once set inside the chimney throat, by means of a strong spring, dilating and contracting to gather the soot around it. No matter if the chimney was crooked or straight, this automaton would find the light somehow. I never heard that it came into use, but it seemed to me it was like man's brain. The sooty problem lies inside it, and of its own accord the answer will work itself to the light.

I fixed the tuggy cloth onto the marble fireplace in Lady Beezer's library most carefully so that not one speck of soot could fly into the room to dirty Lady Beezer's books. This wasn't as grand as her library at Hanwell Place, but it contained much of value to her. Lady Beezer was watching me, though with amusement, not concern.

'I can afford to pay for your services, Tom.'

I was set on sweeping her chimneys for nothing. 'I know that, your ladyship, and much obliged I am. But this is a matter of my using your services, not you mine.'

'You really expect one of those three artists to come here to confess to you?'

I knew Lady Beezer valued me, so I didn't take her doubt

amiss that a gentleman would bare his evil soul to a chimney sweep.

'Yes, your ladyship. He wouldn't come to Hairbrine Court, but a hansom cab to Sussex Square is a different flue altogether. We won't be troubling you, for my plan is to meet him outside.'

I said no more, not wishing to state my beliefs until they were proved right. It could be Laurence Tait about to call on us, with his eagerness to bestow his favours on defenceless girls. It could be Edward Harwood-Jones with his love of painting the darker side of London life and the livid lights of the Haymarket and Cremorne, which he had claimed he never visited. Or it could be smiling Frederick who was the one that forced Bessie and then, because that made her a sullied woman in his eyes, found her no longer pure enough for the honour of marriage. I was certain that the only Angel who could *not* be Bessie's murderer was Valentine Drake. The police might still be unconvinced that the three murders were connected, but Tom Wasp had no doubts at all. The patterer gave out this morning that there'd been an escape from Newgate yesterday, but Drake wasn't the name, so he could not have murdered Polly, or Jenny either.

The kitchen flue was the heaviest in soot in Beezer House, since the fire never goes out there, summer or winter, save for the sweeps' visits. However, I do a good job, and Ned and I were rewarded by Mrs Tiggle with a fine muffin and beer, which set me up for the task ahead of me.

Ten o'clock found us marching out with the soot bag to place it on the cart. We'd left Doshie on the far side of the square, to Ned's surprise. Now I told Ned he had to stay with it, which he didn't like at all. He wanted to come with me to meet the Angel, but I stood firm. Whoever came wouldn't want to talk in front of the boy. I walked back to Lady Beezer's past all the grand white houses, wishing myself anywhere but here, and a few minutes after I reached the house a hansom drew up. A man called from within.

'Come up, Wasp.'

I had been right. I had no intention, for reasons that will later emerge, of being alone with this gentleman out of the sight of other eyes and, once in a cab, he could insist on our going anywhere.

'No, thank you, Mr Harwood-Jones,' I called cheerily. 'A nice walk in Hyde Park is what's needed this spring day.'

I thought for a moment he was going to refuse, but a surly, 'Very well' followed. He paid the jarvy and descended from the cab.

You might have deduced for yourselves that it was Edward Harwood-Jones, and for all the sunshine of that spring day, I shivered when I saw the way he looked at me.

'I have come for one reason only, Wasp,' he looked down his large nose like a balloonist on a black beetle, and made it sound as though he were doing me a favour. 'I am prepared to talk to you, but to no one else. The only reason I have agreed to this ridiculous escapade is that—' He stopped, and continued up a different flue. 'I still believe Valentine may be guilty of murder, and nothing I will say changes that. You may tell Mr Mudgwick what I relate to you, but it is not to be spread otherwise. It would be *my* word against yours, and I would see you suffer for it. You understand?' I nodded, and he continued grandly, 'Very well, let us walk to the park.'

'No need to worry about curious eyes, sir,' I pointed out humbly. 'You are known to be of a clerical family, and folks will assume I am one of your good works, or that you are a Commissioner studying the chimney sweepers' act.'

His face lightened as he considered this, and my chances of falling under the omnibus horses' hooves as we crossed the Bayswater Road diminished.

'You are not a bad fellow, Wasp,' he graciously informed me, which, coming from him, I could not believe to be a compliment. 'Our talk,' he continued as we walked through the Victoria Gate, 'has *no* relevance to Bessie's murder, or to that of the unfortunate girl last evening. It is merely to tell you that I am, or I *might* be, the father of Bessie's son. I cannot be sure, since she had other lovers. She was not virgin when I—'

'Raped her, sir?' I enquired, as if to help him out.

Edward didn't flinch. 'Persuaded,' he amended.

'The Bessie I knew wouldn't have been persuaded by you or anyone. Nor is she the Bessie I heard described yesterday by the Angels.'

'She was hardly an angel herself.' Harwood-Jones smirked, and I wanted to ram his stovepipe hat down over his smug face. I couldn't, because I needed him to talk. He wasn't going to have it all his way, however.

'And that entitled you to force her, sir?' I kept my voice mild.

'I atoned for my sin,' he replied calmly. He sounded at peace with himself over the issue, but I was going to change that one way or another.

'How was that, sir? By refusing to acknowledge or help the child?'

He stared at me with what seemed genuine surprise. 'The child was the product of sin. I am a clergyman's son, and my mother is of the highest principles. How could I continue to contribute to that sin in any way? My mother deserves more than that, and I am bound to her for—' Again, he thought the better of what he was about to say.

'Money,' I finished for him sympathetically. 'And a roof over your head.'

'Damnation to you, sweep. How dare you speak to me thus?'

'In the interests of Valentine Drake, sir, one of the Band of Angels to whom you swore to be loyal.'

That stopped him, and he tried another tack. 'How did you

know it was me in the cab, Wasp?'

'It was simple, sir. You live in Kensington, and yet Bessie came to you first from Holywell Street. The nearest Angel from there would have been Mr Tait. The most obvious would have been Mr Fairfax, who had wanted once to marry her.'

'Valentine still did, the fool.'

'And that,' I said, 'is why she went to him last. He loved and valued her, and she would not take advantage of it. From you three she had the *right* to ask help. Tell me what happened that night, if you please.'

'I will tell you first what happened in that studio in fifty-six. You have to understand we were at the start of our artistic careers as Angels. We had all three dabbled more or less successfully, but we lacked purpose until we discussed our common views and aims. The principle was good and evil in everyday life. It was Laurence who brought Bessie to us, and since Laurence makes no secret of his attraction to and for women, despite his married state, Frederick and I assumed she was his mistress, or that he had at least enjoyed her favours. Indeed, he boasted of the latter, to my natural revulsion. Whether it was true or not, and I believe perhaps it was not, it set up the presumption in all of us that Bessie as a model represented the enticements of sin and evil rather than good.'

'Lust,' I supplied helpfully.

'If you wish to use that word,' he continued coldly. 'I have described however the situation as I saw it. Frederick used Bessie as a model for the sensuous attractions of the world, the luscious fruit in the garden. I was more extreme, seeing her as part of the bright lights that lure man into the darkness. One day we were alone in the studio. She was posing as a Bacchante, in flimsy Grecian drapery—'

'Everyday life, sir?'

He hardly heard me. 'An exception,' he said, and swept on.

'Every artist must experiment. I had to adjust the drapery, walked over to her, my hand mistakenly touched the drapery on her breast, I smelled the violets in her hair, the breast—and, then lower. She pulled away. "No, Edward." I hardly heard her, and it made no difference. She had seduced me by then. It was too late for her to change her mind. I seized the drapery, exposed that breast—'

He was quivering, oblivious of the spring day in Hyde Park, oblivious to the fact I was a chimney sweep, oblivious to the fact I had been Bessie's friend. 'She fought me, but the powers of evil can be overcome, and I overcame her resistance. The drapery was off and Lilith herself was in my arms, naked and beautiful. I took her on the floor, struggling and as slippery as Leviathan, and I rode her in triumph—dear God, it was wonderful as I conquered evil. She was defeated, and slunk out of the studio—'

He was shaking, a crazed man. ' "I'll not be back," she said. There was such venom in her voice that I knew I had done good. I told Frederick and Laurence that she had not come that day, and when she did not return, we all presumed someone from her past life had reclaimed her for their own. It was immaterial. There are models a-plenty, after all. However, in Doughty Street one day Frederick mentioned he knew where she was, and I realised God had still some purpose in mind for me.

'She was reluctant to come back, fearing the powers of good, but I used cunning, and persuaded her I would not attempt to interfere with her wicked ways. I did though. Her evil was too strong for me. I succumbed, but she would not let me triumph this time, and fled in her glee at conquering me. I never forgave her, and would not allow her to model for me again. While she was modelling for Valentine, I had one last meeting with her, although she did not model for me again. She informed me the child was sick, and anxious to be rid of her I gave her money, and shut my eyes to evil by walking quickly away. She pretended she did not want the money, merely advice on a good doctor, but of course she did. That is merely the devil's way when he uses whores as his messengers. The last I saw of her was in the Haymarket that same day, when I was—by chance—passing in a hansom. I hailed her, telling her I had news of a doctor she might approach. I sketched her quickly in the cab, in order that I might work at one further painting to illustrate Satan at work through woman's flesh.'

I was knotted inside at this tale of twisted filth. I wanted to weep for my loved Bessie, and to howl at the hurt done to her, but I could do neither if I was to avenge her. I had to be steady, saying nothing, as his heaving subsided, and his red face assumed more normal colour. It was fortunate we were not in Rotten Row or the more crowded part of the park, and that those here at this time were bent on their own business rather than strollers.

'Tell me—' I thought my voice would choke me at having to address him. '—what happened the night she died?'

He was completely composed again now. 'She came when we were at dinner. I took her into the morning room, aghast at her effrontery at calling, though she was quite calm, seeing nothing in it. She told me, as you know, that she needed my help. She also ordered me to give it to her since her son was my child also.

' "It is not my child," I told her. 'That evening was the devil's work, and, even if my seed had spawned him, as a follower of Christ I could accept no part of him.

' "He is, Edward," she replied. "But even if he weren't, I have the right to ask for your help after what you did to me. Aren't you even curious to see what your son looks like? Don't you even care that he's in danger?"

'She would have ranted further, for she was quite out of control in her twisted mind, but unfortunately my mother came in at that moment, having overheard Bessie's words. Naturally she did not believe for one moment that the child was mine. She is, however, merciful to fallen women. She offered Bessie a place in a house of penitence, having falsely assumed Bessie was with child. There she could earn her keep at useful toil and receive God's guidance, while awaiting the child.'

'And what did Bessie reply to that?'

'She laughed in a most scornful manner,' Edward said angrily. 'My mother was extremely upset, and Bessie departed, ashamed.'

'What happened then?' I waited, curious to discover whether he would admit to anything more. However, when a man's as evil as Edward Harwood-Jones and doesn't see anything wrong in what he's done, he'll see no need to hide anything. And so it proved.

'I finished my dinner with my mother, but later on in the evening after she had retired for the night, I again yielded to temptation. For once I found myself curious to see this boy. Perhaps I might see in him my features. It would be—interesting,' he said jerkily. Perhaps there was some speck of humanity left in him.

'He *is* your son.' The boy was still alive—or so we hoped.

'Bessie would not know I was there, I reasoned. I planned to remain in the hansom. But when I arrived at the place where she told me she had arranged to meet this man of hers, I could see her there alone. She spotted me, unfortunately, looking at her from the cab, and came over to me under the impression I had changed my mind. I had not of course, and told her so. I made the mistake of descending from the cab, which drove off, unasked. I had no intention of remaining where we were to await this ruffian. She agreed to walk a little distance with me, as I pointed out that on the Strand or even by the river, we might find a policeman to whom I could explain the girl's predicament and then leave. Once by the river, and no policeman in sight, we had a fierce argument. She insisted I should come back to see my son. I refused, since this Moonman is clearly a ruffian. We argued on, and eventually I said I would take a hansom from the Strand to go to fetch the police.'

'And did you, sir?'

'Naturally not. The woman was crazed, and I have my reputation to consider.'

And she her life. 'You mean the reputation you no doubt have with the police. Even if they do not know your name, they must know the hansom that crawls down the Haymarket night after night, and the regular appearances at Cremorne you say you don't make.'

He grew pale, and I knew I had hit the target.

'It's not illegal,' he managed to reply.

'No, sir, but it might make the police think you had something to do with the murders of Bessie's sisters. You knew the Haymarket girls well, and Cremorne too.'

He was quick in his own defence. 'There's one thing you haven't thought of, sweep. How would I know what Polly looked like? She was coming to meet you, but you did not send for us. Your apprentice can vouch for that, as well as Frederick and Laurence. And how would I have known who Jenny's sisters were? One does not discuss families with a streetwalker. Only one person could have murdered all three of them, and that's the person Bessie called Moonman.'

'But *you* are Moonman, sir.'

I had the pleasure of seeing him crumple. He had had no idea I'd known his secret, and that was the reason I did not get into the hansom with him. 'You can't deny it, sir. I've pieced it all together. You couldn't leave her alone after she left the studio in Doughty Street. You followed her everywhere, threatening her with what would happen if she did not come back to you. But she wouldn't, and so you hired someone to steal the child, knowing Bessie would come to you immediately. As she did. She thought you had the child with you. She wasn't going to wait till midnight to argue it out on a street corner. She believed you had the child at your home. Have you, sir?'

'You are a madman,' he screeched, to the great interest of two passers-by. 'Of course I don't have the boy.'

'I said I'd find Bessie's murderer, and it's my belief I've found him in you.'

'You're an imbecile and a dangerous one. What on earth makes you think I am Moonman? This is some threat. You wish to blackmail me, no doubt.' He licked nervous lips and his serpent eyes flickered. I was glad we were surrounded by nannies and green grass and May sunshine, for even monsters lose some of their power by day.

'I realised I'd been making a mistake in thinking Moonman had an oddity of face. Bessie called *you* Moonman because deep down you shun the light. By day you lead the life your mother sets out for you, but by night you have different habits. You don't show those night scenes of London in your studio because they reveal too much of you. Most of them show night skies, and when Bessie posed for them, she noticed it, and she called you Moonman. And Jenny knew that too, either from Bessie or because you'd used her services. Polly knew about it as well and was going to tell me before you killed her.'

'No,' Edward babbled, but I took no notice.

'It *was* Moonman who killed Bessie. It was you. You strangled Bessie down by the river in order to stop her revealing your real life to your mother.'

'Even if it were true, my mother would not have believed it. And it is *not*.'

'She would if she saw those paintings.'

'This is madness. Nonsense. Wasp, you are wrong, and if you go to that solicitor with this ridiculous tale, he will tell you so. Look for your murderers elsewhere.'

'How can you prove I'm wrong, sir?'

He stared at me as though at a madman, and then he laughed. 'Why am I even wasting my time with a sweep? Do your worst. You'll find yourself in prison, not me. The police would have no more evidence against me than against you, Wasp, for murdering the girl at Cremorne. It would be your word against mine that this conversation has ever taken place, and I shall deny that I took that hansom cab to the Strand.'

'Cab drivers can be traced.'

'I was not so foolish as to take the cab outside my home. I walked some way, and I shall not tell you where.'

'A photograph shown by the police to the cabbies,' I said, showing my knowledge of the modern world.

'Useless. I wore a hat, an overcoat with collar and a scarf. What would he have seen of me? No, Wasp, I see that the best way of dealing with your ridiculous accusations is to ignore them. Prove Valentine innocent if you can, but not by accusing me. You cannot touch me.'

'Save to tell your mother, sir.'

His eyes glittered. 'Take care, Wasp. You live in a dangerous world.'

He walked rapidly away, and I saw him hailing a hansom in the Bayswater Road. I was even more certain of my ground now. I had a trump card, as they say, which, had I revealed it to him, would have resulted in prompt destructive action on his part. I had seen the painting of Bessie wearing that red scarf, so recently bought. That must have been the last picture he referred to, and was proof of their meeting. He had told the police that she had not modelled for him for several years, and, painting or sketch, it had been done from life.

I was not happy after I had plodded back to the cart to find Ned vanished and the horse unattended and hungry. I gave him the nosebag and led him to the trough, waiting for his lordship to return. An hour went by and no Ned, and I decided he wasn't planning to return. He was off on one of his mysterious errands and would come home in his own good time. I only hoped it *was* a mysterious errand and not a dipping trip. To dip in this part of London might mean he was already in the hands of the police.

I had a last search round Sussex Square, and called into the kitchen at Lady Beezer's house to see if Ned had his eye on more muffins. For once he did not. Then I met a gardener in the square who said he saw a young lad going off with a man, which I didn't like the sound of, although it might not have been Ned. Ned wouldn't do such a thing, I told myself. He's his own man. Even so, I felt uneasy as I took the cart back by myself, although I tried to concentrate on what to do next about Edward. Mr Mudgwick would need to know, but I wanted to have more time to think the affair out before calling on him. Besides, I had qualms about appearing before him while not wearing my number one suit. The trial was coming nearer, and if we were to get the charge dropped, we needed to be quick about it.

When I reached home, I stabled the horse and went to see if Ned was home. He wasn't, and then I realised I was worried. Afternoons aren't the best time of day for our trade, so I decided just to do one or two regulars, after trying all the pie shops and coffee stalls. The pie shop in Wellclose Square hadn't seen Ned all day, which was most unusual, and I gave up any idea of working. I went on searching and asking all the afternoon without success and at last, when the light had almost gone, I had to give up. The gaslights in our part of London are more like good deeds in an evil world than daylight come again, and once out of their pools of light, holes and obstacles wait in the darkness to trip you. I made my way home, but when the silence of emptiness greeted me I decided to go to Rosemary Lane to buy some bread for supper.

Usually the sparsely placed lights are friendly enough, but tonight they seemed enemies, as though they couldn't wait to get rid of me as I left, bread in hand, to make my way back through the maze of dark alleys to Hairbrine Court. From every house came noises of various sorts, but I walked on alone, listening to the crunch of my boots. For the first time I felt nervous in these alleys, for they are mostly honest if poor round our way. Tonight I felt the hounds of hell were on my tail. I heard the sound of water shushing from the bucket of the communal privy and the cries of a child lost somewhere in the dark. I worried even more about Ned, hoping to see his bright young face at any moment.

With relief I reached the familiarity of the door that led into the house where our rooms were. It only had one hinge and squeaked in protest as I pushed it, anxious to be inside. As it yielded, however, a man suddenly stepped out from the darkness of the archway leading into the court, squelching in the rubbish of the yard. He was a large man, burly even, coming out of the darkness and coming for *me*.

'Sweepie Wasp?'

His rasping voice struck terror into me, and I knew where Ned had vanished to.

'The boy's with me,' he grunted. 'We need a talk, you and I, Wasp.'

I saw the menacing eyes, I saw the lopsided face, and I didn't need to be told his name.

Chapter Twelve: In Which I Face the Monster

The bag of soot emptied over me, clogging my mind, paralysing my legs. Had there been two flues in my chimney after all? Had I ventured down the wrong one and taken the dead flat instead of the path to the light? Was George Clare Moonman after all? I'd been so sure that Edward Harwood-Jones was at the top of the chimney, but now he was only a phantasmagoria that had dissolved into thin air. I couldn't think straight about Moonman for fear about Ned, for he was in George Clare's clutches. If he were Moonman—as surely he must be for him to have the wickedness to take Ned—my guts and wits heaved together at the horror of it. How was I going to rescue Ned when I didn't even know where George Clare lived?

I asked the Lord to straighten my brains out immediately, so confused was I by terror, and He obliged. Moonman, He pointed out, didn't want Ned for himself. He wanted *me*, for I knew the truth about him, or thought I did. In the dark of the court, cut off from the lane by Moonman barring the archway to freedom, I was not so sure of truth, for terror plays a London particular with your feelings, until your mind clears the fog away. It wasn't clearing it fast enough, after that one shaft of light. All I could think of was the huge man menacing me, a man who had great reason to do me harm, was half as tall again as I and twice as wide and powerful, for all he must be fifteen years my senior. He carried no weapon but that was of little cheer when I looked at his hands, big, strong and capable of wringing my neck like a chicken's.

'Let's have a chat inside.' He leered at me. 'Can't stop out here all night, can we?'

'I'm not going up,' I declared, so we prowled around one another waiting for an opening. He knew full well I had only to yell and curious faces would be peering out, Mrs Parsnip's would most certainly be one of them, and maybe even a pigman might arrive—though I've never seen one here yet. As Clare's description was probably plastered outside every police station in London, he could not risk it. Or so I hoped, as I pressed my luck.

'We'll chat when you take me to where Ned is.'

'Later, Wasp.'

I told myself that he guessed the moment I saw Ned was all right, his power would be gone, but the fear swept over me he had a different reason for ignoring me. If Ned were dead . . . I had to believe he wasn't, and put my brains to work on his behalf. I had an idea about somewhere we could both feel safe—especially me. If I could persuade him to come.

'The pigmen may be watching the regular pubs round here,' I told him, 'but I know one they'll never think of. Decent beer too. No adulterating it with the Indian Berry like most of them round here.'

'Where?'

I'd got his interest, but I knew who'd be paying for the drinks to fill that fat belly. Mr Mudgwick would not begrudge me this expense, I was sure.

'The Old Mahogany Bar at Wilton's.' It was my hope that Mrs Wilton might be in the bar and remember me and my mission. I explained to the monster giant, 'Folks are too busy drinking and enjoying themselves at the show to think there might be a murderer in their midst. And the pigmen would never guess you were out enjoying yourself at a music hall. They'll be too busy searching the pubs and lodging houses.'

His face grew dark, and I thought for a moment he'd finish me here and now. He didn't, although he took a long time thinking it over. A slowish sort of cove, I realised with relief. All his brain was in his brawn and that boded well for me—and for Ned.

We walked through dark alleyways to Dock Street. I wasn't too happy about this, all the while tense lest I feel his hands about my neck, and breathed a sigh of relief as we came out to Cable Street where human beings could be seen. As we turned into the narrow Well Street towards Gracey's Alley, fear swept back in a rush, for there was little light, and we were approaching Wilton's from the wrong direction for peace of mind. The main entrance of Wilton's lies in Gracey's Alley, although it prides itself on being in Wellclose Square. The square is one of those where rich and poor can stare at each other without having to meet. One looks too high, the other too low. On the east side are swell buildings, but tucked behind them, and even on the western side, are places that make Hairbrine Court a palace in comparison. Well Street, where we were walking, is like that too. By night you feel you walk with all the sadness of history beside you. There's a sailors' home on our right that hides a darker past, for it was here about forty years ago the old Royalty theatre burned to the ground; it was rebuilt and called the Brunswick, but three days after its grand opening the building collapsed with much loss of life and injury. Even as the injured and dead still lay there, the local tub-thumper arriving to seize the opportunity of decrying theatres as Sodoms and Gomorrahs. Tonight I not only had history, but Moonman at my side. The darkness weighed heavy on me, and I reached the doorway to Wilton's with great relief.

Most folks were in the hall, for the evening's entertainment had begun. I could hear the sound of W.G. Ross's 'Sam Hall,' and this well-known song about a vicious murderer on his way to execution put me in mind of Valentine again. The bar was almost empty, which George Clare didn't care for, so I left him in the darkest corner while I fetched (and paid for) our porter.

He drank noisily and lengthily, and the pulled-down mouth made it the worse. Eventually, 'What you doing this to me for, Wasp?' he demanded, pushing the empty glass towards me meaningfully. 'That's what I want to know.'

'What have you taken Ned for?' I countered.

'Because the pigmen are after me, thanks to your meddling. I know all about you. Polly told me.'

'Before you garrotted her?'

He growled like a maddened dancing bear, and I hastily filled the glasses. 'I wouldn't touch a hair of her head.'

'What about their throats?' I asked. 'First Bessie, then Jenny, then Polly. Maybe even Sophie, too.'

From the look on his face, I thought he might kill me with one blow of that enormous fist. 'What's your game? If you weren't such a tiddler, I'd think you did for them all yourself.'

I had to keep things peaceful for Ned's sake, as well as my own. 'Bessie was my friend,' I told him quietly, 'and I swore I'd find her murderer. Now I have.' It was time to get things straight before I met St Peter.

'Me? You're fool-witted, sweepie.' It was hard to read his face, it being so lop-sided. 'It's thanks to you the crushers think I did it. You're going to tell 'em they're wrong, sweepie.'

'If you didn't, I don't need to tell 'em anything.' Fine words, but he and I knew they meant nothing.

'Listen, pal. Do I look like the kind of chap who could have murdered four bloody daughters? Why should I?' His lopsided face looked at me with a kind of appeal.

'Bessie through revenge,' I said quietly, 'and two for fear of discovery once you knew we were on your track.'

He was angry now, this dancing bear. 'Revenge for what? What had Bessie ever done to harm me? I loved the girl, Wasp.' He was roaring and heads began to turn in curiosity, which made him quiet again.

'Because she left you. She wouldn't come back to your bed,' I told him. 'You used Sophie, then Bessie and Jenny and would have done Polly too, if they hadn't got her away from you. But you never forgot, did you? You tracked them down, wouldn't let them rest, then you tried the last trick and the best. You stole Bessie's son to make her come back to you. She wouldn't, and you killed her.'

He was staring at me white-faced, and took a gulp of the beer as though to gain time in his reply.

'Even if you weren't their murderer, you did as bad in your unnatural lusts. You killed them that way,' I added, letting it all out now.

His head was bent over his beer, and I made ready to cry for help, when he raised it to me. His eyes were full of tears. 'You've got it all wrong, Wasp, and you can tell your bloody pigmen pals so. If you loved Bessie, you'll believe me. Didn't Polly tell you how it was?'

'She was murdered before she told me anything. As you well know. You fixed yourself that job at Cremorne once you found out she was to work there too.'

'I got her that job,' he hissed. 'Listen, Wasp.' he licked his lips nervously. 'Jenny and Polly lived with me after Bessie left until I went to stir. After I got out, Bessie looked after us all. *Me?* Think I'd want to kill her after that? Then I went to stir again, and when I came out in fifty-eight, I found out she was working at this music-hall down Bermondsey way, so I went to see her to—' He drank several gulps of beer, and I could see the sweat glistening on his forehead.

'See if she could help you out,' I suggested ironically. 'Seems to me Bessie did a lot of helping out, but no one helped her.'

He looked at me queerly, but did not answer me.

I couldn't bear to look at the huge hands gripping the porter, knowing what they'd done to his daughters. Instead I concentrated, thinking perhaps I was missing something. 'Did Mr Harwood-Jones put you up to it?' I had this idea they might have been in a conspiracy together. It would explain how he came to know Ned was in Sussex Square.

'Wasp,' he interrupted heavily, 'there's something going on I don't understand, and plenty you don't. I've never heard of the cove.'

'The pigmen can make you hear.'

He wasn't always so slow. 'Ain't you forgetting something?'

Of course I was. My wits had been addled. I was forgetting Ned. *Ned.* While George Clare held him, he had the power in *his* hands. And what's more, I'd forgotten Bessie's son. It wasn't only Ned he held, for if George Clare was Moonman, or if he was acting on Edward Harwood-Jones' behalf, then Bessie's son was also with him. Or had been.

'I didn't do any of these things, Wasp,' he grunted. 'It's not rare in the rookeries, I grant you, for beds to get filled in ways that aren't right, but to track them down years after to use them that way—no.'

'If you didn't, who did?'

He licked his lips again with nervousness, and said nothing. He didn't need to, for I knew now.

The show in the hall was over, and the bar was filling up. Who should I recognise, for all the uniform had given way to smart trousers and waistcoat, but Sergeant Wiley who was out for an evening with his missus. You might think I was overjoyed at this turn of events—but I wasn't. I still didn't know where Ned was.

The sergeant's eyes fell on me, then on my companion. In a

trice he was outside springing his rattle, carried with him for all he was not on duty, and seeing what might shortly happen said to Moonman, who hadn't the benefit of my knowledge, I hissed, 'Where's Ned?'

'I told you—*later,*' he snarled. 'I got to think.'

I pushed my glass over to him, feeling like a Judas. Suppose he was right? Suppose he hadn't touched those girls? Suppose it was Harwood-Jones?

There was enough beer left in his mug for the pigmen to arrive from Wapping and burst in, led by a triumphant Sergeant Wiley. They didn't waste time buying George Clare drinks. They jumped on him, all four of them, with handcuffs and big manacles, and carted him out to the Black Mariah like a Smithfield butcher's carcase. I was running at their side, desperate now, and crying, 'Where's Ned? *Where's Ned?*'

He laughed at me, and I saw he'd been playing with me all along. He *was* Moonman. He *was* Bessie's murderer. 'I never took him. I never took either of them.'

'How did you know Ned was missing then? And Bessie's son was your grandson, for pity's sake.'

'Pity?' he yelled from the van, as I stood outside the doors still open. 'You don't know what you're meddling with, sweep.'

'*Where* are the kids?' One of the pigmen gave him a blow with his baton to reinforce my plea, and the second one produced the most terrible yell of pain I've ever heard from man or beast.

'Rotherhithe Street butcher's shop, and may God have mercy on your soul.'

The doors were closed, and the horses moved off, leaving me with Sergeant Wiley.

'I'm going there,' I told him. '*Now.*'

'Take care, Mr Wasp,' he said gravely. 'Leave it till I can get the Southwark police. Rotherhithe's their beat, and there's a station in Paradise Street, not far away. I'll get a telegraph sent.'

'I'm going now,' I said. I'd thought it out. If George Clare was Moonman, he was with the police and no threat to me. If Edward Harwood-Jones was Moonman, he was employing Clare to do his dirty work and would hardly be in Rotherhithe himself. Ned—and Bessie's son—would be alone, or perhaps with a woman to guard them.

Sergeant Wiley still looked worried, but seeing I was set on it, he made no more demur.

There's no bridge to cross our grand river of Thames nearer than London Bridge, and that's a fair way from Rotherhithe on the far side. It would mean wasting time while I got Doshie and the cart out, and so I had a better idea. A great tunnel passes under the river between Wapping and Rotherhithe, engineered by Sir Isambard Brunel himself. It was many years in the building, with many tragedies caused by the river fighting back against the intruders, but it's been open nearly twenty years now. We're still awaiting the building of approaches for traffic on wheels, but all those who pay their pennies and descend the hundred steps of the shaft can walk across.

It is not to my liking being enclosed and poorly lit, but it is a blessing for many. Tonight I would take it. To get there, however, I must walk through the dark of the dockside areas and through the lanes of Wapping. The Lord would guide me, and I still had my brush and iron-tipped rod with me, which show my trade so those that walk by night would know I had no money. There are many such nowadays, for ships from the great land of America seeking arms for the Civil War dock in the Pool of London. Many carry slaves aboard, and it is known to them that any who can escape to our riverbanks are thereby freed from slavery. But free is a relative matter, for who takes care of them then? How can they live but by evil ways?

'Tom Wasp is coming,' I asked the Lord to notify Ned and

Oliver, and stepped out briskly, fortified by a free pie from Mrs Wilton, down to the Ratcliffe Highway. It was nearly twelve and normally being in my bed well before this hour, I wasn't prepared for the crowds leaving the pubs or seeking brothels. Faces of all colours, sailors of all nations lurched by, oblivious to anything but money and drink—even Tom Wasp. The quickest path to the Wapping entrance shaft of the Thames Tunnel was straight through London Docks between the eastern and western basins, and it was not a path I fancied.

I put fear aside by thinking of Ned and Oliver, and carried my brush and rod like a crucifix before me to ward off evil demons. Even though the King's Arms, where the second of the two great murders of the Ratcliffe Highway area took place years ago, had been swept away when the London Docks were enlarged, the atmosphere still seemed evil.

At this time of night I hoped the docks area might be unfrequented, with the sailors seeking enjoyment on the bright streets and the dockyard workers dispersed to their homes. There was little light save that graciously provided by God, but the moonlight produced strange effects, an unreality in which anything might happen. I passed several scuffles between drunk sailors, but they did not bother me, and I walked on, hearing little but my own footsteps and the occasional lapping of the water in the wind.

It was not far to reach the safety of Wapping, but the fear in my mind made me feel I was being watched, and not only by God. I made myself stop to rid myself of night terrors, looked round, but no one walked after me. The noise and traffic were far away, and only a night bird hooted somewhere close at hand.

Nevertheless, I was glad when the lane began to be lined with the houses of Wapping, for at its end lay the river. Just before that is Wapping police station, not that of the Thames Police where Sergeant Wiley reigns nearby, but the Metropolitan Police of Stepney K division. It helps keep the surrounding lanes of Wapping quiet, for some well-to-do folks live round here, in addition to the poverty-stricken casuals.

Even so, I reached the tunnel entrance shaft with relief, although as I paid my penny I realised a new horror now faced me. I had crossed by day, when even though one walked through by lamplight it was busy with other travellers. Tonight there would be few about.

There are two tunnels in one, for Sir Isambard had envisaged traffic travelling in one and returning in another, and at intervals there are arches leading to the other tunnel. The whole shape, however, is *cylindrical,* since they say Sir Isambard had the idea of it through studying a sea worm boring holes through wood. In short, it is like a horizontal chimney, and where the lamplight does not fall, as dark.

'I can do it for you, Ned,' I vowed, having reached the last of the steps and surveyed the tunnel ahead. With a great rush of confidence, like Blondin on his tightrope, I stepped forward. It occurred to me that only last year a female Blondin had nearly been killed at Cremorne, but I put such thoughts from me as I walked into the unknown. I thought of Mr Holman Hunt's picture, 'The Light of the World,' and imagined Christ with his lantern at my side to guide me through.

Twelve hundred feet this tunnel is in length, less than a quarter of a mile, but it seemed like ten miles as it stretched out ahead of me in the gloom, and a black hole ahead waiting to gobble me up, dark archways on either side, where anything might await me.

Like Edward Harwood-Jones, Moonman. The thought came into my head, and would not go.

At the other end, I told myself, would be the shaft of Rotherhithe and at its top the open air and Ned. I plodded steadily on. Was I alone? Dear Lord, let it be so. But ahead of me might appear the monster's clutching hand. I forced myself on, concentrating hard on ignoring imaginary monsters ahead and thinking only of the joy of walking up those steps.

When the clutching hands came, they came from behind, for the monster was real. The world went black inside my head as well as all around me, as the monster clutched my throat, dragging my head backwards. I dropped my brush and rod to free my throat with my hands, but strong though they are, they were no match for the monster's.

With my last conscious thought, I knew I was alone with Moonman. I knew I was dying. And then I heard the voice, a voice I knew.

'I hate you, Wasp. And do you know why? Because Bessie loved you. You, a bloody crippled chimney sweep. You took my ma. You took 'em all, Sophie, Jenny, Polly, Bessie and *ma!* They all belonged to me. They had to, after Ma died. Why did she have to die? She wouldn't let me in her bed, so Bessie and the others owed it to me. She said they'd look after me. And they *didn't.*'

The screeched words didn't make sense. Nothing did. I fastened on to just one thing. Bessie loved me? Me? Could *I* be the only man who truly loved her? Then all was dark as the soot smothered me forever.

I was in a garden, having come through the tunnel, and Bessie was there to greet me. She was smiling so sweetly, her red-gold hair floating around like an angel's, and her gown covered in violets. She didn't say anything, but she didn't have to, for she loved me. Oh, Bessie, what a time we'll have here, with no black walls, no soot, no evil. I put out my hands to take hers, and stepped forward to paradise.

But then came pain, and the sight of walls around me, and the flowers had vanished. Instead of Bessie, I saw pigmen sitting on a giant of a fellow I half recognised. He was in handcuffs by now, and leg manacles as well, for he was a violent man. He stared at me with sneering, evil eyes, as he saw me come back to this wretched life. He gave his evil grin, his thin lips curving sarcastically. 'I'll do for you yet, Wasp. Love *you?*'

I saw then, with my blood cold, my throat cracking with agony, why Bessie had called him Moonman. I knew him as Mr Slit.

Epilogue: All Up!

Half an hour later we found Ned, hungry and cold but unharmed, over the butcher's shop in Rotherhithe Street, where George Clare had been living. He'd taken Ned, as he said, so that he could talk with me, and had treated him kindly. Like Bessie, like Jenny, and like Polly, he had been too scared, it turned out, to tell us about Slit, for all he was his own son. They all treated him as if he were that old Dr Mesmer himself, so strong was his spell over them. Bessie had been the only one to stand up to her brother, and she had been garrotted for her pains.

It turned out Slit was the leader of one of these garrotting gangs terrorising London at the moment, so the pigmen (especially Sergeant Wiley, who is now Inspector Wiley) were most grateful to me, for *nearly* getting myself garrotted so that I could recover to give evidence for them.

But then I had reason to be grateful to Sergeant Wiley, not to mention Mrs Wilton and Mrs Wiley. These two ladies had put their heads together, and guessing how I would go, nagged the good sergeant into suggesting in his telegraph to the Southwark Police that they should enter the tunnel from the other end to meet me. It seems the sergeant himself had had doubts about George Clare being Moonman, and had expressed anxiety to them about my lonely trip. I was much obliged to them all and told the sergeant so.

'You ain't so important, Wasp. It's that old horse of yours we were all worried about.' His squinty eye gleamed. 'If you got garrotted, if Ned starved to death—who'd find and feed her?'

I think the sergeant was joking, although I didn't see a smile—but then I've taken a dislike to smiles at present, remembering Mr Slit's version of it. I'd been wrong all along in thinking the man with the lopsided face was Moonman, and taken many other false flues too. It just goes to show a man should stick to his own trade, and let the pigmen get on with theirs. And yet, if I hadn't made all those mistakes, Valentine might still be in prison, and so might George Clare, which proves that God works in mysterious ways His will to be done.

When we found Ned in Rotherhithe, I was so choked with feelings, all I could croak out was, 'You're safe then, Ned. We'll have a pie back home, shall we? I can't eat, but I'll look at one.'

'Don't worry. I'll eat yours, Gov.' There wasn't a quaver in his voice—not then.

The pigmen wanted to take me to hospital, but Ned wouldn't let me out of his sight, so they took me home. Lady Beezer, when she heard next day, sent her doctor, which was most obliging of her, and later tried to persuade me to move into one of those model lodging houses at Bethnal Green. It might have a laundry room at the top of the house, but there's a lot of steps to climb and it's a long way from the pie shop Ned and I favour. So we shall stay here, but take an extra room or two, which Lady Beezer paid for. What's more, her ladyship has paid for them to put in an indoor privy of our own!

Mr Mudgwick, when he heard next day, sent round his doctor too, and so did Valentine as soon as they let him out of prison. I didn't hear that George Clare wanted to send me his doctor, but he has reason to be grateful to me for ridding him of the nightmare of his son Slit. Slit's woman was grateful too—she didn't send her doctor either. She just wanted to move in and be my woman.

I thought hard about that, but Bessie was too close, so we got her a job at Wilton's instead. You see, I still couldn't believe the wonder of it that it was me, not one of the Angels, who Bessie said was the only one truly loved her. She was right, for I did. Bessie had looked under the soot. Perhaps if I'd realised—but no. Don't think that way. Look up the chimney, Tom, not down.

And talking of dear Bessie, you'll have noticed there's something I've omitted to tell you. What of Bessie's son?

Oliver wasn't there in Rotherhithe, and all the pigmen in London couldn't get Slit to speak. Not even his woman knew what had become of the boy. He had stayed with them a day or two and then he'd disappeared. Slit had arranged it. The pigmen assumed he was dead, of course, but we still hoped for better than that. There's money in live boys and none in the dead. His silence about Oliver was Slit's last hold over me.

Two days later when I was feeling better and Ned decided he could leave me alone for a minute, even without all those doctors around, he vanished on another of his mysterious errands. He wasn't back with pies in half an hour or so this time; he was away all day. At last I heard his voice shouting from the stairs.

'Gov, Gov . . .'

I went to the door, being on my feet again, curious at the excitement in his voice. I opened it and in shot Ned, dragging in a small child, black from head to foot, by the hand. Did I say the head was black too?—ah, no, for some of his red gold hair was shining through the soot.

'Come in, Oliver lad,' I said, tears running down my face. 'Let's send Ned for an extra pie.'

Well, the arrival of Oliver, after determined searching by Ned amongst the chummies of London, gave my well-wishers something else to think about than doctors for me. His grandfather George wanted to take him, but when he heard about all the other offers, he said the child deserved the best he could get, though it's my belief he was sad at heart for this sacrifice. Mr Valentine wanted to take him. Mr Harwood-Jones suddenly decided he'd like a son after all. Mr Fairfax made an offer, and even Mrs Laurence Tait turned motherly. George Clare said I should choose. I knew Ned wanted him to stay with us, and my heart yearned to take him. Deserves the best? Who was I to decide whether I could offer that?

So I chose Mr Valentine, but then our Lord took a hand in the proceedings. He pointed out to me that Mr Valentine isn't married, and Oliver needed a touch of mothering. The long and short of it is that Mr and Mrs Mudgwick have a new son.

That settled, my well-wishers all turned thoughtful eyes on Ned. Luckily, Ned noticed and guessed what was in their minds.

'*Naaaaah!*' He rushed screaming behind me. 'Gov, don't let them take me.'

No one said a word. Quietly they departed, one by one, and left Ned and me to our pies and porter.

ABOUT THE AUTHOR

Amy Myers worked for many years as a director of a London publishing firm and became a full-time writer eighteen years ago. She is known for her Auguste Didier series of crime novels, in which a Victorian master chef takes to solving crimes as well as producing culinary triumphs, for her short stories, and currently for a modern series featuring Peter and Georgia Marsh, who investigate crimes from the past. (See her Web site for further details, www.amymyers.net.) She and her American husband currently live in Kent, UK, about forty miles from the scenes of *Tom Wasp and the Murdered Stunner.*